Titus and Roni

Gregory Dark

First published by O Books, 2010
O Books is an imprint of John Hunt Publishing Ltd., The Bothy, Deershot Lodge, Park Lane, Ropley, Hants, SO24 0BE, UK
office1@o-books.net
www.o-books.net

Distribution in:

UK and Europe
Orca Book Services
orders@orcabookservices.co.uk
Tel: 01202 665432 Fax: 01202 666219
Int. code (44)

USA and Canada
NBN
custserv@nbnbooks.com
Tel: 1 800 462 6420 Fax: 1 800 338 4550

Australia and New Zealand
Brumby Books
sales@brumbybooks.com.au
Tel: 61 3 9761 5535 Fax: 61 3 9761 7095

Far East (offices in Singapore, Thailand, Hong Kong, Taiwan)
Pansing Distribution Pte Ltd
kemal@pansing.com
Tel: 65 6319 9939 Fax: 65 6462 5761

South Africa
Stephan Phillips (pty) Ltd
Email: orders@stephanphillips.com
Tel: 27 21 4489839 Telefax: 27 21 4479879

Design: Stuart Davies

ISBN: 978 1 84694 341 6

A CIP catalogue record for this book is available from the British Library.

Printed by Digital Book Print

Titus and Roni

Gregory Dark

BOOKS

Winchester, UK
Washington, USA

Dedication

To my parents, all four of them,
without any one of whom I would not have been possible.

Acknowledgements

Napoleon would never have considered me for the post of general. If for no other reason than for the fact that, normally, I am unlucky. Even conscientiously so. ... In all bar one way: the people who come into my life.

When my path crossed **Anne Piper's** my luck was not only good, it was spectacular. Her diligence, support and general good-eggness are aspects of both my professional and personal lives which are alchemical. And this 'thank you' is completely inadequate to express my gratitude.

As it is to express that which I feel for **Dr Teresa Parrott**, who urged me to finish writing the book, and to **Julian Day** for assuring me it was worthy of submission. I am (as ever) grateful to **John Hunt** for having then published it. Thanks are also due to **Jim Marshall** for having edited much of Roni's Scottishness; the thanks are ongoing to my brother, **Daniel**, and **Stuart Davies** for their ongoing help in my ongoing struggle against the I-Tyranny.

Writers in today's world (except for a very few) have a rough time of it. Nevertheless most are incredibly generous with their time, advice and encouragement – at least, they have been to me. All the below have selflessly given substantially of themselves. I hope they feel that at least some of their seeds fell on fertile ground.

I separate **Edward Bond** and his wife, **Elisabeth**, because their help and support was simply extraordinary. Not just to a wannabe writer but to what was then the very young man. I also separate **Jonathan Hales** for similar reasons. Again 'thank you' is inadequate.

As it is to recognise the help of:

John Antrobus; Catherine Barry; Michael Bywater; Colette Caddle; Richard Carpenter; Bruce Crowther; John Gordon-Davis; Maurice Gran; Wilson John Haire; Laurence Marks; Paul Mayhew-Archer; Roger Singleton-Turner; Sam Snape; Paul Thompson; and **Ray Villis.**

Gregory Dark, Nérac, 2009

'Titus'

"Owww! Christ! Christ Almighty! Owwww, for Christ's sake!

"For God's sake. For *God's* sake – ow! Gerry, you okay? You okay, Gerry?"

"I'm an old man, you bastard. Can't you see? Have you no eyes a-sodding-t all? *Yo ... alt. Vieux. Vieux homme, je. Yo.* And the boy? *Niño*? The *niño's* young. *Jeune*, for Christ's sake.

"Gerry? Gerry? You hang on in there, tu'penny. You'll be alright. You're going to be alright."

Dear God, please let this not be happening to us.

"That how you get your kicks, is it, from bullying the old and the young?"

Please, dear God, please let it not be happening. Not to us.

"Don't push me. Do not push me. I'm moving, for God's sake, as fast as I can. Do not push me.

"Where are we going? Where are you taking us? Where the hell are you taking us? *Où ...*? No ... *dondé*? We don't have money, you know. *Nous, uns ... no dinero. Pas d'argent.* Not a bean, old bean. Not a sausage. Nothing. *Nichts. Nada.*"

It was the flash of a spark, the burst of a gun. The rat-tat-tat of Gatling. The blink of a cobra's eye. One dead. A hundred dead. In the blink of a cobra's eye. After the first death, there is no other. *Not* death. Not *sensations.* Flashes of sensation. Vivid colour. A streak of scarlet fear. Primary colours. The smell of indigo. All rushing in a whirl. A black-hole of a rainbow. A rainbow of a spectrum all of black.

"*Por favor, amigo*: I cannot move any faster. *Por favor.*

"Oh, thank God. Thank God for that. A rest. Thank God. Gerry? It's going to be alright, Gerry. We'll soon have this mess sorted out. Soon be on our way home.

"What was that? Sound like a bolt to you, Gerry? Sounded like a bolt to me.

"Oww!"

Get me out of this, God. *Please.*

"You do not – do not, for Christ's sake – need to shove me everywhere. I respond, you know, and quite well, just to a simple urge, an indication, a nudge in the right direction."

I can't cope with this. Gerry, he's young, fit. He *can* cope. He's healthy, God. Please. *Please.*

"Sit? Sit? Are you asking me to sit? I don't understand."

Keep Gerry if You must, but, please – *please* – get me out of this.

"Okay, okay, I'm sitting; I'm sitting, okay? It's not that easy, you know. Not at my age, not all the way down to the ground. Not in handcuffs. Okay? Okay? I'm sat now, okay?"

For Christ's sake, Titus. *For Christ's sake,* lighten up.

"Gerry? Gerry, that you, Gerry?"

Only way, old mate, you're going to get out of this – *only* way –, you're going to have to *charm* your way out.

"Oh, thank God. Thank God. Okay, tu'penny, alright. It's going to be alright. Gramps's here. He's here, old mate. It's okay, Gerry. It's alright. Just snuggle up to me tight. Yes, that's the way. Tight, Gerry. "Any moment now they'll have these handcuffs off us." Don't have a bean, old bean – where did *that* come from? "Any moment now, Gerry.

"*Scusi? Pardon?* Handcuffs? Cuffs *de main? S'il vous plaît.* Please. If not mine, then the boy's. *Du garçon.* The boy, he's not going to run away – *PLEASE* – not without me. For the love of God, please.

"What's that? What's that?

"Are they releasing you, Gerry? Is that what I can hear? *Have* they released you? That's it, you just hold onto your old grandpa. Grip me tight, old darling. Hold me really tight. *Gracias. Gracias.*

"Oh, they're unlocking me now, Gerry, as well. They're unlocking me.

"There! A proper cuddle. There, that's better, isn't it? Hugging like this, there's nothing – *nothing*, Gerry – we can't face. As long as we have each other, old tu'penny, we'll be alright. We'll be okay. Any second now they'll let us take the blindfolds off. Any second now.

"Okay, they slammed the door. That's okay. That probably means we're being held prisoner somewhere.

"No, NO.

"Don't take the blindfold off. Don't even think about it. Not yet." Err, about what I said just now, God, ... "Not just yet." ... about what I, as it were, well, you know ... about keeping Gerry, letting me go ... Could we, do You think, draw a delicate veil over that? Delete it, as it were, from the record? Tape over it? Go back to: 'please, *please*, get *us* out of here'? If You'd be so kind. Sorry to keep troubling You.

"Please, Gerry. Don't whine like that, don't simper. Just hold on for a few minutes more. There's a good chap."

"Well, we don't know, for example, whether they might not just have left one of them in here to guard us.

"Now, I'm sure they're alright, these guys. Sure of it. But, just till we know that for *sure* sure, as it were, we've got to treat them as being very dangerous. Very, *very* dangerous, old mate. You know, like unattended baggage at airports and things. Potential bombs. Possible bombs. Till we know better."

Second thoughts – third thoughts, rather ... about my going and Gerry staying ... could we, do You think, just 'stet' my earlier prayer? He snivels – You may have noticed – and he simpers. Just maybe, Lord, he should be given something, Lord, to simper *about*. I remain, Sir, Your obedient servant et cetera, et cetera.

"No, that doesn't mean we just sit here like lemons. That's not what I'm talking about either. You alright now?"

"Sure?"

"There's no brave face involved here, Gerry. You know, there's no competition involved for machoness or anything."

"Alright, 'machismo', then. You sure you're alright? Well, if you're sure, then I'll have a hunt around. Try and work out the size of the room, see whether there is indeed someone in here guarding us."

May the saints preserve us! And just who, pray, Titus, do you think you are? James Bond? Indiana Jones, maybe? I mean, armed with the invaluable information about the size of room, what precisely are you going to do with it? Extract the nitro-glycerine from your 'Q' designed loafers?

"No, I can't hear anyone either. No, or smell anyone." Calculate the force needed in the karate kick you're going to need to break down the door with? "But ... well, remember what I said, about them being bombs and such ... we have to be careful, Gerry. Very, very careful. Not only walking on egg-shells, old mate, walking on quails' egg-shells."

"Well, they're even more delicate than hens' shells."

"No, it doesn't sound big, you're right. Sounds in fact very small. A cell-like sort of size. Will you be alright if I let you go?"

Please let me go. They are so terribly sticky, those little fingers of yours.

"Sure?"

"Sure you're sure, Gerry?"

Space. Please, Gerry, give me some *space*. Stop sticking to me, child, like some superglued treacle.

"Okay, I'm letting go of you ... now.

"Okay? Still okay?"

"It's got nothing to do with being a baby. It's a frightening situation. A very frightening situation. Christ, even Superman would be frightened."

"Well, you know what I mean. If you're in a frightening situation, it's sensible to be frightened. And not sensible not to be. In fact, downright stupid not to be. Downright idiotic, in fact. And you're not stupid, are you?"

No, not even like treacle ... like one of those leeches, more like – those slimy, slithery, black little leeches – those leeches that Bogart so hated in 'African Queen'.

"Yes, I'm sure that does mean that Tommy Corbett will never ever be frightened, but it's you here, isn't it, and not Tommy Corbett?

"Okay, I'm going to stand up now. I may have to sit down again in a hurry. So don't move, will you? Or I could sit down and squash you." What's the betting you've never heard of 'The African Queen'? "Hear anything?"

"No, neither can I.

"Let go of my leg, Gerry."

Now, there's a thought. That would be something that could make this whole experience something altogether more pleasurable: A statuesque and nubile African queen! A nubile, *Nubian* African queen!

"Well, if I'm going to investigate the dimensions of this room, I need my leg. You want another hug, another cuddle? I could sit down again."

"In that case, yes please, let go of my leg."

"Okay, that makes sense. Yes, we could examine the room together. Yes, why not? Good thinking, Batman. I need some *space*, kid. "Well done. Take my hand. I'm waving it round. There? Got it? Up we come, then. Upsa-daisy." There we go. That's the way. Keep hold of my hand, we'll be okay. We'll be alright."

Tight grip, Titus. You've got to keep a tight grip. It's this, this experience, this you've been in training for your whole life, what your whole life up to now has meant to prepare you for. Clear head, sunshine, that's all that'll save you. And him. A clear head, and a tight grip.

"Concrete floor would you say?"

"Yes, that's my guess. Concrete. Still, good for the back, isn't it, a hard surface? Sleeping on one, I mean? Your great-grandmother always slept on a board, you know that? Slipped a disc when she was a lot younger, slept on a ... Ow!!"

"Banged my shin on something. God, that hurt. Ow. Oof.

"Aha! What have we here? A bed, is it? You never know. Never know your luck. Say the magic words, 'Abra Cadabra'. One bed indeed. Only a single one. Still, we're neither of us exactly giants, are we? Not that we'll be here probably by the time night comes. I should think already they've realised their mistake and they're trying to figure out ways of letting us go. Without losing too much face or so. That sort of idea. But ... well, if it does take them till tomorrow to figure that one out, at least tonight we won't be sleeping on a concrete floor, will we? We'll be in a bed. On a bed, anyway. Snug as a bug in a rug. Snug, I should say, as two bugs in a rug."

Oh wow! Aren't I the lucky one?!

"Okay, let's just sit on it, shall we, the bed? That's it. That's the way. Well, I've felt worse mattresses in my life. Not many, that's true. Still, I have felt worse.

"Just let go of my hand, Gerry, for a moment."

"Well, I want to try an experiment. I can't, as you said, hear anyone in here or smell anyone. I can't believe that if there'd been someone in here with us, they wouldn't have said something. I'm just going to try easing my blindfold off. Just as an experiment. Just to see."

"Yes, you're right, just to 'see' in that sense as well.

"No, Gerry, don't you do yours. No, tu'penny. Remember what we said? Suspicious packages, unexploded bombs – remember? You have to believe me, Gerry. You understand? You *have* to believe me."

"Good. Alright."

"No, it's okay."

"No, I'm not cross with you."

"Why would I be cross with you? I'm frightened too, Gerry. I told you earlier, only an idiot wouldn't be frightened in this situation."

"Well, alright, yes, everyone might very well know I am an idiot, but I'm not that much of one.

"Okay, I'm easing the blindfold off, Gerry. Ea-sy. Oof. That hurts. No, wait a minute. Just let my eyes get acclimatised, just let me make sure it *is* clear, the coast, the room, whatever.

"It's really painful, the light, Gerry. Be careful when you do take your blindfold off. NOT YET, I told you."

"You have to wait for me to tell you, Gerry. You have to.

"Unexploded bombs.

"It's not like normal life. You have to, Gerry, *have* to do what I tell you. When I tell you. And not do anything I *don't* tell you to do. Okay? *Okay*?"

"You understand?"

"You sure you understand? It's not any kind of power trip, matey, or anything. It's just ... Well, it's just what has to be, that's all. That's the way it must be. Till this is over, anyway."

"Okay, well, it seems we *are* alone. Inside the room, anyway. It is a room. Hell, you might as well see it for yourself. You want to take your blindfold off?"

"You need a hand?"

"Take it easy, Gerry, very easy. The light will hurt your eyes to begin with. What I'd suggest, take the blindfold off, but keep your eyes closed. Let the light first of all filter through your closed eyes. The view's not breath-taking, that I can promise you. You're not missing much by keeping them closed. Tight shut, Gerry? Scrunch them up good and tight. Okay, take the blindfold off, then. Keep them scrunched up. Really scrunched up. That's it. Okay, now slowly, slowly, start to unscrunch them. Gently, Gerry, that's the way.

"Okay, now blink them open. Right. Okay? They okay?"

"No, the spots probably come from the scrunching, Gerry. Don't worry about them. They'll go in a second or two. Okay? Okay?

"Well, welcome to the Ritz. Now, don't be intimidated, will you, by all its sumptuousness and grandeur? I mean, I know you're not used to luxury quite on this scale, but ..."

We're going to die. We're both going to die. O dear God, help us. O God, o Christ, please help us.

"You alright?"

"Well, if you *are* alright, I'll go over and see what's behind the curtains. I mean, I'm sure the window's been boarded up, but it's got to be worth the try. No. On second thoughts, no.

"First of all, Gerry, let's listen. Listen. As hard as we can. Listen for anything, anything at all that might give us a clue where we are."

"Well, two reasons: first, because – you never know – one of those clues might just give us some kind of clue how to escape; second, because it might help the police later. After we've been released. Help them catch the crooks, the bad guys, those that are terrifying the living shit out of us. Out of me, anyway.

"Sorry. Language like that. What on earth would your father say? Don't tell him, okay? Christ, I'm in enough trouble with your father, anyway. Will be about a millionly more so once he hears about this mess without ... Well, you know very well without what."

Fuck you, Ewart. Yes, fuck you, and fuck too your intolerance - your bigotry, Ewart, your fucking, Ewart, priggishness. Yes, and fuck your unfairness too. You are so unfair. *So* unfair. So *unbelievably* unfair.

"Listen, Gerry, closely. Tightly. You know how you scrunched up your eyes, well scrunch your ears up like that." Fruit of my loins? Fruit, Ewart, of my loins? If any fruit, the rotten bloody apple that curdles the whole barrel.

"Well, I know you can't do that literally, clot. I keep telling you: I'm not that stupid. Well, perhaps I am, as a matter of fact. But let's – just for the moment – ignore that fact." 'Curdles': is that the right word? "Listen, Gerry, for anything. Anything at all ... a bird singing, a train clacking in the distance, the hooter from a factory, anything."

"Yes, a dog or a chicken. Anything like that. Anything too you can smell."

Son? Son of mine? Sharper than a serpent's tooth? Sharper than a surgeon's bloody scalpel.

"No, I know what you mean, I can't smell anything obvious either. It smells ... hot. That's the only word to describe it."

"Yes, it does, doesn't it? A bit dusty. A cobwebby sort of musty smell."

"Yes, a musty, dusty smell. Well done, Gerry, that's the way. Laugh as much as you can. Keep your spirits up, old chap, just as much as you can.

"Right, so ears and noses scrunched up? Let's have ... oh, I don't know ... a minute, say, maybe two, of just listening for the tiniest thing, smelling the most delicate ... what? ... pong, I suppose."

"Yes, ping's twin brother, you're absolutely right. Okay?

Okay? Ready, then, steady, go."

* * *

O dear God, o please God – God, if You're there, God – please, PLEASE, get us out of this. Christ, even I'm too young to die. Gerry? Gerry, God – 'case You hadn't noticed – he's barely started to live.

* * *

"Well?"

"Yes, I heard that too, a cock crowing. Some way off, though."

"Cicadas, yes."

"Yes, I heard that whatever it was somewhere else in the ... house, do you suppose it is?"

"Yes, it *does* feel like a house, doesn't it? What do you suppose that was? Pot falling, was it? Something heavy, anyway. Something like a saucepan or something."

"A radio, yes."

"Yes, also a long way off."

"A car radio. Yes, I think you're right. Anything else?"

"Smells?"

"That's onions, I think. Maybe someone's preparing supper. I hope so. I'm starving."

Starving? I couldn't eat a sodding thing.

"Okay, well, I didn't hear anything more than you. The wind, maybe, at one point. But that's not too helpful. As for smell, there *is* something, but I can't put my finger on it."

"Of course you can't put a finger, clot, on a smell. You know what I mean."

"There *is*, isn't there? And I mean something that's not

just the hot we were talking about earlier. Not just the musty dusty either."

"Or even, as you say, the *justy* musty dusty." ... Yes, you could eat, Titus. In fact, you *are*, Titus, starving. Mind over matter, old mate. To survive, you've got to eat. And Gerry's got to eat. You've got to get Gerry to eat. *Got* to get him to eat. He's not going to eat unless you do.

"Okay, next game: What do you remember of the trip here?"

"No, from the time they grabbed us."

"Same reasons as before, Gerry."

"How *many* men?"

"Only two, you think? You don't think they had someone else keeping watch or anything?"

"Well, fair enough, not that you saw. Fair enough. What about the men? Remember anything about them?"

"Big, right. Both of them?"

"Yes, that's what I remember too. Sort of Colombianly, yes. One had a moustache. Yes, a sort of droopy Guevara moustache, wasn't it?

"Anything else?"

"Scars? Tattoos? That sort of thing? Distinguishing features, they call them on passport do-dahs ... applications."

"No, me either. Not that I saw. We didn't really have a lot of time, did we? Bundled into the car as we were. And away. Handcuffs on. Blindfolds on. It was all so quick. Anything else? Jewellery, for instance?"

A second. Two. And all life has changed. The seconds it took between the bomb falling through the bay doors and landing on Hiroshima. The salmon wrenched from the water by a bear, the rabbit grabbed by an eagle. The violence of death. The second that divides it from life. The nanosecond, which was also the Big Bang.

"Watches, yes. Anything else? Well, rings, say? Or identity bracelets?"

"I know it was quick, Gerry. I was there, remember? Well, if you do think of anything else, don't keep it to yourself. And I'll let *you* know if *I* think of anything else. You never know, you see, what might be nudged by our memory in the memory of the other. And then, who knows?, that might be the very thing which helps us to get out of this place."

"Escape, yes, or persuade them to release us."

"Well, we'll never know, Gerry, unless we confide in the other one absolutely. I do mean, absolutely, old mate. Absolutely. We won't know until we're well out of this place what was useful information and what was useless." ... How many times did I promise myself that next year – definitely – I would start learning Spanish? ... "Which, by the way, is probably true of most of life. Okay, lecture over."

He doesn't need this crap, Titus. He needs loving, holding, reassuring. He doesn't need your philosophy on life. Be nice, Titus. For once in your miserable bloody existence, think – will you? – of someone other than yourself.

"I know you're hungry. And those onions certainly aren't helping. Never mind. Soon be eating. I'm sure of it. They smell, those onions, almost done to me."

"Alright, alright, yes, 'like I'm such a great chef', okay. Still, I *am* used to the smell of onions cooking. And those onions, they smell pretty nearly done to me. Just right for the eating."

"I'm sure there'll be other things, Gerry, as well as onions."

"I know you don't like onions. There'll be other things. Please don't go on about it. I'm *sure* there'll be other things. Please don't whine, there's a good chap."

"Sorry." ...Oh bravo, Titus. Well bloody done. That's

'reassuring', is it? And 'loving' and 'cosseting'? You really are, aren't you, so good at this thinking-about-other-people thing? ... "It just sounded ... well, just for the moment ... well, you know. Sorry. We're going to have to be so strong, Gerry, to get through this. So grown-up and so strong. Strong and grown-up like we've never been before – ever – in our life."

"Of course me too."

"Well, let me tell you a secret about grown-ups: Most of them, Gerry – most of *us*, I should probably say – aren't very. Grown-up, I mean."

"Yes, strange that, isn't it? Maybe, even a bit scary. But they're not: Most grown-ups are not grown up. Or rather, most grown-ups are grown-ups only some of the time."

And there are some like you, Titus, who, even grown-up, are only grown-up dolts, Titus. Grown-up imbeciles. Grown-up, Titus, arse-holes.

"Me? Oh, I'm afraid I'm a not-very-often a grown-up. There is a very rare species, getting rarer, known as the more-often-than-not grown-up. But they're highly endangered. Likely to become extinct any day. Likely, more like, to become eradicated. Extincted. By the pretend grown-ups. Because the pretend grown-ups, they're the most dangerous grown-ups of all. They don't like the realer, the more honest ones. They do everything in their power to try and eradicate them, the more-often- than-not grown-ups. They try to extinct them." He does not need to hear this, Titus. Will you just shut up for while! He does not need to hear this. "And they're succeeding.

"But what there isn't, Gerry, nowhere on the planet, there is no such thing as an always grown-up. Or a completely grown-up. Nowhere. That creature does not exist. Except in the fantasy of those selfsame pretend grown-ups, the really dangerous ones. The ones you have to be on your guard against before all others. The ones who will, if they suspect you may grow up to be a more-often-than-not a grown-up, will seek too to extinct *you.*

"Okay? Feeling a bit better now?"

'Course he is, genius. Exactly what you need when you're terrified out of your bloody skull: someone lecturing you about how rickety the bridge is on which you're crossing the bottomless chasm. In future, Titus, when I tell you – please – to shut up, will you *please* shut up!

"Shhh! Listen a second, old chap. Shhh, Gerry, for Christ's sake. Footsteps coming closer. I think, maybe, we should put these blindfolds back on again."

"Just do what I say, Gerry. PLEASE. Do it NOW."

* * *

"That sounds like a heavy old lock. Try to remember that, Gerry. That could be significant. Try to remember everything. It could all be signifi- ...

"Ah, *Beunas días. Bonjour. Sprechen Sie Englisch*? *Parlez Anglais*? *Inglés*? *Obrigado*? English? Anyone speak English? American, at a pinch? Rhyming slang? Australian?

"The blindfolds? These? We can take these off?"

"Okay, okay, okay, the blindfolds stay. Okay. You've made your point. Alright. Not a problem. *No problemo.* The blindfold, she stays. Fine. It's staying, see. See, my hands are miles away. *Manos.* Miles. Away."

"What's this? What's this? Ah, water. For me? Gerry, have you had some water? *Niño*, has he had some?"

"Oh, that's good. That is so good. You have no idea how good that is.

"No, don't take it away. Please. There was another swallow. Please don't take it ...

"Oh, you've filled it up again. Have you given Gerry a

second cup? *¿Niño, uno cupo más?* Have they given you a second cup, Gerry? Oh, thank you. *Merci. Muchas gracias. Obrigado. Grazia.* Just wonderful. Just delicious. *Dos vidanya. Efharisto. Danke, danke, merci.*

"Maybe a third cup? Please, sir, I'd like some more. You know, more? *Encore, encorra, noch einmal,* that sort of thing?

"What do you want me to do? You don't have to kick me, just tell me what you want me to do."

Do that again, you lump of shit, I'll throttle you with your own testicles.

"I think they want us to stand, Gerry."

"Gerry, are you standing? Yes, that's definitely what it is, they want us to stand."

"Okay, they're taking me some place. Gerry? They taking you too?"

Maybe if I'd studied judo or karate, or something ...

"Okay, okay. Icy-calm now, sweetheart. Icy-calm. Could be, could just be, they're taking us to the bossman or something." Oh right, Bruce Lee! God, Titus, when does the fantasy end?

"Gerry, you there? Could just be – ow! There's a step coming up, sweetheart, watch out for it. Shit! Make that two steps, Gerry. Okay, harsher light here. Linoleum floor is it? Something softer anyway. – Could just be the whole mess gets sorted out right there and then. They realise what a terrible mistake they've made and send us packing on our way.

"Okay, they're opening a door now.

"Jesus, what a smell!

"It's the loo, Gerry. They've taken us to the loo. I'd try to use it, tu'penny, if you possibly can. God knows when they'll let us out again. And I do mean 'use' it, Gerry, you know what I mean? Your tummy's bound to be a bit upset." The ultimate humiliation, the ultimate nightmare, the ultimate indignity reserved for old age: crapping in public. "All this excitement and things. All that jiggling around for hours in the back of that jeep or whatever it was."

I'd always thought, that'd be a torture, I'd always thought, reserved for the Old People's home. Incontinence bags, senility, the final impulsion to hurl you from the mortal coil. Not when I was hale. Not when I was sane. O God.

"Oh, thank you. *Merci.* All that. *Gracias.* They given you paper, Gerry? Loo paper? They could be telling us something, sweetheart. I know it's not easy. But do try.

"Even a flush. That's good, isn't it? Ah, and a tap. Very much more of this royal treatment and luxury we'll think, won't we, we really are at the Ritz or something?"

See how noble I'm being, God? How I'm thinking of others? Loving my neighbour, that whole bit? I do trust You're taking a note of all of this, reckoning I'm a really good egg, sort of idea, who deserves to live, whose death would be needless and premature. Just thought I'd check in with You.

"Did you manage, Gerry, to ... you know ...? No, I'm not going to ask that question. That's a question you ask a child, not someone who's now a young man. It doesn't matter, anyway. Whether you did or you didn't, you did well. It's very, very hard to meet humiliation with dignity. Very few people can do it. Read Oscar Wilde describing his journey to Reading Gaol. You did that, Gerry: met humiliation with dignity. And you deserve to feel very proud of yourself.

"This feels the same way back as the way we came. Does it feel like that to you too? Yes, I'm sure of it. Oh well, I guess no bossman, then. Not on this trip anyway. They're taking us back. Err, *scusi, le général? Führer? El Generalissimo? Il Duce?* There's been a mistake, see. Mistake. *Une erreur.* *Ein Mis*-something or other. What's

Spanish for mistake? Uno fuckupo. Oh, shit. *Vous ne voulez pas nous. Uns nicht. No* enemies ... *no enemigos. Amigos.* My *grandhijo* and *yo. Niño* and *yo*: *amigos.*

"Bastards! Son-of-a-bitch bastards!

"Heavy lock, what did I say? So, quick, details. What do you remember? Now. Whilst it's still fresh in our minds."

"Bright lights, that's one. A linoleum floor. How many guards do you think? I'd say four. Two each. Did you have two people touching you? How many people could you hear breathing? Or did you sense around you?"

"Certainly two guards, then, maybe four. One was wearing cheap aftershave. I mean, is there no *end* to these indignities? Did you smell that aftershave?"

"Hold that smell in your mind for a moment, Gerry. Or in your nose. Wherever it is you hold memories of smells. It could be significant. It could all be significant. There was that squeak on the floor. That probably means rubber-soles. Trainers, maybe. But was that rubber soles that I heard coming towards us down the corridor? Perhaps some of them have got boots. And boots, that probably means soldiers. But trainers, that probably means not-soldiers. Or does it? Christ, I don't know.

"Another thing I flunked at school: 'Things to remember when you're being kidnapped'. You didn't happen to take that course, did you?"

"Atta boy, that's the way. A good laugh, that's what'll always do it for you. Pull you through the awkwardest situations, see you through the toughest times. 'Awkwardest', where did that come from? English: something else I flunked at school.

"Flunked most things at school, point of fact. In fact, flunked school."

Flunked school? Flunked, Titus, the lot. The whole shebang. Flunked, Titus, life. Don't flunk this. Do not, Titus, flunk this.

"I don't think somehow I'm designed for living. Not in the conventional sense. I think when God was allocating tasks, He should, I don't know, probably have made me an abstract. You know, something wafting around in the ether somewhere, without having to concern myself with, oh I don't know, cooking breakfast and making the beds and stuff like that. I should have been, say, a thought. Yes, I'd have made a good thought. Or beauty. Better even, that, than a thought: The concept of beauty."

"Now, listen, Gerald, when I said that a good laugh was good for one, I did not mean when such laughs were at the expense of your beloved grandpapa, do I make myself clear?

"Go and listen at the door, tu'penny. See if you can hear anything. '*See* if you can *hear* anything'? Does that make sense? You know what I mean."

"Your ears are a lot younger than mine for one thing, Gerry, a lot sharper. If you can't hear anything, I was thinking we might take these blindfolds off again. But not till we know the coast is clear."

"Well, they didn't tell us, did they, to take them off? Unexploded bombs, Gerry, remember? And I think they would have done. If they'd wanted us to. Or, not even if they'd wanted us to, just if they'd allowed us to. Don't you think?"

"I'm sorry, Gerry. I'm getting a bit cranky. Sorry. It's been a long day. And I'm tired. I'm too old for this kind of carry on. Too old, Gerry, far too old. Just have a listen at the door, there's a good chap. See whether we can't take these blooming blindfolds off."...

"Well?"

"You can't hear anything. That's good enough for me.

"Oof, that's a relief. Must be awful, mustn't it, being permanently blind? It's bad enough being blind part of the time. It's horrible enough being blind part of the time.

"And still the onions simmer on.

"Sorry. I shouldn't have reminded you. I'm starving too. Can't be long now, though, can it?"

Oh Jesus Christ, will you stop fucking snivelling?! It's not my fault, you know, this. Any of this. Well, it *is* my fault. Of *course* it is. But, even so, it's not exactly, you know, a stroll in the park for me. Not for me either.

"I want to go home too, Gerry. But remember what we said? About us both, Gramps and Gerry, being stronger and grown-upper than we ever have been?"

"Well, we have to be.

"Gerry, come here. Sit next to me on the bed. That's it. Atta boy.

"Look at me, tu'penny. Gerry, we will get through this. You have to know that. We will get through it. We will survive. Know that, Gerry. Know that deep, deep, *deep* within you. Know that ... oh, I don't know ... like you know two and two equals four or that Jimmy Corbett is a real idiot."

"*Tommy* Corbett, I beg his pardon. Know it, Gerry, like you know I love you.

"And that your parents love you."

"Of course they do. Of course, tu'penny, they do. Know it at that kind of level. And if a moment comes when you lose that knowledge or forget it, then take a moment – take *another* moment, I should say – to remember it or reinforce it. 'I will survive this, Gerry,' tell yourself. 'I will come through it.'"

"It's not silly, old mate. Quite the contrary. It's important. It's really important. Try saying it now."

"I want you to say it, Gerry. I want you to say it now."

"What's there to feel silly about? There's only me here."

I'll kill you, you little shit. Break the habit of a lifetime and just do what I fucking well tell you, will you? Break the habit, you little shit, of an entire bloody lifetime.

"Okay, I'll say it first if that'll help. I will survive this, Titus. I will come through it. I *will* survive this, Titus. I *will* come through it. I will. I will."

"JUST SAY IT."

"Don't cry. I'm sorry, Gerry. Don't cry. Please don't cry. I didn't mean to shout. I told you I was feeling rattled."

Bravo again, Titus. Is there really no end to your parenting skills? Your patience, your insight, your acumen?

"Cranky, was it? Alright, cranky. I told you I was feeling cranky. Sorry. No, you don't have to stop crying. You just let them come, those tears." *No-one* ever did as they were told. Not your father. Not your aunt or your uncle. Certainly not your grandmother. No-one. Not one of the sods – not one of *you*. "They're not about me shouting at you. Not *just* about me shouting at you." Only time people did as I bid them? Work. Only place where I was boss. Which is why, I suppose, I used to like it so much. Why, anyway, I did when I *was* the boss. "That sounds as if I'm making excuses. And I'm not. I'm sorry I shouted at you." That's probably too why I made the money I did. Till your vultures, Emily, managed to spirit it all away in the settlement, of course.

"I shouldn't have shouted at you." So that all those sods – all *you* sods – could live the life of Reilly whilst never, ever, doing anything I asked them to! "But what you're crying about, that's not just about being shouted at. It's a bit too of being hungry, and being scared and hot, wanting to be home, wanting to be with your mummy, your daddy, all that."

Is that irony or is that irony?

"Of course you're scared. You'd have to be idiotic, as I said – you'd have to be *mad* or Tommy Corbett – not to be scared." ... O God, I really am not cut out for all this crap. Face it, Titus, you do not like children. It's not just a figment of your cynicism, it's *really* that you do not like children. And you *really* don't like them, what's more. ... "It's alright to be scared, Gerry. Really."

And to think this is how I'm going to die. It's like a vegetarian dying in an abattoir!

"Blindfolds, Gerry. Quickly. Quickly, for God's sake. Tie it tightly. Tightly. Okay, good boy. Well done. Icy-ca- ...

"Now, look here, my good man. I have, I think, been patient long enough. This situation is intolerable. Ah, water. Well, thank you. *Gracias* for the water. Gerry, you had water? *Gracias* too for Gerry's water. But the thing is this ...

"Ah!

"Ouch!

"Thank you. *Gracias*. Allowing me to take the blindfold off. This. *Gracias*. Hello, there. The name's Titus. No, not Oates, as you'd be expecting. Still less Grant. McLaughlin, point of fact. Which is a Scottish name. And you're right, there's not one syllable or decibel of Scottish in me. Still, what's in a name, eh?

"Really nifty, those balaclava helmets of yours. I hope you don't mind me being personal. Yves St Laurent, are they?

"See, the thing is, well, if it wouldn't be too much trouble, do you think, and at the risk of sounding too much like a Martian, you could – possibly – ... Take me to your leader?"

"No, it was a bad joke, that's all. Just a bad joke. What's this? I don't understand. What do you want me to do? I don't understand. What is it you want me to do? No, hold it." ... Shit! You berk, Titus! You total prat. ... "One second. Just one moment. The boy. You know, *garçon*, *niño*, can he, you know, take his blindfold – this: blindfold

– can the boy also take his blindfold off? Please? Blindfold off, like me, the boy? *El niño*?"

"Better, Gerry?"

"Thank you. *Dos vidanya. Efharisto.* Whatever. Thank you. *Gracias.* Remember, sweetheart, give your eyes time to adjust. Remember what we said: ten seconds closed, ten seconds open. The blindfold, remember, has been on an awfully long time.

"Yes, dear boy, I *have* noticed this grubby scrap of paper. You've jabbed me with it now at least a dozen times." ... **Careful, Titus. Really careful, sunshine. Can't afford to lose your temper. Can't afford to snap. ...** "What, I repeat, would you like me to do with it? You want my autograph, is that it? Am I supposed to compile a crossword on the back of it, blow my nose with it, eat it, what?

"Ah! A tape-recorder. You know what I think, Gerald? I think this paper contains a message I'm supposed to record on the tape-recorder. See, Gerry, you're supposed to say, 'Remarkable, Holmes' and then I reply ...?"

"That's right. 'Elementary, my dear Wat- ...' I can't make this out. Err, excuse me, I'm not Colin. Me, *moi, io* – no Colin. *Nicht* Colin. *Pas* Colin."

"Okay, okay, I'll be Colin. What's in a name? Just keep that gun, will you, away from me? Away from him as well. Particularly away from him. I jest not, my little freedom fighter, whatever the hell you are. You keep that gun away from my grandson. *Capische*? ...

"See, they *capische*.

"Seems we're Colin and Wictor, sweetheart. I think they mean Victor. Well, that's cleared that up, at any rate. They'll soon realise they've got hold of the wrong people, we'll be out of here within a matter of minutes. Certainly not more than an hour or so. A case of wrongful arrest, or something. Whatever it's called when the bad guys do it.

Wrongful abduction. ... Is there a rightful abduction?

"I read? You want me to read? I read this into this? Right, I read this into this. Thing is, Signor Marconi, not that I claim to be a technical wizard or anything, not an engineer of your brilliance and understanding, but I think the machine – the *macina* – before it can work, it has to be switched on. *Voilà. Bravo.* See, the little red light is on and the Geiger counter thingy, it swings backwards and forwards when I talk.

"Don't you ever dare criticise me again, Gerald, my lad, when I'm unable to set the video.

"You want me to talk now? You know talkie-talkie? *Parler? Sprechen? Maintenant?*

"Why is it, do you imagine, that I imagine they'll understand pidgin English any better than they'd understand proper English? BBC English, even? Would I understand pidgin Bengali better than BBC Bengali?

"The good old BBC. Right, right. This is the BBC Home Service with the ten o'clock news and this is Alvar Ladell reading it. No, can't be Alvar Ladell. You ever heard of Alvar Ladell? Alvar Ladell, young Gerald, used to read the news in the war – that's the Second World species of war – wearing, mark this, a bow-tie. I kid you not. Full dinner-suit and a bow-tie. For the radio. It's not that eccentricity's accepted by the English, it's more that it's endemic. A radio presenter wearing a dinner suit. Not today, mind. And there's a sort of sadness there ...

"Okay, okay.

"I think they want me to record now. Studio time, you know, it's so expensive, you've no idea.

"One for level?

"I saw this programme once about Broadcasting House and its workings. They were always asking for 'one for level', whatever that means. They went to the canteen, asked for a cup of tea, and the canteen lady asked for 'one for level'.

"No, you're right. Serious, serious. Okay, my man. We have lift-off.

"'Estimated Alan Dance...' He's a footballer, isn't he? Isn't he a footballer? Well, *why* don't you know?

"'This is I, Colin, your father. We and boy Wictor is safe. We is been well accommodated. You have needless to be fearful. Howsoever, captivators are not stupid and must have money. They need one million U.S. dollars in small dominations. Twenty and fifty dollar notes. If they do not have money they first kill me, then Wictor. Instructions will follow about where to leave money. This am serious. Do not telephone police. Your loving father, Colin.'

"Mark Twain could scarcely have written better.

"*Finito, mon Capitan*? You know, finished? *Das Ende*? All that? You can switch the machine – the *macina* – you can switch it off again now. Sorry. So-rry! Won't touch the precious thing, okay? See, I'm walking away from it.

"My actual name is Titus McLaughlin. I'm here with my grandson, Gerald. We desperately need help. Urgently. We don't know who are the abductors ...

"Oh, you've switched the machine off. Well, so I should think. In these days of energy conservation and things, no sense, is there, in being profligate? None at all.

"Excuse me. *Excuse* me: what about my fee? I understand they can command big bucks, people who record for commercials and stuff. Well, this is a sort of commercial, isn't it?

"Any chance of a book? You know, book? No, not book. A book in Spanish would be about as much use as a television in a power cut. Cards? You know, playing cards? We'd be so grateful for cards. Any old cards. Even not fifty-two of them. Maybe some paper. Some paper, you know, *papier,* like this – *comme ça*. To write on. *Ecrire*.

"Well, been nice seeing you. Don't be a stranger. Next time you're in the neighbourhood, you just make sure you ring our bell. You know where the front door is. Toodle-pip.

"The one wearing the after-shave he's the taller one. How tall would you say he is?"

"What's that in feet and inches?"

"Just over six feet? Yes, I'd agree with that. And the other one? About five nine, five ten, yes?"

"Right. Anything else? Let's call the taller one Robbie and the shorter one William."

"What's so funny about that?"

"Well, it's because it's a pop singer's name that I chose it. I thought, being a young man of very little brain, you'd find a pop singer's name easier to remember. Not as complicated as, say, Ludwig and Wolfgang. What did William smell of?"

"Well, besides B.O., let's say. Did you smell nicotine on him?"

"Well, I did. I'm sure he's a smoker. Sure of it. And they were both wearing trainers, right? So, who has the boots?"

"Still, we're out of the blindfolds. Officially, I mean. That's one good thing, I suppose. That has to be one good thing.

"Christ, boots again. I can hear boots again. Christ, coming towards us. That lock, it's like an alarm bell. Who is it wearing boots?"

"Okay, okay.

"They want us to put our blindfolds on, Gerry. Do it, Gerry. Do it now. Don't try to be clever, sweetheart, leave peep-holes or anything. Something's happened.

"Ow!

"They want to handcuff us again. Put your hands out in front of you. Do it now, sweetheart.

"Alright, alright, I'm coming. Please don't push.

"I think they're taking us somewhere, Gerry. Maybe

they've realised their mistake. They're going to take us somewhere away from here, from their hide-out, somewhere well away so we can't let the cops know where we've been, and then they're going to release us, Gerry. Yes, that's what's going to happen: they're going to release us, Gerry. Going to let us go.

"Gerry? Gerry?

"*Gerry*?

"Where is my grandson? *El niño, donde es? Mon grandfils? Grandsohn? Ragazzo*?

"I'm not going anywhere, sunshine, that I can promise you, not without my grandson. You can push me and shove me as much as you like. *Gerry*?

"Me, not go fucking no fucking place, man, not without boy. Capische? You'd better fucking capische. You fucking capische you fucking son-of-a-bitch heap-of-shit son-of-a-bitch?

"Gerry? Gerry, that you?"

"Okay, sweetheart. We're okay. We're back together. Alright. Okay, sweetheart. It's alright.

"That how you get your kicks, is it, big boy? Frightening someone half your size half to fuc- ..., half to death? Make you feel good, does it? Make you feel like a big, brave freedom fighter or something?

"Whatever you're fighting for, sunshine, whatever morsel of justice or retribution or whatever the hell else it is you just lost it. Don't you understand that? You just completely blew it.

"You know something else?, I don't care. I don't care any more what you intend to do to us or with us, or whatever it is, the use we're supposed to fill. It doesn't matter. Whatever it is, it's got to be worthless.

"And I don't care either any longer that you can't understand what I'm saying. You understand that? Because maybe, just maybe, my tone of voice will get through to you, penetrate those moronic muffs you call ears. You ever – you hear me? – *ever* try to separate me again from my grandson then the hell you'll have to pay, my friend, will make the hell of Calvinist legend seem like a tiptoe through foam-rubbered tulips.

“Okay, Gerry. You're okay. We're going to be okay.

“Don't you prod me. We'll go when we're ready. When *we're* ready, you understand? You frighten us half to death. We need time to recover, we need time to adjust.

“Okay? Okay, Gerald? You say. You just say. We won't move till you say it's okay to do so. Alright? You sure you're alright? Alright, then.

“Very well, my good man, lead the way. ‘Lead on, Mac-...’ No, better not. It's supposed to be unlucky, isn't it?, quoting from ‘Mac-...’, from ‘The Scottish Play’, as the luvvies call it. Normally I just think of these things as fanciful nonsense. Well, you know that. I've said it often enough. Just right at the moment, though, I see very little point in pushing our luck. Not in any direction. Want me to convert me to the cult of the Incan god for Finding-lost-cufflinks? Now would be a good time to approach me.

“We're a bit like a gherkin, really, in a jar of vinegared walnuts: hard to think how we could be more in a pickle. But somewhere in the world there's a bloody great vat of piccalilli. And with our name on it. Why push our luck, eh, Gerry? Why, my dear boy, push our luck?

“Try to keep your ears open. In the truck, I mean, in the jeep, whatever it is. It's not easy, I know. It makes so much noise, the damn thing, it's hard enough to hear yourself think. But do try, Gerry. When we're idling, say, at lights or stuff. Anything like that. It could be important. It could be *vital.* A factory hooter or a train whistle, water falling into a fountain, anything. And keep your nose open too. Hard when all you can smell is petrol. But you never know. A good healthy whiff of cow manure or something, or freshly baked bread extracted from a supermarket. Anything, sweetheart, anything at all.

"Have I told you yet how well you're handling all this?"

"Well, you're doing brilliantly, sweetheart. Just brilliantly. Better than brilliantly – super-brilliantly. You always make me so proud of you, Gerry. Always. But this, how you're handling this, *that*, sweetheart, is something else again.

"Fresh air!

"Don't worry that they're putting a gag in. Really. It's uncomfortable, I know, tu'penny, but they'll take it off again at the other end. You know that.

"Listen, Gerry. Smell."

* * *

Ow! Jesus, if this truck jolts one more time ...

What, Titus? What are you going to do about it? What the fuck are you going to do about it? Write an indignant letter to 'The Times'? What?

Well, I think I might be sick, that for a starter.

You are not going to be sick. You cannot be sick. You just can't afford to be. Mind over matter, old mate. You've got a gag in. If you gag with a gag, you could drown in your own vomit. – Yeah, and that, dear Titus, is a gag to gag *on*! – Or choke on it, your vomit, you pillock. You are not going to be sick. And you are not going to die. You're too young to die, for God's sake. And for Gerry's sake. You've got to keep alive for Gerry, Titus. You've just got to. If for no other reason, then keep alive for him.

Sod that for a row of soldiers. I've also got to keep alive for numero uno here, for yours truly, for li'l ol' me. 'Gag to gag on'! I cannot believe I said that!

* * *

"Shhhhh!

"Sorry, sweetheart, I wanted to listen for the lock. Shh!

"For footsteps. Hear the footsteps. You never know when we might not need an alarm system. Some sort of alarm system. No, not alarm system, that's not what I meant: early warning system, rather."

...

"Okay, they've gone. I think they've gone. How long do you think the drive took us? No, that's a pointless question. We don't know where we came from, so it's completely irrelevant. Motorway-y roads for, what'd you say, twenty minutes?"

"Okay, fifteen, twenty minutes.

"Hold it. Shh! Yes, they're coming back. Christ! You can barely hear them. We'll have to be a lot quieter here, a lot more careful.

"Thank you. Thank you. *Gracias. Muchas gracias.*

"There, that's better, Gerry, isn't it? Out of those horrid handcuffs, that awful blindfold. How's my hair? In a right old state, I'd imagine. A right old 'two-and-eight', as the Cockneys say."

"Well, two-and-eight was tuppence more than half-a-crown in the old days of money. Before decimalisation, all that. You won't remember. Probably, your father, even he won't remember. God, you know *I* can't remember. The date, anyway, of decimalisation. Was it the '60's? Yes, late '60's. No, your father wouldn't remember it. The oh-so-much-less-swinging '60's than they were vaunted. For me, at least. The '60's for me managed a few feeble oscillations, but they never got close to a swing. Not a swing, anyway, worthy of the name.

"Err, *scusi*: cards? And paper? For *écrire*, for *escribir*, rather? You remember, cards? Cards, you know, for playing and things. 'Alice in Wonderland', all that bit. Or was it 'Through the Looking-Glass'? You know, pay 21's, pontoons and five-card tricks. Cards. 'Cincinnati Kid', you know. 'Bridge Over Troubled Water'? That was meant to be a joke there, Gerry. Funny, there's no great bridge novels, are there?"

"Yes, alright, 'funny' unlike my joke."

"'Bridge Over The River Kwai' was a film, clot."

"That doesn't count, that's plural: 'Bridges ...', my dear, '...of Madison County'.

"Robbie? Robbie, my friend, a word in your shell-like. Robbie, me Titus. *Io* Ti-tus. Me. You? Me, *io* Colin. *Vous*? *Usted*? *Was hessen du*?

"About as talkative as a Trappist monkfish. Yeah, yeah, thanks for the ride. A cup of tea would go down well. Earl Grey with a slice of lemon. Cooking tea for the young man. About three kilos of sugar. Water? You know, water? *Agua*?"

"What?"

"I don't understand. *What*?" ...

"We——ll, en suite bathroom, no less. Well, well, luxury indeed. Real luxury. I suppose it'd be too much to hope, something to drink the water with. *Basa*? *Un varre*?"

"No. Slurp. We'll slurp, Gerald, you and I. Slurp."

"Yes, straight from the tap."

"Well, that's just a risk, Gerry, we'll have to take. You have to drink, tu'penny. You just have to. You're a good slurper, no?"

"Well, let's see you do it, then."

Jesus! What's this pain in my back? Christ, that hurts. It's from being cooped up like that, that's for sure, trussed like that, like a Christmas sodding turkey. Christ, does that hurt!

"Alright, I suppose. An okay sort of a slurp. You want to

see whether you can do any better. Well, I don't want to show you up. I was considered in my youth, well, quite something when it came to slurping.

"There, that's better, no? A quick rinse of the face and hands too? I don't think that would do any harm."

"Just wipe them on your shirt, or your trousers. Don't worry about it. In this heat, it'll soon dry by itself. Okay, now make way for the master." **This should be interesting, bending over a basin with this back. This could be the moment the whole thing seizes up. Mind over matter, Titus. Here goes nothing, I suppose.** "I did warn you, did I, that I used to be pretty good? Well, some things, you know, never die. Some habits, some aptitudes....

"There! What d'you think of that? Was that a slurp or was that a slurp?" **Christ! Made it. All the way down *and* back again! Well, well, things are looking up.**

"Nah, that's just jealousy talking. I told you: I was the school champion. Slurped for the county once. People said of my slurping, if I disciplined myself, if I took the training schedule, like, really seriously, it wasn't beyond the bounds of possibility that one day I might slurp for England. I might even represent Britain in the slurp Olympics.

"You want another go?"

"Well, now it's right next door, we really don't need to bust a gut, do we?

"Very nice, my man. We'll take it. Oh and if you'd be so good as to have Room Service send up, oh I don't know, say a small Filet Mignon, *saignant*, maybe a Salade Niçoise, a bottle of Burgundy. A good one. I'll leave the choice up to you. Oh, and a few lettuce leaves for my hedgehog friend here. Thank you so very much.

"Food. Seriously, *amigo*. Food. *Comida*. *Essen*. Anything. *Paquette de* crisps. Uno Marso baro. Anything.

Locusts dipped in honey."

"What's the matter? You don't like locusts dipped in honey? What's the matter with you, kid? How has your mother brung you up, for goodness' sakes? A million housewives every day/ Pick up a tin of food and say: 'Oh, yummy: It's locusts and honey.' Actually that worked rather better than I would ever have dreamed it would. Think I could sell it to Heinz?

"Oh, going so soon? Well, don't rush back. Or, if you do rush back, rush back with food. *Ciao-ao-ao-ao.*"

Shit! This back. I think I've really done something to it!

"Okay, only one rather feeble lock. My guess is that means they've got another one of them sitting the other side of the door. It'd be too easy otherwise. Your ears are better than mine. Put your ear to the door. See if you can hear anyone, I don't know, breathing or anything. Scratching his head. Or farting."

"What's gross about farting? As a general principle, I mean? There are some specific farts, that I grant you, grossissimus maximus. Remember Ezra? Maybe you were too young. He was my dog. Died when you were ... what? About four, I suppose."

"Why Ezra? Because we got him from the pound. Another bad joke, I'm afraid. And which sort of stuck."

"You've never heard of Ezra Pound? Well, you should be ashamed of yourself, young man." And how much Ezra Pound have you actually read, Titus? What was that? One whole poem, did you say? Maybe a poem-and-a-half? "Well?"

"Yes, that's what I thought. They'd be bound to leave someone there. Just to discourage us, kind of thing.

"What a farter he was, dear old Ezra. Especially, so it seemed, after Winalot. Or was it rabbit? Poor Ezra. I still miss him. Oh, I know people sneer at a pet's death, but those that do – I can't help feeling – have never had one. I doubt it, anyway. And people who've never had pets ... well, there's something lacking in most of them. They end up as very peculiar people. Prime Ministers of England and such like.

"So? Back to the trip. What do you remember?

"These are shutters. Fastened – yes, they would be – from the outside. Oh, and hark: a tweety bird. We must be in Berkeley Square. What are you talking about, Titus? It's only nightingales sing in Berkeley Square – and then only in Fred Astaire songs. See, Gerry? Me, heap big ornithologist. Me know all things pertaining to feathered friends. Like when birdies cheep that usually means garden. And garden usually means not-town.

"God, Hollywood owes Indians ... owes Native Americans one great big apology. A huge great big apology. And why, young Gerald, my lad, did I just start talking in that nonsense way? Me heap big thick as a plank sort of numbskull.

"The trip. We must remember the trip.

"My guess is we're on the first floor ..."

"What do you mean, 'Oh, well done, Gramps'?"

"Well, we could have climbed up from a basement, couldn't we, smarty-pants?"

"Okay, okay, point taken. Whatever. The first floor of a fairly big suburban house. There's none of those ripe country smells, are there? No cocks crowing, or any of that. You know, country noises. It's probably been rented. It's in good decorative order, as the agents doubtless said. But, see, it lacks titbits. Pictures on the wall, ornaments on the bedside tables. It's all very clean, very antiseptic. Very bland. To be rented.

"Trip.

"About twenty minutes or so ..."

"Okay, fifteen minutes or so motorway or, anyway, fast

road. Then, what? Ten minutes slower road? You think that was traffic lights we stopped at or a 'Give Way' sign?"

"I agree. Too long a wait for a 'Give Way' sign.

"One roundabout, definitely."

"Two, you think?"

"Okay, certainly one, maybe two roundabouts. Then a track for ..."

"Well, yes, it felt like hours, I agree. What do you think actually? Five minutes? No more than ten."

"It's important, Gerry. Say, somewhere between five and ten minutes. And then road again. Which is a bit curious. For, what, about another five minutes?"

"Right, and then we were here."

"Did you hear gravel? When we parked, did you hear gravel?"

"No, neither did I. Not a pavement either. It's some kind of tarmacked drive, then. Quite posh, in that case.

"Like this room. Quite posh without being super-posh. Sort of middle-of-the-road posh. Not Bentley posh. But not clapped-out Cortina posh either. Sort of Saab posh. Would you agree?"

"Right. Smell?"

"Me either. That blooming diesel fuel, all I could smell was that. All I can *still* smell, come to that.

"I suppose none of that's very helpful. Not really. But I suppose too we won't know how helpful or not it's been until we're helping, as they say, the police with their inquiries. I suppose the good guys can do that as well. Help the police, I mean, with their inquiries."

...

Hush! I hear dew stippling a marigold, I hear a rain-drop cascading down a daffodil. And I can hear you whisper, Valentine, that you love me. And just for an instant, lover, I have the taste of you upon my tongue, and have you infusing within me like tea-

leaves in a pot. And, just for an instant, lover, the world again is a haven, a place where cares are kissed away and pain becomes the crackling of the Sunday roast. Just one touch, Valentine, and I have again the strength to keep on fighting. Good night, sweet lover. Dream of me.

"Sorry, I was just thinking. Remembering, more accurately. Ezra's farts. Yes. God, they were lethal. They could kill a man, they could, at a hundred paces. We should have sold them to the Ministry of Defence. Think what the country could have saved on Trident and Exocets and all those other monstrosities. One quick fart from Ezra, old Saddam would have had his hands up in the air, pulled out of Kuwait, given back his private collection of Bruce Lee videos – or, even more treasured, the copy his mother gave him of 'Little Women'.

"I am starving. Starving. How about you?"

"There's nothing like a good kidnap to get the gastric juices going. I am *starving.*

"Definitely an improvement on the last place. Definitely. A big improvement. Bed's more comfortable as well. A lot more comfortable. Won't be the first time we've shared a bed, will it? You still wriggle as much as you used to?"

"You *didn't* wriggle?! *You*?! You made the average python look like a Grenadier Guard laid into cement. You made the wriggly worm of song seem like a steel girder."

"Wiggly, wriggly, what's an 'r' between friends?

"Well, in that case, thinking about it, friends would become fiends. But, hey? What's an 'r' between fiends? 'Wiggly', on the other hand, and 'wriggly' are pretty, I'd have thought, interchangeable. And 'wiggly' or 'wriggly', you, my dear friend, were the world champion. In supremis. Wigglius maximus.

"Blindfolds. Now. Squeak. Trainers' squeak. *Now,* Gerry.

"What did I tell you? They're getting sneakier."

"What?"

"Yes, *squeakier* and sneakier, very good."

"You're quite right: They did say we could take them off. Good thinking, Batman. You're absolutely right. Blindfolds off, Gerry.

"Do you smell anything?

"I think they may be bringing us food. Not before time, you're telling yourself. You hungry, Gerry? I'm starving, me. You hungry?

"Ah, *buenas* ... whatever. Evening, I suppose. I'd always been led to believe Room Service knocked at the door prior to entering, but far be it from me to squash local traditions, trammel them or question them or anything.

"No, that's alright, just clank it down anywhere. No, *gracias, gracias.* Oh, and paper! Treasure trove indeed. Even a pencil. Thank you for that. *Muchas, muchas gracias.*

"I trust the champagne has been properly chilled, and that the caviar has indeed sturgeoned its way here all the way from Beluga. I'll just give you one global tip, if I may, at the end of our stay. Which reminds me ... If you could just ask Reception to prepare our bill. What I should have said, of course, was at the imminent end of our stay, at the extremely imminent end of it.

"*Gracias, gracias. Scusi. El generalissimo*? *Parler* with *el generalissimmo*? Hablar*! Hablar* with *el generalissimo*? *Yo* and *generalissimo hablar* together, *si*? *Por favor*?

"No-one ever tell you it was rude to slam doors? Peasant! Brought up in fields, some people.

"Okay, then, let's see what delicacy they might have brought to tempt the jaded palate. It has got some onions in it, Gerry. I can smell them. Still, we can scrape round them or something.

"Well ...

"You know Esau sold his brother his birthright for a mess of potage? I think Esau might have left them his recipe. Still, it probably tastes better than it looks. Look at it this way – look at the bright side – it could scarcely taste worse."

"You are eating it, Gerry."

"I don't care what it looks like. You are eating it, tu'penny. On this there is no debate. There can be none. You have to eat it."

Oh God, I am so tired. *So* tired. And this sodding back's not getting any better! Suffer the little children? *Suffer* the little buggers? Wasn't that what You said? What about the suffering the little buggers cause *us*?

"We're going to need our strength, all our strength, Gerry, to get us through the next hours, maybe even the next day or two. Look, *I'm* eating it. It's actually *not* as bad as it looks. You have to eat it, Gerry. You *have* to eat it."

Hey, you guys. Ho, you guards out there. You want to come back? Take the little fucker out and shoot him? Just so you know, that'd be okay with me. Perfectly okay.

"Remember I said earlier these are not normal times? There would be times, remember me telling you, when you would just *have* to do what I said? Remember that?

No, maybe shooting's too quick. Make it preferably a lingering death. If you'd be so kind. Don't throw him on the pyre, but on the barbecue. Even better, dip him in honey, plonk him on an ant-hill!

"Remember the considered tones in which I told you that?"

"Well, this is one of those occasions, Gerry."

"JUST DAMN WELL EAT IT."

Please don't cry. I can't bear it when you cry. It rips through me, your crying, like a carving knife. One with a serrated edge ...

"You can cry as much as you like. You have to eat it. You have to eat. You just have to. It's about surviving, finally. It's about knowing, yes, we will get through this. We will survive. Remember that?

"And we will survive it, Gerry. We will. You have to remember that. But we do have to help ourselves. It's not going to happen by magic, or by *wanting* it to happen. We have to *commit* to surviving and then do everything in our power to ensure it happens. That's our end of the bargain, if you like."

"Well, even if you don't, I'm afraid.

"Go on, keep on crying. I'm not going to bend. I'm not going to soften. Not on that. You are going to eat, Gerry, even if I have to force-feed you. You are, Gerry, going to eat."

"I may very well be a bastard. Your father seems to share that opinion. Pity your great-granny's not around any longer or we could get it straight from the horse's mouth. And whether or not I'm a bastard does nothing as far as your intake of food is concerned. It doesn't alter the case one jot, Gerry, not one bloody iota."

"Yes, you probably do hate me. That's okay. Hate me as much as you like. Only you will hate me, Gerry, you will, with a full tummy. That much I promise you. Understood?"

"Oh, I think you should. I think the NSPCC would be very interested. They'll probably be fairly interested in why I thought taking a child for a walk in downtown Bogotá was a sensible thing to do as well. I'll tell you something, Gerry: I'll be delighted when the NSPCC throws the book at me. Know why? Because that'll mean we're at home again. And you won't have died of starvation or anything. JUST EAT."

See the thing is, Ewart ... well, I needed some time alone with the boy. I mean, it's not much of a relationship you've *allowed* us to have. I wanted ... I just wanted ... it's not unreasonable, as a thing, to want, is it? ... even to expect? ... 'Quality time,' as I think they call it. Today. The Oprahmans. 'Quality time' ... it's not unreasonable to seek some quality time with your grandchildren. Your grandchild. -son. Mine.

Oh God, Ewart, I am so sorry.

"No, of course it's not very good. Look at it. How could it possibly be good? But it isn't – and this I assure you – as *bad* as it looks. Not nearly as bad as it looks."

"I don't want to alarm you, but just think, what if this is the special treat they've prepared for us as a celebration or something of our first night? Me, I think you might well be well advised to eat whilst the going's good. God knows what fare we might receive on the morrow.

"There. That didn't kill you, did it?"

"Well, it hasn't killed you yet. Swallow it, Gerry."

"I don't care *how* you get it down, but swallow it you will."

"Even if you *are* sick. In fact, if you're going to be sick it's important to get even more into your stomach. Food is energy, Gerry, and energy is strength."

"Yes, I did, as a matter of fact, flunk science at school. You're quite right. Clever clogs. But, even in those subjects we flunk, something sticks. Like mud, I suppose. Mud is supposed to stick, isn't it?

"That's the way, tu'penny: Shovel it in. See, you've eaten half of it already. See, it'll all be eaten before you know it.

"Try not to bolt it, though, there's a good chap. I mean, no point in being sick, is there, just for the hell of it, as it were? If you don't have to be, I mean? Just think how much better Mummy's food's going to taste after this."

Hang, draw and quarter the fucker.

"No, I wasn't being rude about her cooking. It's very

good, your mummy's cooking. *She's* very good, a very good woman. She's very precious to me, Gerry. Just because your father and I can't get along together any longer, don't think – *ever* think – I don't love your parents. Because I do. It's just ... Well, you know what it's just. No need to lay it on with a trowel, eh?"

I never wanted to hurt you, Ewart. Never. I never wanted to hurt anyone. I didn't choose to be gay, you bastard. It's not like I sought it out, turned myself inside out or anything to be gay. And it wasn't anything either that I'd consciously repressed. To begin with, all it was, it was *just* a friendship. I didn't know how it was developing – that it had already, in fact, developed. Cut me some slack here, Ewart. For Christ's sake.

"'Mum'?"

"Since when?"

"Oh, childish, I see. And does 'Mum' know about this?"

"And how is she about it?"

"Well, if 'Mum's' okay about being 'Mum' and not 'Mummy', I suppose it would be churlish of me not also to be. Alright about it."

"No, just kidding. 'Mum's' fine with me. Absolutely fine. Not that it's got anything to do with me. I mean, if that's what you want to call her and that's what she wants you to call her then my opinion on the matter is, as they say, completely irrelevant. You could call her ... oh ... 'baggy bum' if you wanted."

"Well, I know she hasn't got a baggy bum, Gerry. It was a joke, Gerry, that's all. A figure of speech, a bit of fun." **For Christ's sake, kid!!!** "An attempt to levitate the atmosphere. Do I mean levitate? Lighten! An attempt, rather, to lighten the atmosphere, to lift the mood. A random phrase, one I just picked out of the air. I didn't mean anything by it.

"I think you're getting tired, Gerry, getting – as you said of me – cranky. I think, as soon as we've finished supper, we should get ready for bed." ... Maybe I could just murder him in his sleep! ... "I have not been picking on Mummy – on, excuse me, Mum. I have no reason to pick on her. She is, for the hundredth time, a very good woman. I would have no reason to."

"No, you haven't had enough. You've just been pushing the food round on your plate. I'm not that stupid, Gerry. Or that blind."

"Okay, five spoonfuls more and we'll consider it done. But I do mean *real* spoonfuls, Gerry, not just a couple of grains of rice."

"Yes, that's a spoonful. Well done."

"And that's another spoonful. You're doing well, old mate, doing very well.

"That's a third, very good."

"Just try one more, then. We'll forget the fifth spoonful, just have one more. Bravo. Well done.

"Okay, now you can have the orange. See, I even peeled it for you.

"Well, they can't make an orange taste yucky, can they? Here it is. Fresh from the peel.

"Good?

"Juicy, anyway. The way it's running down your chin. You want the other one?"

"No, we'll just keep it for breakfast, then. Just in case, sort of thing. We don't yet know what their routine is, do we? Maybe we only get one meal a day."

"Oh, old crocks like me, we don't need vitamin C. Not in the way that you young people do."

I'd kill for that orange, you little shit. *Kill* for it. It's not only that the young are so selfish, it's that they're also so bloody prodigal with their selfishness!

"Tell you what, you go and wash your face and hands, get all that orange juice off your chin, and we'll talk about it. Try and scrape your finger too across your teeth. You know what I mean? Pretend your finger's a toothbrush. It's not very effective, truthfully, but it's better than nothing."

'And now I lay me down to sleep/ I pray the Lord ...' What made me think of that? What on Earth made me think of that? Jesus, *I* want Mummy. My mummy. I want Mummy to fix it all for me, make it all alright. I'm an old man.

No, no, you're not, Titus. You're five years old and you want your mummy to make the bogeyman go away. It's the body that's an old man's – an old queen's! Not the courage. Certainly not the wisdom. Oh God, wisdom. The quotes 'wisdom'. Yeah, whatever happened to that?

"Better?"

"I think we should get ready for bed now, tu'penny. They don't seem to have supplied any pyjamas, I'd suggest you sleep just in your pants."

"Yes, I think that's how I will sleep. Who knows how cold the night might be? We may need our clothes as sort of blankets."

"Like the food, Gerry, they might be better than nothing. You remember the commitment we made to our survival? Well, remember too that that commitment requires us to do *our* part."

"Okay? How's it feel?"

"It's been a hard day, Gerry. A tough, tough day. Very few people ever had to get through days, Gerry, like the day we've had, Gerry, you and I, today. And you've done well. You've done wonderfully well. And I'd imagine you'll sleep like a log. But if you don't for any reason, then wake me up. Don't be lonely. Not on top of everything else. I won't be cross with you. That I promise. You just wake me up."

Please don't wake me up. You have no idea how desperately I need to sleep. Please just let me sleep, Gerry.

“I hadn’t forgotten. I was coming to that.”

“Well, I keep thinking – the situation’s so absurd – I keep thinking they’re going to come to the door, apologise for their ghastly mistake, drive us into town somewhere and release us. I keep thinking, in two or three hours, all this, it’ll just be one hideous memory.

“But, yes, we also have to face up to the fact that that might not happen, that their fantasy will continue, that we are indeed Colin and Wictor. Father and son of some unknown footballer ... ”

“Of some *well-known* footballer, I stand corrected. I thought you’d never heard of him.”

“Oh, teasing, is that right? Oh great, and just to put the icing on the cake, now I just heard a mosquito! Presumably, therefore, this Alan Dance is worth a bob or two. We have to be ready for the long haul, in other words. Hope for the best, but be prepared for the worst. Which, thinking about it, is no bad recipe for life in general.”

“Don’t even start down that path, Gerry. Just excise it. Do you know what ‘excise’ means?”

“Cut it out. Cut it out of your thinking, old mate. There’s no way of knowing how long we’ll be here. You’ll just drive yourself bananas.

“At least *we* know we’re *safe*. Think how it must be for those people – Mum and Daddy and the like – who have no idea. How much better off are we, Gerry, than they are.”

‘And now I lay me down to sleep ...’ Help me, Mummy, help me. Help me, God. For God’s sake, something out there, please – PLEASE – help me. Jesus, my eyes are closing. I just can’t keep them open.

“Remember what I told you earlier, remember to tell yourself that: ‘We will survive this, Gerry. We will come through.’”

* * *

Day 6

Dear Gerry,

There is the merest sliver of moonlight, so my writing - never good - may be completely indecipherable. I'm sure it'll be a struggle for you to decode it. You'd better make that struggle, though, you little bastard. It's hard work, this. Bloody hard work, actually. On top of which the night is sticky, the air full of mosquitoes. I'm trying to kill all those seeking to bite you, and you just snore on, oblivious. I haven't shaved in days, and this beard is both incredibly itchy, and ... well ... magnetic: I can't stop stroking it, tugging at it, scraping it along my fingers. It's driving me CRAZY – crazier even than the sodding mosquitoes. *I hope the struggle is worthwhile.*

still

You're sleeping now, Gerry. It's / such a pleasure to watch you sleep. If there is anything to pray to (and I guess I'm soon going to find that one out!), then I pray that one day you too will experience the joy - no, the ***rapture*** *- which is watching your grandchild sleeping.* Lay it on with a trowel, why don't you, Titus? Make sure your loving is as eloquent as it was invisible! Go for it, my man! *When your father was a child, I was always too busy.* Oh, very hip, Titus: 'Go for it, my man!' Very street cred. *Sure there were times (not too many, but certainly* ***some*** *times) when I saw him asleep. But I never* ***watched*** *him sleeping. My body was there, but my head was out doing deals or wondering about new premises or finding fault with my business partners or the local authorities* *or the tax people or a recalcitrant client or whatever.* Yeah! That's what's called 'living', kid. And *making* a living. Providing a home, a homestead, putting food on the table. It's something grown-ups do.

A painter I know (actually not a very good one, but that's by-the-by) once told me that the only way to appreciate a work of art is from the inside out. What was that? Someone coming? What? Quiet now, Titus. Quieten your thoughts, those as well. Shhh now. ... No. Something outside the window. A night bird or something, maybe a bat. Okay? Listen, damn you. ... Okay. ... *You can observe a painting from without, but in order to appreciate it, you have to be inside it, and let it wash all over you, let it - Gerry - absorb you. It's the difference, if you like, between sympathy and empathy. Well, I think that's true of a lot of life. We notice things without seeing them. I noticed your father sleep as a child. But it has only been with you, Gerry, that I noticed sleep. The sleep of a child. The sleep, in your case, of a young man. Which seems to be such total peace. And yet ...*

As a child of ... about 7, I suppose, maybe even younger, certainly a lot younger than you are today, I used to have nightmares. I was in a tunnel, running I have no idea where. 'Jogging,' it'd be called today. The term then didn't exist. But it was an easy run. I'd call it a 'fun run', except (as you know) physical exercise has never been something from which I have derived any 'fun'. Then either. Be that as it may, I'm lolloping along when suddenly, and terrifyingly, out springs a lion. All teeth and snarling and enormous claws - enormous claws on enormous paws - all intent on killing me. Oh, writing it like this, it appears to be nothing. Funny, even. But it was terrifying, the dream, a full-throated nightmare. The lion kept chasing me till, screaming, I awoke. It was probably, thinking about it now, probably the screaming that awoke me. 'Full-throated' was, thinking about <u>that</u>, even more of an appropriate adjective than I intended. I was drenched in sweat. ... I mean, I was <u>drenched</u> in sweat. I had that dream many times.

I wonder (and this is the point) whether anyone watching the 7-year-old me asleep, Gerry, would have thought there was someone basking in perfect peace. Oh, I know, during the nightmare I'd have been thrashing about. But there would have been a point, prior that that, when (as it were) I was <u>preparing</u> for the nightmare, that I seemed to be at perfect peace. And how far into the nightmare had I wandered before I started thrashing? And how true is that of life itself?

Having now written that, I cannot count the numbers of ways in which that is a bad analogy. First of all, there <u>would</u> have been indications of fretfulness in my sleep before I got to the complete horror of the nightmare. Secondly, I had no idea then, and continue to have no idea to this day, what caused the nightmare. When I was asked, in other words, how I was and I replied "fine", I wasn't being evasive. I really thought I <u>was</u> fine.

What I was trying to say, what that analogy singularly failed to say, the question I was trying to pose was this, Are we all of us like the famous swans: on the surface serene, but underwater flapping frantically - like demented and half-starved fledglings?

I suspect we are. I suspect, I mean, that that is something common to almost all of us. And I further suspect that the biggest single communal sin we have committed against our own species is in not acknowledging that. Honesty, you see, is less about stealing sweets from sweet shops (not, you understand, that I would be condoning, or even countenancing, such larceny) than it has to do with being truthful to ourselves about ourselves. Because finally it is only about that that we can be truthful.

* * *

"Ah, *buenas días, amigo mio. Bien? Usted bien?*"

"*Bien, bien. La cosa es, amigo mio*, it's been a week – *una semana* – and still we haven't *hablar*-ed *con el generalissimo. Hablar, generalissimo y yo, no.*"

"*Mañana*, eh? Yea, *mañana* and *mañana* and *mañana*, the pace it creeps on, it really is pretty petty, let me tell you. Okay, what delights have you brought us this morning?

"Well, well, is that mangoes? Oranges? Oh, and bananas. Well, yummy, yummy, yummy. Not bad, eh, Gerry?

"*Momento, momento*. The boy – *el niño* – he needs exercise. You know ... exercise? Go walkies?"

"Well, what's the Spanish then for 'walk'?"

"*Football! Niño football. Necessita football.* Or *volleyball.* Or ping-pong. You know, ping-pong? P*ingo-pongo*? Tennis *de misa*? No, not '*misa*' '*mesa*'. Tennis *de mesa*?

"What's this? What's this?"

"Ah, cards. *Gracias, gracias. Muchas gracias. Amigo mio.*"

* * *

Day B

(I've now lost touch with how many days we've been held. My beard has stopped itching. I suppose that's one thing.)

Where was I? Ah yes: Honesty and self-awareness ... Neither of them, if I'm honest (ha!ha!), my longest suits. Important, though, both of them ...

A lot is talked, Gerry about being honest, particularly honest with ourselves. As if being honest with ourselves were the most natural, the easiest thing in the world. Well, I've got news for you, kid: Most of us lack the kind of self-awareness that will even allow us to be honest with ourselves. Even to get close to it. If we are truly honest with ourselves, then the only thing we can aspire to being is to try to be honest with ourselves. Honesty does not come naturally to us humans. We have to work at it. We have to choose to work at it.

There is so much I want to tell you, so much I need to. The cliché parent wants for their children all the things he or she never had in their childhood: three meals a day, historically, a clean bed, holeless shoes in which to trudge to school. It's a sadness that the cliché is more about material welfare than spiritual welfare, or ethical - even educational - welfare. But, I suspect because we have for generations lied about the kind of pain we've been in, material comfort is so much easier to define and thus recognise than emotional or spiritual - or ethical or educational - comfort.

Me, I've always hoped my experience would mean that my progeny stretching out into the *future would never need to make the same mistakes that I did. And yet I made the mistakes of my parents. Apparently (or a-parent-ly!) we all do. All of us. We make the same mistakes - enormous mistakes - and we make them over and over and over again, one generation after another.*

Apparently we have yet to learn even that wars kill. And that killing is a painful process. And maybe particularly for those who survive.

* * *

"You want a game of cards, Gerry? You want, Gerry, to play 'Patience', do you think? With me, I mean?"

"Well, I thought maybe we could."

"Do we *need* to bond, then, do you think?"

"No, I don't think so either."

"It wasn't for any ulterior motive. I just thought it might be nice ... well, just to do something together. Besides eat and sleep. And me natter.

"The nutter natters! That what you're thinking?"

"Oh, did you? I thought it was rather good."

"Well, what *are* you thinking, then?"

"You will get out of this, sweetheart. You will."

Oh God, please do not start on this again. Please, Gerry, do not start on this again. There is a limit, you know, even to Job's damn patience.

"Well, no, I can't *promise* you. It's not in my power to promise you that. I'm not God, after all. I mean, a bloody great meteorite could come crashing through the wall. Nothing can be a hundred per cent certain."

Notice that bit of humility, God? "I'm not God," I just said. Just in case You missed it. I mention it, on the off-chance ... well, you know, there's a brownie point maybe looking for a home ... maybe even two brownie points?

"I am, though, as certain as I can be you'll come through all this. And I'm only a tiny bit less certain that I will."

"Well, ninety-nine per cent that you will, and ninety-eight per cent that I will. That do you?"

What happened to thinking about other people, Titus? Not only your New Year resolutions, is it, lover, that last about twenty-three seconds?

"We've been harmed already, Gerry. Well, haven't we?"

"So, no, I don't think we'll come out of this totally unharmed. Or unscathed. Without a psychological scratch on us, or anything. But sometimes – just sometimes – there is some good in being harmed. In being scathed.

"Is that a word, 'scathed'? What I mean is, if the harm that happens to us teaches us empathy, then the harm – although still harmful – has been mollified by the good that's come from it."

"If, let's say, I were killed in a car crash, I'd like to think my organs would be handed on to someone who needed them."

Whoever You deem to send to this young man, God, as his offspring, please – *please* – let it be someone impossible.

"Okay, that's probably true. Still maybe there's someone else somewhere equally as old as God who *would* want them. Life – as I'm sure, Gerry, you've already discovered – is full of surprises."

Tom Sawyer with attitude, say.

"Okay, you're right, that's not the same thing. Not the same thing at all, you're right." Make him suffer, Lord. Oh, please make him suffer. Let the boot be on the other foot. Let him, God, deal with an emotional hooligan. Let him know what that's like. Even a physical hooligan would be alright. Just so long as it causes him *trouble.* "A really duff example. Sorry."

And I do mean, Lord, a whole heap of trouble. Trouble with a capital 't' sort of trouble. Bart Simpson without the charm.

"Is it me, or has it suddenly gone cold? There you go: that's a perfect example, of the surprises there are in life: You don't expect Colombia to be cold, do you? Well, alright, *I* didn't then. Mind you, in my school report once the geography teacher wrote, 'He is wasting both my time and his.' Strange, really, because I love travelling. Well, you know that.

"Me, I think that's so much more an indictment of my teacher than it was of me."

"Think about it, tu'penny, for a second.

"It *all* starts in school.

"Well, no, of course it doesn't. It all starts at home. That's the first school – the nest. And it starts on Day One. Second One, in fact. Get that right, Gerry, when you come to be a parent, and the rest of child-rearing will be ... well, as much of a breeze as it's possible for it to be."

Which is not a lot, dear boy. Which is colossally not a lot.

"I've always loved you, Gerry. What on earth are you talking about?" Or, God, Pollyanna with permanent toothache, or Rip van Winkle with insomnia ...

"Always."

"Oh God, tu'penny, you had nothing to do with it. Nothing at all. Yes, I promise you. That I can promise you."

"Well, we just didn't see eye-to-eye, your father and me, that was all. It's a difficult relationship, Gerry, father and son. You're maybe beginning to experience that yourself. He thought I'd betrayed Granny. That was pretty much the nub of it. It had *nothing* to do with you, Gerry. Absolutely nothing. It was all about my conduct, sweetheart. It was about me."

"Of course Daddy loves you too, Gerry. Just as much as

I do. Probably even more. As does Mummy. Mum. What happened between your father and me wasn't his fault. I don't think it was my fault either, but, yes, he'd disagree with that. *I* think, it's just the way it was. Just one of those perverse little tricks which life so enjoys playing on you. But not for a second did any of that affect our feelings for you. Any of us, in any of our feelings for you."

Was ever child born as needy as this one? As cloying? Get real, kid. Grow up. Deal with it.

"So? Cards? What do you say? While away a few more minutes, a few more hours before they release us?"

"They're bound to release us, Gerry. They've learnt we're not who they thought we were. We're costing them – and plenty – in terms of resources and man-hours and safe houses. If they were going to kill us, frankly they'd have done so already some time previously. So, what else is there for them to do?

"Who knows? It might even be today."

And, of course, Titus, you – aged nine and a spit – you would - *of course* – have handled yourself with such dynamicism and fortitude and James Bondism, would have been laying out the abductors as you escaped with your backpack jet.

"So? What do you say? 'Patience'? What do you say?"

Why is it only ever you, o great one, who is allowed any slack? *Allowed* any? Who claims slack as his right! Why is it only *ever* you? Ever think that others, they may need some slack too? Those, let's say, for instance, under the age of ten? Who have been kidnapped? Are frightened out of their senses? A hundred miles from home, from anything familiar?

"You know how to deal them out? ... Oh, God! If looks could kill! I *was* only asking, Gerry. So, seven cards along the top ... You know that. Sorry. Jack of Diamonds. Do you play using every third card in the pack? Or each one?"

"Well, me, I prefer to use each one. I work on the

principle, you see, that getting the game out is quite hard enough of itself. You don't need to add to its difficulties. Like life, as a matter of fact. Ace of Hearts.

"Life is difficult enough. You don't need to make it any harder than it already is. Nor do you need to make anyone else's life harder than it already is. That's my philosophy of life, old darling, wrapped up in one sentence. Well, three sentences, if you want to be pedantic. But only little sentences. And who's counting, right? Finally, the four of Clubs.

"Not a lot there, is there?"

"You could dump the Ace."

"Sorry. *You're* playing it. Sorry. Queen of Hearts. Could go on the King there, of Spades. Sorry. ...

"That's it, then the Jack on the Queen. And that nine – that's it – the nine of Hearts on the ten of Clubs. Why are you moving the King?"

"Well, I'd keep that column open if I were you. Before you've started playing the deck you don't know when that hole, it might not be useful. Another lesson for life, Gerry: Always keep as many possibilities open as are possible. And for as long as you can. Never enter a cul-de-sac willingly. There'll be quite enough times when you have to; enough times when your choices are limited: You're forced to go in a particular direction. In that case, go with it. Accept the inevitable, and hope for the best. You never know. The game's never over, Gerry, until it's over."

Just before you get totally carried away, Titus, by the brilliance of your pedagogic skills, may I be allowed to point out, old bean, that your beloved grandson is not listening? He's simply not listening. So if you thought it was thus, Titus, that you would impart to him your legacy of experience, think again. 'Cos this, sunshine, ain't going to work. Nope, not going to work, not nohow, not no way.

"Missed it. There was an eight. Of Clubs, I think. It could have gone on the nine of Hearts."

"No, you can't do that."

"Because it's cheating, that's why. And it's the worst kind of cheating, Gerry, the very worst: It's cheating yourself. And cheating yourself is exactly that: *cheating* yourself."

Oh do please excuse me whilst I snort contemptuously. Who the hell are you, Titus, to lecture *anyone* about cheating themselves?

"There was a really good sitcom some time back, 'Taxi'. It's where Danny de Vito, as far as I know, started making a name for himself. In one of the episodes, I think it was Judd Hirsch – he was the actor who played the central character – turned to one of the others and quoted an aphorism he'd learnt, I don't know, from his granny or something. 'The liar's tragedy,' he said, 'is not that he is not believed but that he cannot believe anyone else.'

"If you lie to yourself, you cannot believe anything you hear. If you cheat yourself, Gerry, you cannot trust anyone else. What a horrible way to live."

Never in our all too short time together, never, Valentine, did I lie to you. And I don't think you ever lied to me. And the relief of that was just enormous.

"'Course the cynics would tell you, given the moral fibre of today, that that's the only way *to* live, by lying and cheating, that anything else is only hopeless and romantic nonsense, that such ideas are so saccharine they make you feel that there is not enough vomit in the world. I suspect that's usually because such people need an excuse for their callousness or duplicity. And thank God they do still need that excuse – anything less would be the thin end of a wedge where barbarianism would simply take over. That day appears to be not too far away. And that prospect really frightens me, sweetheart."

They always start, lies, with the good lies, the kind lies, the beneficent ones: the surprise you're keeping for a birthday, how pretty your hair looks – but it ends – with me, anyway, it always ended – with the blackest of lies, the most malignant ... yeah, maybe the most malicious. Those same lies that kept me away from home, that stopped us, Emily, looking at the truth about ourselves. The same lies that were intended to save you pain actually hurt you far more, my darling one, than the pain they were designed to shield you from. And they hurt you so much. I'm beginning to see that now. *So* much. And I am *so* sorry.

"It's staring you straight in the face, tu'penny. There's a move you can make, Gerry, staring you straight in the face. Look. Look. 'Look,' as the Bible says, 'and thou shalt see.' ...

"You got it. That eight on the nine, that's it."

"No, I'd move the whole lot, if I were you. You've got the other hole now. Three of Diamonds, that's a bit of a bummer. No, I don't think there's anything else you can do, not for the moment."

* * *

Day C

I have a toaster at home. You'd have seen it, Gerry, if you'd ever been allowed to visit. Sorry, that sounds rather bitter. Sorry. It's not one of those pop-up ones, but one where you pull down the sides each side of the grill and wedge the bread in that way. Its advantage is, it can cope more easily with awkwardly sized bread. Valentine , anyway, had a thing about it. He wouldn't let me throw it away! I cannot tell you the amount of times I've burnt my fingers, getting the toast out of the damn thing, turning the bread over to toast the other side. Nor the amount of times others - yes, including you, Valentine - *have burnt theirs. It takes an enormous amount of pain for us to learn from our mistakes. A huge amount.*

* * *

"I don't think you've got a choice, sweetheart. I think you'll have to use that spare column, see whether you can't release that ten of Clubs. Otherwise – and I don't want to baffle you here with the use of jargon – but, otherwise, my dear friend, you are what's known in the business of 'Patience' as buggered. There you go.

"It was obviously meant to be! With the Queen and Jack available so quickly afterwards.

"Okay, this is it, the moment of truth. Ace of Diamonds, that's okay. Next? Ten of Hearts. Not wonderful. Have you seen the two of Diamonds in the pack? Well, if not, to revert again to that technical expression ..."

"Quite. Buggered, quite. No, I wouldn't, old mate. Well, if you put that two on the three, you could trap it.

"What lousy cards, eh? What a load of rubbish! What a load of old rubbish!"

"What do you mean, like I talk? That's extremely cheeky, young man."

"It *may* be true, but it's still cheeky."

You're bristling, Titus! This is a nine-year-old's banter, for God's sake! It's not that you're the Emeritus professor, or something – or that *he* is –, and your lifework's being challenged. For God's sake, Titus, for God's sake, man.

"I probably do talk rubbish, Gerry. I certainly don't want you to think of me as any kind of oracle or anything."

"Well, okay, fat chance though there may be of that."

But if I do talk rubbish, Gerry, I mean you no harm. ... Oh God, Gerry, this is big stuff. I need to tell you this. It's important stuff. I need to tell you this, matey, and I need you to allow me to tell you. And for you to listen. "Anything you hear," I need to tell you, Gerry, "*anything*, you need to analyse it. You need to filter it. 'Is this true?' you need to ask yourself. 'Or is it a convenient hypothesis designed to safeguard some kind of vested interest?'" You need to ask yourself that. You have to ask yourself that.

Day D

You're not sleeping well, Gerry. Your fingers are twitching, you're murmuring stuff under your breath. I should probably be relieved I can't make out what it is you're saying!

I want to hold you and take away your fear. But I can't. I can't even do that. No, no 'even' attached to that. None of us can do that. Not really. We can help. But we cannot do it. How much of our pain comes from not understanding our limitations, I wonder.

I am cross with myself for my reticence. I find it incredibly hard to be serious around you, Gerry. That's to do with me, I suspect, and me wanting you to like me. Apparently, at any cost - even to you.

I've been writing about how we fail to learn from experience. And here we are roller-coasting on a learning curve of Hawaiian wave-like proportions, and I'm neglecting the opportunity to point all the lessons around us. Because I'm scared such will lead to you not liking me. Which means I'm neglecting you. Which means, of course, that I'm just as culpable, just as guilty, as all those I so readily criticise.

I <u>am</u> just as guilty as all those I criticise, by the way. Let's be clear on that point. I'm not any kind of moral paradigm.

You said earlier today that I talked rubbish. Oh, it was just a joke. I'm not getting all huffy about that. God, I really hope I'm not that precious - or preposterous.

Of course I talk rubbish, Gerry. No human being doesn't from time to time. You'll hear a lot of rubbish in your life - whole landfills of the stuff - a thousand times more rubbish you'll hear than wisdom. And it's not only right that you question whether what you're hearing is rubbish or wisdom, it's <u>essential</u> that you do. Absolutely essential. And when you're analysing that, Gerry, always ask yourself one thing: Does the person so informing you have your best interests at heart?

I do, for instance. Although I certainly sometimes talk rubbish, I mean you no harm. The world's plutocrats, though, they do wish you harm, Gerry. They wish harm to all they subordinate. And they prove that they wish them harm by the simple fact of subordinating them.

A plutocrat, Gerry, (and forgive me if you already know this) is someone who believes that government should be controlled by those with money. Oh, there's a terribly witty axiom: 'It's the golden rule:' it goes, wittily, 'Those with the gold make the rules.' An enormous amount of us appear to believe in it.

America, as a for instance, maintains that, because it contributes more to the United Nations than any other country, it should be allowed to dictate UN policy. Well, of course America 'per se' does not believe that, but, if the polls are to be believed (and that's a bigger 'if' than I care to think about), there is a body of opinion in America which does think that. And that body is, well, substantial.

Again IF the polls are to be believed, there is in the States also a national opinion that contributing to party funds is an exercise of free speech. And of course it is - at the level of the man-in-the-street giving up some of his hard-earned cash to further a political cause. But that precept has been distorted into a gargoyle of itself, some kind of grotesque misrepresentation of its intention. Because now giant corporations are paying enormous sums into the coffers of both political parties - in order that their corporate interests will be protected whichever party gains power. Even if those corporate interests are against what are perceived to be 'national interests' and certainly if the perceived interests are extranational.

What was that? What was that? Someone walking over my grave? It's not that chilly. Not cold enough to cause that kind of shiver. Maybe it's *me* walking across my grave. This *is* going to be my grave, isn't it? ...

Free speech does not mean that the man with the most gold talks the most truth. Nor that he is entitled more to his opinion being heard. Those are the politics of feudalism and barbarism.

Snap out of it, Titus. Right now, I mean. ... But this being my grave, that is the reality, old chum. ... *Snap*, Titus, out of it.

And it's not just Americans, Gerry, let me tell you. I used to believe that, for God's sake. I used myself to be believe in that golden rule. That's the worst of it. Not that long ago either. And for most of my life, I used to believe that. A lot of people do. It is a sacred cow axiom, and like all the other sacred cows, it has become lodged - should I say corralled? - in some kind of aspic of folk-lore or myth or folk-truism or something, never to be dislodged.

My own belief in it only started crumbling - my belief, that is, in that golden 'rule' - when I started to face all the stuff around Valentine and me - the bigotry, the hostility, the bare-teethed aggression and hostility. The whole fabric of my existence started breaking down at that point. But, no, you're quite right: that's scarcely the point, not at the moment.

But there is a point, Gerry, and the point is: that plutocrats do wish you harm.

Would you like to be a bit more impenetrable in your writing, Titus? The boy's nine-years'-sodding-old. He's not studying for his PhD. ... Yeah, but,Titus old fruit, I'm not writing for the nine-year-old, am I? Not any more. Shit, know *what* I'm writing here? I *am* writing a legacy, my legacy. I'm writing my fucking legacy here.

Mohammed Ali has always been a big man. And I never did fancy him, Valentine. Whatever you thought. Whatever you accused me of. I didn't even fancy him in fancy. In Nancy fancy. Not even in fantasy. You are such a baby sometimes. There's only ever been one man I've fancied, lover. In the entire of my life. *A BIG man. In a lot of senses. But he became a giant, know when? When he started to encourage everyone to believe we are all the greatest. He encouraged those of us with hearts less robust than his to start believing that: That every single one of us contains the seed of greatness within us. But, know what?, that's a hard thing to believe in. It takes energy to believe in that. Great dollops of it. It seems to fly in the face of the evidence. Those of us with less robust hearts, we need encouragement - not so that we can believe it initially, that's the easy bit - but to continue believing that. We all need that encouragement sometimes. It's so hard to keep finding the courage to reach within us and to keep willing that seed to grow.*

Yes, it is, this, some kind of legacy. I suppose somewhere I know – I must know – I'm going to die. Here, I mean. Legacy, that's not the right word for it. Some kind of intellectual will-and-testament. God, not chilly any longer. Cold, so cold.

Ali was always hated by the plutocrats, will always be hated by them. Because his message has never been one they want us to hear. When he was young, they didn't want us to know how appallingly black people were treated in the United States - in the Western world generally -, nor that the war in Vietnam was a particularly immoral one. Today they don't want us to know we are all the greatest. They want us to subordinate our potential to their comfort. They want us to stifle the potential within us in order that we will more peacefully work for them.

That is not someone with your best interests at heart. And if someone does not have your interests at heart, he is capable of harming you. Indeed it's almost certain that, if the opportunity arises, that person will harm you. And therefore the apparent sense he's talking is that much more likely to in fact be rubbish. Not only rubbish but toxic rubbish - intellectual nuclear waste, in fact.

Sleep. I must sleep.

* * *

“There, got the eight that time round. Well done. Shame it wasn’t the red five instead of the black one, you could have released that entire column there. Yup: four on the five of Spades, good. You’re not going to move the three? Certainly I would. You’re beginning, sweetheart, to run out of options. ...

“Finally: the much vaunted red five. Let’s see whether that does the trick. That’s often the way. We think we want the Aces and the Kings. But, nine times out of ten, it’s actually where the fives are or the sixes which determines the outcome of the game. Quite often, the twos and threes. If you ignore the importance of the numbered cards, tu’penny, more often than not, the game won’t come out. Same with life. Any system – remember this, Gerry – any system of any kind which does not look after numbered cards as well as the picture cards is a system which finally has to implode.

“Whatever it is the system in control of the world today does not look after any of the numbered cards. Only begrudgingly does it even notice the nines and tens. And I fear, tu’penny, for the inevitable implosion. Fear for it? I’m totally terrified of it – and by both its prospect and its size.

“Would you believe it? The other blooming red five. Whoa, Gerry.”

“Well, look, sweetheart. Look at the deck. Is that not the four of Spades? And that could go ...?”

“You got it.

“Followed by the Ace of Spades. And? The eight of Spades. Less good. But okay. Everything’s okay until the last card is played. Only then can you decide whether or not the game was played well or not.

"Whoa, whoa, whoa. You're going too fast. You're going to miss something. 'Patience' isn't about the speed you play it at, Gerry. It's about getting it out, about playing the hand as well as it's possible to play it. Again like life.

"Speed can be an illusion, Gerry. Remember the magician: 'The speed of the hand deceives the eye.' We need undeceived eyes today, Gerry. You do. Eyes that will not let themselves be deceived.

"Got it! That bloody great mosquito. I finally got it!"

* * *

You do not have to make your own mistakes, Gerry. Learn from history. See through history. Read the sub-text of the history books. The sub-text is considerably more relevant - and revealing - than the text. Most of the text is written by barbarians for dolts. Such barbarians describe history at their masters' behest. They care considerably more about the concerns of those masters than of their fellow man.

You can almost define the barbarian as someone who wants others to be subject to his rule - or hers. (Whatever political correctness might dictate, there are plenty of female barbarians around. Barbarians too who are black, blind, or poor. Barbarians of impeccable ethnicity. Even some that are gay!) The civilised man is one who wants to encourage others to celebrate their otherness, and wants them to cherish themselves. The civilised cherish variety. And the barbarians want sameness and subordination. And will stamp out all who thwart (or who seek to thwart) that desire - the civilised, in other words.

Avoid the barbarians, Gerry. That's sometimes very hard to do. And getting harder with each passing day. Nevertheless, try to do it. Stick with the civilised. They may soon be wiped from the face of the Earth - such, anyway, seems to be today's ambition. But at least you'll die surrounded by a better quality of corpse!

* * *

"Yeah, that's it. The seven of Hearts on the eight. And then ... Got it: the six of Spades on the seven. Jack of Hearts: not the greatest. Still ...

"I was going to say, 'It's only a game.' And it *is*, tu'penny, only a game. 'Patience'. Life, in fact.

"No, not life. Not *all* life. Yours. Your own life, it's that which is the game. As much as it is the lives of others which is not."

What I need to tell you, Gerry, what I need to say, what I need you to hear: It took over five hundred million years for life to arrive at human beings. Five hundred million years! For you and me to be sitting here. Five hundred million years!

And we're prepared to threaten all that effort, all that myriad of miracles, the incalculable odds against us, just so that Mr Gates can make yet another billion? Or Mr Murdoch can promote to editorship some rather unpleasant toady? Or Mr Blair can spin contemptuously through the Downing Street door? Or Mr Bush can ... I don't know. What *does* Mr Bush do all day long? Apart from break the Geneva Convention and curtail the human rights of his citizens?

I know you're not interested in any of this. And I'm sorry, but in a year or two's time, you're not going to have a choice: You're going to *have* to be interested in this. You're just going to have to be, Gerry. Because, as things are going at the moment, by then your very survival will depend on it.

"Yes, I think that would be a good idea: Go through the pack again. See what else happens. Ah, there's the nine of Diamonds. Which means you can plonk the eight of Spades on it. That releases another column. That takes some of the pressure off."

Mankind, I need to tell you, mankind desperately needs to learn from the Buddhists. We need to start respecting all life among us, and beyond us. As the Buddhists do. We need to learn their humility. And we need – rapidly – to shed the arrogance of so much Christian practice.

"See, you *have* got the Queen. Now you can put down the King with impunity. And there, you've revealed the Ace of Clubs. You see, it doesn't matter what the rules are, tu'penny. Just so long as you play by them. That makes you an honest person. And an honest person is one with integrity. Today's world seems to hate people with integrity. It demands of its doyens that their morality is malleable.

"It sends representatives to oversee the elections in so-called Third World countries or countries with suspicious democracies. And yet when its most avowedly 'democratic' country elects a President by let's say a ... 'debatable' majority, the appointment is sanctioned by that country's own Supreme Court. Even by the losing candidate – the candidate who should have won. And when several of that 'democratic' country's Congressmen protested that their constituents had thereby been disenfranchised, not one single member of the Senate – not one, Gerry – would sanction their appeal. Yet still today they hold themselves to be the champions of democracy. International objections? Not one."

His eyes, dear boy, have glassed over. They're well past

'glassed over', actually. *Well* past it. He stopped listening about an hour go. Why don't you just stick to playing cards, Titus? Being nice? Leave all the philosophy – if that's what you want to call it –, leave your 'legacy', Titus, to the letter?

"Sorry, Gerry. Sorry, tu'penny. Well, I say 'sorry' and a part of me means it. You're too young, I know, to be expected to be handling all this. But all this, tu'penny, is all – and I'm sorry, Gerry, to keep harping on about it – all stuff you're going to *have* to handle. It's not just going to bite you on the bum, Gerry, this – all this – it's going to consume you. It's going – and you have no idea how painful it is for me to say this – it's going, sweetheart, to *devour* you.

"Does that smell like coffee to you? I think breakfast may be on the way."

* * *

Day E

There are apparently two things true of every generation in history. First, that each discovers sex. And secondly, that each generation has to make its own mistakes.

The first is fun!

It's one of the few bonuses of aging: smiling (usually, condescendingly!) at the innocence of the new generation, which imagines its forebears forbore sex - well, not quite forbore it (they themselves are there, after all), but indulged in it as a sort of copulation-by-numbers.

The present batch of 20- and 30- somethings would claim to have taken sex out of the closet. They flaunt their sexuality in a manner unprecedented in history. I think it thinks, because it is honest about sex, it is being truthful to itself. Without seeing the subdued desperation of all of it.

There has, of course, never been too much laid back about getting laid, but today's obsessional, even neurotic, insistence about sex and its benefits has a ring about it of 'Methinks the lady doth protest too much'. ... Yeah, yeah, you're absolutely right: That could just be the old man in me, carping at pastimes no longer available to me (at least, so you young 'uns like to think!!!) I'd concede that. Be happy to. If they only knew, huh, Valentine? If they only, Valentine, knew! *Much of my intellectual makeup today is the old man carping at pastimes no longer available!*

But know what, lover?: if you were here now, it's not the fucking I'd want. Not straight away, anyhow. (Maybe I should have said, not 'right' away!) Not even for a bit. I'd want you first to hold me, lover, kiss my brow. Make all the badness go away. All the badness and the madness.

Less whimsical, though, is this inability we have to learn from history. It is one of mankind's most devastating weaknesses. I fear it will end up killing him. The personal extends into the public.

How many generations have burnt themselves turning over the toast in antiquated toasters?

How many children of abusive parents find themselves in abusive relationships as adults, and in turn start abusing their children? It's not sexual abuse, you understand, that I'm talking about - not just (I should rather say) sexual abuse. And, yes, you're right: that is, I would concede, a dramatic example. Okay, how many children of, let's say, the chintzy become misers themselves? Or spendthrifts? Because the opposite behaviour is also as a result of received treatment.

...

And this has now a dimension of global importance, of importance now, Gerry, to our whole species. Personally, I think it's as much a reason for today's invasion of Iraq as cheap oil.

There is no still in still. I thought I was still; thought I was floating in an ocean of still. But I became aware of the mosquito's buzz. The Lazarus mosquito, the one I'd thought I'd killed. And then the cicadas, the crickets, whatever they are. Then the glass rattling gently in the window-frame. A floorboard creaks as you snuffle, Gerry, in your sleep, and snort. The sheets rustle as you wriggle into a new position. And now I can hear the thousand voices in my head: the massed bands of doubt and guilt and self-recrimination. There is no still in still.

I really hope you will know who I mean when I say David Attenborough. Because that will mean that you, like me, will have enjoyed his breath-taking work about this incredible planet - the one we inhabit. Mr Attenborough is a Natural Scientist, he's not any kind of a political being. <u>Sir David</u> (I beg his pardon!) in one of the last programmes I saw of his said: "Mankind now faces the greatest crisis in its existence." The greatest, Gerry, crisis in the entire of its existence. You see around you any evidence of that crisis being addressed? I mean <u>any</u> evidence of that? In any, I mean, but the most derisory fashion? And how much of that inertia is caused by us not learning from history?

I saw another wildlife programme - for once nothing to do with Sir David - about releasing gorillas back into the wild. The exercise was extra-

ordinary - both in its complexity and its cost. As serendipity would have it, a few days later I watched a documentary about the parole board - the exercise, if you like, of releasing prisoners back into the wild. It started me wondering about the cost of putting right our mistakes, as against the cost of not making those mistakes in the first place.

How much is it going to cost us, our lack of investment in education today? Global dimming masked the problem of global warming. How many problems today are being masked by other ones? When we start dealing with the crumbling sewers of London, what other problems are we going to unearth? If we ever get round to feeding the Earth, what problems will starvation have hidden from our eyes?

You know what, Gerry? I shouldn't be writing only to you. Not just to you, tu'penny. Of course I love you. You know, by now I hope, how very much I love you. But there are others too I love. Others too I need to speak to.

* * *

I'd kill for a shave. Kill for one. A good night's sleep. A fuck. A passionate, energetic, huffing-and-puffing fuck.

"Are you going to discard that Ace?"

No, a gentle fuck. A long and languorous, sensuous, feel-every-nook fuck.

"Sure, go back to the deck. I think that would be prudent. Eh voilà, the King of Clubs. Kind of answers the question, doesn't it? And the two of Clubs. That rounds it off nicely, too: the Queen on the King."

"Now, now, Gerry, don't be vulgar.

"Six of Hearts. Hmm. All we've got in the deck, the seven of Clubs, the four of Diamonds. Okay, okay." **And a bath. A long bath.** "Well, let's see whether we can't open up a hole, discarding onto the Aces. The five of Hearts. To reveal? The eight of Hearts!"

"No, I don't think you are buggered." **And a *shave*. My kingdom for a shave.** "Well, look closely, Gerry. You've got the five of Spades available to you. Lose all those and move the six of Clubs across. There you go. Jack on the Queen. That's it. Only two to go. I think you're going to get it out, sweetheart. Five of Clubs onto the other Clubs. Last one: seven of Diamonds. Well done, señor. Very well played. Another?"

"No, I'll shut up this time. Well, I'll try and shut up, at any rate. You sink or swim. All by yourself. Try, yes, to shut up. Give them a good shuffle, sweetheart. Well, otherwise it'll be too easy. There's scant satisfaction in achieving the easy. *Very* scant satisfaction in that.

"If you ever have a memorial service for me – not that I'm dropping hints, you understand, or anything – there are three or four pieces of music that I'd like to be included: the fourth movement of Beethoven's ninth symphony would be one, the so-called 'Ode to Joy'. Because joy should be oded to; because life should be about joy; because, Gerry, there is joy to be squeezed from every situation – do you know how much joy I'm getting just talking to you like this? I know it's not very joyous for you, tu'penny. But you will find joy again. That I guarantee you. There will also be a time – and this I guarantee you as well – when you will find joy in this. *Some* joy in this."

It *could* be joyous, Titus. Don't you think, part of Gerry's joylessness might be that he knows your 'joy' is a sham, an act – a not very good act, even? Couldn't you make the effort, Titus, to sense for real the joy around you? To feel it for real? *Really*

sense and feel it?

"It's also, Beethoven's ninth, one of the most beautiful pieces of music ever composed."

***

Day F

Dear ... well, everybody, I suppose,

You'll have to forgive the tiny writing. I have no idea whether I'll ever get more paper. For which reason I'm forced too to write a communal letter, even though there will (if I am given time!) be parts of it which will be deeply personal to individuals amongst you. As far as it is possible, I know that you will respect the privacy of those sections which don't concern you. I appreciate that, if you open the door on a couple having sex, you cannot unsee the sight. But news of it, I know you all agree, need not be broadcast. x

I have no idea how much longer I have to live. Each time I hear footsteps outside the door, I am convinced that it is to lead me to my execution. That's the way, Titus, old bean. Go for the sympathy vote. *Where I have marked the letter with an 'x', it's because I have been interrupted. I don't guarantee I will pick up from where I left off. x* Interesting what you're *not* telling them: that sometimes you're *hoping* they're coming to execute you. But, hey, all the best lies, they're the ones of omission.

My chief anxiety at the moment (as I'm sure you can imagine), is to try and secure Gerry's release. I'm not going to say that with his release I'll be able to relax nor that I will die 'a happy man'. But I will be a deal <u>more</u> relaxed and would die a deal <u>happier</u>. I do want to live and perhaps (if I'm *honest), that's why Gerry's safety is so fundamental.* No, I'm not going to spell that out for you. If that is really so difficult to understand, there really is no hope for you.

Ewart, you first. I do love you, you know. You've known me for a number of years now. And in all those years, I have loved you. Even when I was mightily pissed off with you, I still loved you. I can still see the first smile you gave me. You were only weeks' old. We were in the 'Mad Hatter', just behind Queen Charlotte's, there in Stamford Brook. In the garden, of course. You were blowing bubbles, those fragile bubbles of curiosity that all babies seem to blow. And I was bursting too, just like those bubbles of spit, bursting in my love for you. I leant into the pram to wipe away the excess spit that had dribbled onto your chin. And you smiled at me, Ewart. A chasm, a Grand Canyon of a smile. And I toppled into an abyss of love, my darling Ewart, from which I never did – fully – emerge. *And it is al right for me to have been pissed off with you, Ewart. It is and was. Just as alright as it was for you to have been pissed off with me. The reasons don't matter any longer. We've gone way past that.* The reasons do matter, Ewart, and we're a long way yet from being even past that, let alone *way* past it. You hurt me, you unmitigated shit. Hurt me badly. And for no reason at all – certainly none that I can see – beyond your personal agenda, beyond your own bigotry. *I need you to know that I also love the rest of you - no less than Ewart. I separate Ewart only because the love I feel for him is, apparently, contentious.*

Shit! What about Valentine? What the fuck do I do about Valentine? Whom do I hurt? Him or the family? If I don't acknowledge him, doesn't that make a lie of the whole of 'us'? Doesn't it give credence to all Ewart's fucking bigotry? Would it also not aggravate, exacerbate Emily's pain? That too?

Talking of contentious love, I also want you to

know, Valentine, that, yes, I love you too. Deeply. Love you and want you, my darling one. I want you here. And that is what I do: I want you. Here. I want to fuck you. Here. Now. I want to feel myself deep within you. *I want there to be no doubt about that. x And I'm really sorry, Ewart, you might have a problem with that, but I cannot change facts just to protect sensibilities. And if that too offends you, then for that too I am sorry. x*

* * *

"I don't understand. *No entiendo.* I don't understand."

"*Don't* prod me like that. *Por favor.* Not with the barrel of a rifle, whatever it is. *Por favor.* I'm standing, I'm standing. Okay?"

"I don't understand. *No entiendo.*"

"Ah, *generalissimo*! Ah, *bien, bueno. Muy bueno.*

"And the boy? *Niño? Football para el niño, si?* Important, *importante*, sport, *esporto para el niño. Muy importante.*"

"Okay, okay. I think they're taking you to play football, Gerry. Me, I'm going – I think – to talk, like, to the boss or someone. Let's see whether we can't – finally – get this bloody thing resolved. I'm sure – sure of it – that finally they'll see sense.

"You'll be alright, will you? Whilst I'm away, I mean? 'Course you will be. Righter than right, I should think. Kicking a ball around, feeling the sun on your face. Just what the doctor ordered, I'd say."

"You have to let go of me, Gerry."

"Well, you have to, tu'penny. I won't be away for long. I mean, why would I be? But I can't negotiate our release, can I, unless I'm *there* to negotiate it?"

"*¿El niño puede venir con yo?*"

"No, I thought not. They won't let you come with me, Gerry. You just go outside, kick a ball around, work off some of that excess energy of yours.

"*Si, si,* I'm coming, I'm coming. *Yo* ... come .... *Yo voy – vengo*. Gerry, please let me go.

"Don't even think about using that rifle on the boy, you understand? *¿Entiende usted?* Don't you even so much as think about it. *El* gun – *el* ... bang-bang – *con el niño, no, entiende? Muy, muy no*! *¿Entiende?*"

"I'll only be a few minutes, Gerry, I'm sure of it. Please don't whine like that, grizzle in that way. Please. I'll be back soon. Before probably you've even known I've gone."

They're taking me to shoot me. Look after yourself, Gerry. I do love you. Please God, they don't kill you too. Please God.

"That's it. Well done. You go and play football. *¿Football, no, el niño? Si, si, football.*"

I won't ever see you again, tu'penny. Remember me with fondness. Try to. I suspect it'll only be you who might. Somewhat sad, no, as an epitaph? Maybe Valentine as well.

"*Si*, you're going to play football, Gerry. You'll be alright, tu'penny. I'll be right back."

* * *

"I'll be alright. Don't fuss. I'll be alright. I just need to lie down."

"I need to lie down, Gerry. I'll worry about the blood later.

"I'm sorry you should see me like this. You should see the other guy, though. Please let me lie down, tu'penny. Please."

* * *

"Sorry. I think I must have blacked out there for a moment. Sorry."

* * *

Hold me, Valentine. Hold me sweet. Hold me dear. There's a lion. A lion chasing me, lover. Running through the tunnel. Running towards me. Gaining on me. Getting closer. Ever closer. I can hear its paws behind me now, pounding on the shingle of the tunnel floor, the gravel slithering, the pebbles clinking like cut-glass crystal in a toast to the bride and groom. I'm running, running. The sweat is coursing. Now I can hear the lion's breath, can hear its heart beating, can *feel* its breath on me, can sense it tensing for the pounce. Still I run. I run pell-mell for the match-head of light I can see ahead. Run like there is no tomorrow. Because, if the lion gets me, there will be none. No tomorrow. No more tomorrows. I'm drenched in sweat. Covered in it. I hear the absence of clinking pebbles. The lion is mid-pounce. His weight hurls me to the ground. Now I'm under the lion. It's almost as if it's raping me. Huge paws pinion me to the ground, a syrupy mane slavers into my neck, feather-dusters it, but the so-called 'feathers' are in fact shards of broken glass. He's tearing at me, shredding me, about to eat me. Alive. I can see his huge jaws, opening ... opening some more ... gaping now, stretching into an infinity like the night sky, can see shreds of zebra caught in his teeth, can see speckles of his spit glistening on his sandpaper tongue. I'm going into a blackness, lover. Diving into a void. *The* void. Not an emptiness, no: a blackness, a whirring blackness, a *whirling* blackness, a spiral staircase of it, a liquorice anaconda crushing me with its coils, suffocating me in folds of girdered blackness ... a rainbow of a spectrum all of black, a sea of blackness, a pitching sea, both drowning me and making me sea-sick, spluttering and gagging at one and the same time. Making me violently sea-sick. The retch of the forlorn. The retch of the wretched. ...

"They're going to shoot me, Gerry. The next time they come through that door, old mate, that'll be to take me away and shoot me. Oh God!"

That's it, lover. That's the way. Stroke my brow, Valentine, just like that – my cheeks, my brow. Make it all go away. Magic the lion into a kitten, make the pitching still, let there be dawn in the blackness – a Northern lights dawn, a twilight chorus of colour. Let darkness be silenced by the fanfare of light. By the light that is you, lover. Hush now, my sweet. Hold me sweet. Hold me dear, my dear. My 'Just So' dearest dear. My Valentine.

* * *

"God, how long have I been out?"

* * *

"Gerry, you there, sweetheart? Oh God. Gerry? Tu'penny? Water, Gerry. Please. Water, please. Hello? Oh, there you are. You alright? What time is it? What *day* is it? No, first of all water, sweetheart. Please. *Please.* I must have water."

You are such a bastard, Ewart. Such a twenty-two carat shit. Just as long as your precious life isn't disturbed, hey? Just so long as nothing about it is ever questioned.

"You'll have to improvise somehow. Just right at the moment I can't move. I can barely talk – as you can hear. My throat's so dry. Like sandpaper. All of me, the whole inside of me, like sandpaper. *So* dry. Please. Find something. If necessary use your hands. One drop at a time. I must have water, Gerry." ... You're not angry with me. It's yourself, you shit, you're angry with. The only reason you hate me, Ewart, you hate me – *hated* me – because I made you question. Yourself. Your life.

"Thank you, thank you. O God, thank you."

But even more than hating me, you hated yourself. For never having done so of your own volition. For needing me to lead you to the questions. For knowing, without me, you'd never have found the guts.

* * *

"Hi, there. Feel like filling your shirt, sweetheart, with another load of water? That'd be really good. Then I'm going to need you, I'm afraid, to walk me to the loo. God knows how. God knows, I mean, how we're going to manage that. But I need to pee, I'm afraid.

"No, water first. Water. Please. That first."

Oh God, stop me hurting this much. Please God, stop me hurting this much.

"It's good, this shirt. Clever of you to think of it. Clever, yes, of you. Necessity, all that sort of stuff, mother of ..., all that. God, no champagne – ever – has tasted as sweet. Could you, do you think, drip some onto my forehead? We're going to have to go to the loo soon. Pretty soon. I'm bursting here, busting a gut, sweetheart.

"Could you give me a hand, Gerry, do you think? If you could just help me to stand."

"No, I'm not kidding, Gerry. I need you to help me. I need you to help me stand."

"Gerry, please. It's not the moment, old mate, for wisecracks and stuff. Please, Gerry. Help me. Please."

"No, sorry, it can't be rushed. It just can't be. I'm afraid if I burst, then I just burst. I'm sorry and all that – would be sorry – but I can only do what I can do. Just as *you* can." ... Keep it together, Titus. You've got to keep this together. It's not only Ewart, you know, who's been a twenty-two carat shit. Pay-back time, old darling. ... "If you could just help me up. Upsa daisy. Gently, Gerry. Gently, gently. God, it hurts!

"No, that's not going to work. Try not to jerk, eh, tu'penny? Try just to pull in one smooth movement. I'll push down on the bed at the same time. On the count of three, maybe?" For once – *once*, Titus, in your whole miserable bloody existence – think of someone else.

"Remember, old mate, nice and smoothly does it. Nice and smoothly. Okay ... two, three." 'Bloody', that's even quite funny in the circumstances.

"Oh, wow. Still, I'm up. No, don't let me go, Gerry. Let me hold you. Bit giddy." Even if, Titus, that miserable bloody existence is about to end. "Bit ... if you could just let me lean on you. Till I get to the bathroom, at least." No, not 'even', 'because'.

"I need to lean on you, Gerry. This is not a game. Please don't be difficult." *Because* it is going to end, Titus, prove to yourself you can think of someone other than yourself.

"I cannot go on my knees to beg you because I wouldn't get up again. I'm begging you, though, Gerry, *please* to help me. Please."

Please, God, just let me die. *Please.* A heart-attack, a stroke. Something quick. Get me out of this pain. *Please.* Now!

"Thank you.

"And that's a lesson worth remembering: Don't get on your knees to beg if you don't have the strength to get up again.

"I need to talk to you, Gerry, about stuff that's worth remembering. That can be the first one. No, no, sweetheart. I'm not a greyhound, you know. Easy does it, tu'penny. Make that: extremely easy does it. Hell's bells, that's a bruise or something, right there by the shin bone. Every time I tread on it, it's like treading on a glass splinter.

"And here's the second: We can only do what we can do. It's the codicil – I can only do what I can do – to Mr Wayne's famously drawled adage – easy, sweetheart, easy – that a man's got to do what a man's got to do. Which, interestingly enough – you do find this interesting, don't you, Gerry? – is very similar to what Gandhi used to say. The codicil, though, the thing worth remembering – too *fast*, tu'penny – the thing worth remembering is that a man can *only* do what a man can do. *I* can only do what I can do. It's so important to remember that. And, yes, I think I can make it from here. I know I can, in fact. I *can* make the *can*. Joke, Gerry. I'm going to be alright. You mustn't fret. We're both of us, both going to be alright. I'll just close the door, if you don't mind. Don't go too far away. I'm going to need your help getting back. ..."

* * *

"Okay, sweetheart. Gerry? You there? 'Course you're there, what am I talking about? I mean, where else do you have to go? Okay, I need a hand again. Sorry. Getting back to bed. I would slurp some water, but I can't. I just can't. We'll have to use your shirt again. I just haven't got the strength.

Just a thought, God: Do you answer *anyone's* prayers? I mean, I know it's not only mine You ignore. I've known about prayers of Valentine's You've ignored, of Louise's when she was younger, of Ewart's and Justin's. I don't believe it's only our family. So, the question remains, God: Is there *anyone's* prayers which You listen to?

"Gently ... easy ... I'm pulling a face, Gerry, 'cos it's tender. Sore. I'm sore all over. I'm aching in places, Gerry, where I didn't know I had places. That's an old joke, I'm afraid. Older even than I am."

"No, you're right. Nothing's older than I am, sweetheart. Even Time itself, next to me, is a mere stripling. Nice and gently, then. Onto the bed. Very gently, tu'penny. Don't worry too much if I 'oof' and 'ouch'. I'm fine, really. Really. Well, not right now. But I will be. Right now, though – sorry, sweetheart – I need to sleep. I just have to sleep. Sorry."

'If I should die before I wake ...'

* * *

"'Morning, Gerry."

"Well, good evening, then. How long have I been asleep?"

"Oo!

"Not a clever move. Gently does it still, I think. I wonder ... do you think I might prevail upon you again, kind sir, to lug me into an upright position?"

"*Really* black, are they? Both of them? Well, if they come in brandishing steak, let's do a deal. We won't put it on the bruises, we'll just eat it."

"No, the steak, clot. Not the eye."

"Yeah, I think you're right. Fat chance, as you say."

"Easy does it, Gerry. Oof. Easy, easy does it, old tu'penny. Okay, that's one leg. Now the other. Gently, gently. Right. And now the big one. Getting up. Just a slow and even pull, remember?

"Good boy. Okay, on three. ... Two, three.

Mummy, please make the pain go away. Please. Please kiss it better.

"Well done. Well done."

"No, let's see if I can get there by myself. Can you see anything I might be able to use as a stick?"

Kiss *me* better, Mummy. Kiss me all-over-me better.

"Well, maybe if you put the chair in the middle of the room, and left the bathroom door open. And if I inch my feet forward thusly ... Okay, okay. That's the chair. Halfway there." **Mummy, *PLEASE.***

"What have you been doing with yourself all day long?

"More 'Patience'? Right, the bathroom door. No, don't help me, tu'penny. I have to do it for myself. They taken you for more football?"

"They *never* took you? Oh dear, I'm sorry to hear that. **Don't cry, Titus. You are not to cry. You cannot cry. You must not, Titus, cry.** "They really are bastards, aren't they? And, no, I don't care if you tell Mummy I called them that. That's what they are: bastards.

"Made it!

"I'm just going to close the bathroom door, Gerry. I'll be alright. If I'm not, I'll just yell, okay? I know I should have called her 'Mum'. Sorry. Thank you for not having reminded me." ***You* kiss me all over, Emily. Valentine, I mean.** Some habits are difficult to break. Make that, *all* habits are difficult to break." **I meant Valentine. Of course I meant Valentine. Valentine, you kiss me all-over-me better.**

* * *

"Is it going to come out? The 'Patience', is it going to come out?"

"A lot better. A whole lot better, in fact. Thank you for asking. If it wouldn't be too much trouble, though, I would *really* like some water. I'm desperate for water."

"Oh, they did, did they? And have you eaten?"

"Well, you should have done, tu'penny. Now both our meals've gone cold. I think we've gone past that sort of politesse – whatever it is – in our relationship. Of waiting,

I mean, for the other to be ready before we eat. It's going to be pretty hard, isn't it, getting back to civilisation? Getting back, at least, to that place so many people like to call 'civilisation'. They brought a cup?!

"Could you use the cup, tu'penny? Bring your old gramps a cup of water? You have no idea how parched I am. Still parched."

Why did I say Emily? Why – let's face it, Titus – did you *want* Emily? A Mummy-substitute, was that it?

"Thanks. Thank you so much." No, it wasn't. It bloody wasn't. "Wonderful. Keep 'em coming, Gerry." I wanted her. It was her I wanted. Emily I wanted. It was her all-over kisses I wanted. Her touch, her body I wanted.

"Wonderful. ... Please, sir, I want some more. ... I've got a sort of biley taste in the back of my mouth, somewhere in my throat. Somewhere not reachable." No, it wasn't. It was you I wanted, Valentine. Please don't be jealous. I wanted, lover, you. "If you could just fetch me another one. I'll just keep it here. Sip at it, rather than glugging it." I *only* wanted you, lover. *Your* body, *your* touch. Have only ever wanted you.

"I'll just take the tomato. I want you to eat the rest. Please, Gerry, don't argue with me. I haven't got the strength to fight you. I *need* you to eat it. I'm not going to be able to. I'll just sick it up again. And they'll simply take it away. Throw the food away. You know what they're like. I couldn't bear to see that food going to waste. Please, sweetheart, for me."

"Thank you."

...

* * *

"*Ah, buenas días.*" Please don't hurt me. Please God, don't hurt me. I wouldn't survive another beating. Please, Joaquín, *please*, don't beat me again. "*¿Es café que huelo?* Shake a leg, Gerry. Stir your stumps." God, I'm still shaking. Still so scared. So shit scared, it's pathetic. ... "*Nuestro amigo, Joaquín, nos he traido café.* Joaquín's brought us coffee, Gerry. Smells good, I just told him. Look lively, then. There's a brave soldier. There's a good chap."

Titus, Titus, will you please stop putting on this front, this fucking Bruce Lee act or something! They hurt you, Titus. Of course you're going to be scared.

"Smell that? Smells good, no? God, I'm hungry. You hungry? I could eat a horse. I could eat a *rocking* horse, come to think about it.

"*Gracias. Gracias, Joaquín. Muy amable.*"

"Well, I'm trying to be nice to him, Gerry, to *stop* him beating me again. Does that make sense?

"It's hot. Drink it whilst it's hot. It'll cheer you up.

"It's also good and strong. Put hairs on your chest, old tu'penny. At least the coffee's good, huh? Had to be some advantages, didn't there, to being kidnapped in Colombia?

"You wiped away a lot of the blood, cleaned me up. I noticed when I went to the bathroom. That was a very grown-up thing to have done. That took a lot of courage. Well done, Gerry. Well done and thank you."

"They're not going to hurt you, Gerry. They are not going to hurt you. Please stop going on like that. *Please.*"

"Well, think about it: If they were going to hurt you, they'd already have done it. I mean, they were still trying to get me to say we were Colin and Wictor. I'm just going to lie down for a bit, tu'penny. Close my eyes. It hurts less with my eyes closed."

"No, I've no idea why. There. That's better. They thought, Gerry, a bit of 'persuasion' might help. Well, what greater 'persuader' could there be than for me to witness you in pain? Could there possibly be, Gerry?"

"Hurting children, it's been a ruse, sweetheart, of torturers for as long as there've been torturers ...

"Okay, a 'for instance': There was a general of Chile, Gerry, name of Pinochet. At the behest of the then American Secretary of State, a man called Kissinger, Pinochet was funded by the CIA to mount a coup against the elected president, a man called Allende. Are you eating?"

"Is it any good?"

"Well, okay's better than not okay, isn't it? That coup also happened, by the way, on September 11th – it's the September 11th that a lot of Americans don't talk about. And a whole lot more don't even know about. Allende is a name that probably doesn't mean very much to you yet. He was, I think, Isabel's uncle. Isabel Allende's."

"No, okay, you don't know that name either.

"It shames me now to admit this, but at the time, I was all for Pinochet. It was my terror of Communism, I suppose. I thought then that anything – pretty much *anything* – was permissible if it kept the evil of Communism at bay. I'd been to Moscow, you see, been to what was then Leningrad, various other cities behind the Iron Curtain, Bucharest, for instance. I'd been to Warsaw and to Prague. I'd experienced the repression there – Christ, you couldn't not! –, seen what Communism had done, what it was capable of doing.

"I'd also seen what the trades unions had done at home. The destructive nonsense of wildcat strikes and so on. Not forgetting what they'd done to me personally. I was creating a business, for God's sake. I was supplying work, people with an income. You'd have thought I was ... I was trying to institute some latterday droit du Seigneur, or something. Or re-introduce it. Bed all their daughters. I mean, how wrong can you get? It was the unions which created a division in my work-place, not me. I was *not* playing golf all the time. I worked harder than any other man there. And most of the work-force knew it. So did the shop stewards. But they chose to ignore that fact. As they chose to ignore any facts unpalatable to their cause.

"I was also getting attacked, about then, by the feminists. For no other reason than that I was a man. I was outraged by their attacks, outraged. I felt abused. I'd done nothing to offend women, indeed largely I'd championed them, why should they be targeting me? Or lumping me in with all the real male chauvinist pigs there were around?

"So I understand – I do really understand – the American man-in-the-street today who becomes uppity and defensive. He thinks he's done nothing to hurt the world. Indeed he thinks he's done plenty to help it – *plenty* to help. He's been told often enough, with his breakfast and his lunch and his dinner (and with his elevenses, and bar snacks, and late-night cookies!) just how much he's done – he's *doing* – to help. They're so seldom told the truth, Americans, that's such a large part of the problem. That Fox News is allowed to call itself news beggars belief.

"For years I kidded myself that then I didn't know the truth about Pinochet, but, of course, it was more to do with my *preferring* not to know the truth. I wanted to believe Kissinger was a good man. I needed to believe that. I needed to believe that Pinochet was curing the ills of the Chilean economy, was keeping freedom going.

"The point I'm trying to make (although at the time I would – true – have ascribed this to so much Bolshevik propaganda), Pinochet, in order to get their parents to talk, he used to torture the children of his opponents. So did Saddam Hussein – who was also at the time receiving extremely large cheques from the CIA. Hussein was not always America's Number One enemy. The story that does not get told is that the same people who denounced him as a tyrant had originally sold him his weapons of terror. Of course that's another story, Gerry. Of course it is. But it's also – and so much – the same one.

"The unscrupulous, Gerry – and this *is* the point –, always threaten children first. They are the Achilles' heel of any parent or grandparent. Joaquín and Oswaldo, they *didn't* hurt you, tu'penny. And they could have. They didn't and therefore they're not going to.

"'We will survive this, Gerry.' Remember? 'We will get through it.'

"Have you been eating?"

"Good. Well done."

"Well, he's never really been a contender, has he – not a serious one – for the Chef of the Year award? Try and eat more when it comes.

"I have to close my eyes now, tu'penny. Sorry, Gerry, I just *have* to rest."

I'm toppling. Toppling off a cliff. Into darkness. Into black. Is this death? Am I toppling into death?

* * *

"'Patience'. That's an idea! You must have got pretty good in the last couple of days. Thank you, you know, for having looked after me and things."

"Right, 'Patience'. You going to deal?"

"You've been grown-up, shown yourself to be grown-up, Gerry, and that's great. That's wonderful. Remember I told you you'd have to be more grown-up now than you've ever been? Well, I need you to be super grown-up now, Gerry.

"No, carry on dealing.

"*Super* grown-up, do you understand?

"Gerry, tu'penny, my old mate, the thing is this – and this is so hard for me to say you cannot imagine – but the thing is this: If they take me out again, Gerry, and beat me again like they did the last time, I'll die. I know it. I'm sorry to have to be so stark, but that's the way of it, that's the fact of it, the fact of the matter.

"I'm not just your old man's old man, Gerry, I *am* an old man. An old man in fact and in years. I simply will not survive. ...

"No, don't cry, tu'penny. Not now. And *no*, please don't touch me. Sorry, but I'm still too sore. Too delicate, too fragile. Delicate little flower that I am. You have to listen to me, Gerry. You have to. *You* must survive. You *must.* Do you hear me? You *must* survive, Gerry. That is an obligation that you have. You must listen to me, Gerry. You must, Gerry, hear."

Christ, Titus, what *are* you talking about?

"No, you mustn't. What am I talking about? You don't, Gerry, have to do anything of the sort. You don't *have* to do anything. You don't even *have* to survive. If that becomes an issue for you I won't be around. Doubtless Mummy – *Mum* – would like you to survive. But that is only a consideration. It does not make it into something you *must* do.

"No, don't touch me. Sorry, tu'penny, sorry. You have no idea how sore it still is, how sensitive."

"As you say, 'delicate little flower that I am.' I'm not saying they *are* going to kill me. It's more that, living, I've got to know that I've said as much as I can in the event of my dying. If you get my drift. If there's a drift to be got.

"You see, I've spent almost all of my life in a lie, Gerry. Believing a lie, or inventing one or spreading one. I'd like you, Gerry, not to do that. I'd like you to live your life in truth. I think that will make your life a happier experience, tu'penny. I can't give you that, can't give you truth. No-one can. Even you can't. But what you can give yourself, you can give yourself permission to hunt out the truth. And to hunt for the truth, Gerry, you have to start by getting rid of the lies. How can I explain this?

"There was a book, Gerry, an extraordinary book: 'Fingerprints of the Gods'. I read it when I was still with Granny. Its author argues that there was a civilisation on Earth predating ours by twenty thousand years or so. It's a fascinating hypothesis, well worth the read. I have no idea whether or not it contains a germ of truth, but it certainly, in my opinion, seemed to warrant further investigation. But if he's right, the author – Graham Hancock, I think his name is –, it means that Egyptologists, almost for as long as there has been such a thing, have been mistaken. He's re-dated the Sphinx, for example. And, scarcely surprisingly, it is therefore those selfsame Egyptologists who are the book's most vocal critics.

"I remember feeling for those Egyptologists. What must it be like, I thought, at the end of your career to be forced to recognise that your entire career was based on a false premise, that the entire foundation of your professional life was faulty?

"And then, Gerry, well, it happened to me. I fell in love with Valentine. And that started a domino effect which caused me to question everything I'd ever believed in.

"And I realised I had been wrong. And about so very many things.

"Oh, not that Communism was an evil – not, anyway, as practised in those countries which I had visited. But certainly in my belief that, because Communism was evil, Capitalism was good.

"Capitalism today threatens the whole of humanity, and a not inconsiderable chunk of the planet itself. It is Nero fiddling whilst Rome burns, and the band on 'The Titanic' playing up-beat numbers as the liner sinks.

"Greenpeace is derided, Friends of the Earth lampooned. The policies of governments and multinationals tittered over, like they were the peccadilloes of teenage children.

"It's extraordinary to me that people should laugh about their children being abused, but there we go. Nor about the slaughter of their grandchildren. There is, finally, none so blind as those who will not see.

"And that's why people like us, tu'penny – people, rather, like Colin and Wictor – get taken hostage. It's the last sentence, if you like, of an enormous book. Yes, a 'War and Peace'-size book."

"'War and Peace'? It's a novel by a Russian author called Tolstoy. It's a wonderful book. Read it, Gerry. Enjoy it. I so envy you your first time of reading it. It's beautiful. And exciting. And eye-opening.

"Tolstoy was appalled by much of what he saw around him. But what Tolstoy did have – and in abundance – was hope. Hope for mankind. Hope for life. Hope is slowly being confiscated from us, Gerry. Not so slowly either any longer.

"Don't allow them to confiscate hope from you, tu'penny. Just don't. Just say 'no'! Finally, without a tomorrow, there is no today.

"Sorry, I've got to go to the loo again."

* * *

My hand still hurts violently. My already indecipherable scrawl will become fairly hieroglyphicky - sorry. I'm also not too sure how much of my scrambled brain is yet back with me - so the thoughts too could be fairly hieroglyphicky. I will have to write in a higgledy-piggledy way, concentrating on what seems to me at that moment the most urgent thing that needs to be said.x

I'm not sure whether this is allowed or not, this letter-writing. The slightest noise outside the door, therefore - which is often noise that I've only imagined - and I've got the paper folded and hidden. That doesn't do much either for coherence of train of thought, or cohesion. But, if I'm honest, I must (also) confess that the clandestine nature of all of this does add a frisson of sort of DIY Mandela: the spindly writing, the listening for the shuffle of the guards. It appeals to the 'hero' I'd always like to have been, a latterday Hornblower or someone. Certainly not Bond. What a charmless oik is James Bond, when you cut through the crap. And also about as tasteless as his vodka bloody Martinis. Yes, I digress, you're right: I digress.

It was the flash of a spark, the burst of a gun. The rat-tat-tat of Gatling. The blink of a cobra's eye. One dead. A hundred dead. In the blink of a cobra's eye. After the first death, there is no other. Not death. Not sensations. Flashes of sensation. Vivid colour. A streak of scarlet fear. Primary colours. The smell of indigo.

I also, of course, don't want Gerry to find out about this. (If you're reading this, Gerry, I'm sorry for that deception. I hope the fact that you are reading it may help to explain to you why I felt I did need to keep it secret from you.) This letter may well smack to him/ you of Last Wills, all that. I don't think the fear that he lives with daily, and that he's conquering magnificently, needs compounding. I could also tell them, Gerry, what a snivelling little shit you can be at times. See how nice I am to you? See? *So, also, of course, any time he stirs, I have to hide all this. Any time he stirs? He stirs all the time.X And then some of the time he's at peace. At perfect peace.*

The most urgent thing I need to say to you is that which I've already said. But it could stand repetition, I think: I love you, all of you. With my heart and body and soul. As I approach death I see that love as having been - by far - the most important thing in my life.

My biggest regret is that I was not able to demonstrate the depth of that love. But, then, I'm not even sure about that. Do you need to build a Taj Mahal in order to express love? Is a love that needs that kind of tangible expression even love? Doesn't love, for love to be love, need to be a secure love?

The love, Valentine, I have for you.

The second most urgent thing to say is that, to quote O'Casey's Joxer Daly, 'the world is in a terrible state of chassis'.

Maybe you'll remember, Gerry, me talking to you about honesty, about the need we have to be honest with, at least, ourselves. That the lack of honesty today has a world dynamic. Well, almost the principle reason that the world is in the state of 'chassis' it so undeniably is today is because there is so little honesty.

Rudyard Kipling, perhaps most famously, wrote a poem called 'If'. For all its gung-ho stoicism, it's a rather good recipe for life. Kipling is, in fact, rather a good writer. He was, however, also a staunch imperialist. And so much of an advocate for the First World War that he pulled strings so that his otherwise ineligible son, John, was allowed to join the army. John was killed. It is said that Kipling never recovered from the grief. I suspect, even more than the grief, what he never recovered from was the self-recrimination. Take it from one who knows! I have lived that pain here in a thousand manifestations and in a million imaginings.

You know, all of you, how terrible my memory is. I'm not quoting exactly, I know. But later Kipling wrote a couplet something like:

'If asked why 'twas the sons have died,
Reply: "Because the fathers lied."'

I'm told that over the door to the Centre Court of Wimbledon, there is another quote from Kipling - from his 'If', to be precise: 'If you can meet with Triumph and Disaster/ And treat those two impostors just the same'. Know what? I rather fear that over the portal that leads to Armageddon will be engraved: 'Because the fathers lied.'

You have to see through the lies. If I have any last words to you, let them be those. You must see through the lies. And expose them.

* * *

"Not now, Gerry, huh? I *really need* to sleep, *sweetheart*. Please stop jabbing me like that. Please. ...

"*Oh, es usted, Oswaldo. Bueno, estoy listo.* ... It's alright, Gerry. Just relax, sweetheart. It's going to be okay. ... *Es que no puedo mobermi. Si me pegan de nuevo voy a morir.* ... No, don't cry, tu'penny. I'll be okay."

"Sure, I will. They're not going to beat me again. You

just heard me: 'If you beat me any more,' I said, 'I'll die.' They don't want me to die. Look how useless I am alive. How much more useless would I be dead?"

"Well, I shouldn't have said that. ... *Momento,* for Christ's sake, *por Dios. Estoy hablando con mi granhijo – con, perdón, mi nieto. No puedo* – What's walk, Gerry?

"*Caminar. O sea, van a tenir que* ... 'Help me', tu'penny?"

"*Que ayudarmi. Con dos no es suficiente* ...Well, I do need two of them. I can't walk by myself, can I? I do need help."

"Sweetheart, if I did say that earlier, about being shot, I was just rambling, just delirious or something, some kind of bad dream. Sorry. I'm so sorry. I really shouldn't have scared you like that."

"Of course I didn't do it on purpose. Didn't scare you on purpose. Still, I shouldn't have done it – not even in a dream – and I apologise. I'm truly very sorry."

"I'm sure they're taking me away, just to talk or something, take some more pictures of the battered me – they can't possibly want to beat me any more. I mean, where is there left to beat, right? Right? But, just in case ... no ... no 'just in case' ... *¿Esperan un minuto, no? ¿No pueden ver que estoy hablando todavia con mi nieto?* ... I'll be back – I'm sure of it – in two shakes of a lamb's tail – sure of it.

"*Bueno, caballeros. ¿Muy tranquilo, no? Muy tranquilo con migo, muy suave, muy delicado.* What's 'slowly', Gerry?"

"*Despacio, despacio ... okay ... despacio, amigos, suave* ... I'll see you, Gerry, in a bit. Two, as I said, shakes of a lamb's tail."

* * *

"What did I say? See, here I am, back again. *Tranquilo, por Dios. Tengo que sentarmi.* Can I lean on you too, Gerry? Sit me on the bed, tu'penny. *Tranquilo, Joaquín. Despacio.* Gently, sweetheart."

"No, they didn't beat me any more, sweetheart. It's not that. It's just the physical fact of walking. I'm going to be sick. *Voy a vomitar. No voy llegar hasta el baño.* Bring me something. *Traemi algo. ¡Por favor!* Is there anything I can be sick into, Gerry? They're obviously not going to bring anything. Bastards. *Por favor, Joaquín. Por favor.* See anything, Gerry? *En la cama, por sopuesto. Tranquilo. Tranquilo.* Anything at all? Take my shirt off me, tu'penny. You can wash a shirt. *¿Voy a sacar mi camisa, no? Para vomitar a dentro.*"

"*Si, si, si, muy comico, muy comico.* Go ahead, Gerry. Just do it, sweetheart. Just put it down on the floor. *Si, si, hasta luego* to you too. Arseholes. Sorry, what would Mummy say, heh? 'Mum', sorry. Sorry, sweetheart, I have to ..."

"I knew that had to happen. Sorry. Good job you put the shirt there. Just leave it, sweetheart. I'll cope with it when I wake up. I just have to rest now. Sorry, Gerry. Sorry, tu'penny."

* * *

Still. A perfect still. It must be death. The advent of death. Nothing in life is perfect. Not perfect as this is perfect. And nothing is so still. So completely, voluminously still. It must be the still, this, of the Buddhist Nirvana – the still that is absolute. Absolute nothing, and thus absolute everything. The still that is God and the life-force ... and death. The perfect still.

* * *

"Water, Gerry. Sorry."

"If they've taken the cup again, use your shirt. Anything. I must have some water. ... Oh, God bless you. God bless you, sweetheart. I've just got to close my eyes again. Just for a bit.

"Where's *my* shirt? Well, thank you. Thank you for washing it. Just leave it on the floor, though, would you, sweetheart? I think I'm going to be sick again. I think I might be. Quickly, Gerry.

"No, false alarm. Still. You might as well leave it there now. Might as well. I know you're going to think I'm terribly wet – do they still use that word at school? – wet: a weed, someone puny, inadequate."

"Sort of like a nerd, yes, I suppose. I've just got to sleep, though, tu'penny. Just got to ..."

"It's only a little finger, Gerry. And on the left hand. Don't worry about it."

* * *

"Oops. Sorry. Sorry, Gerry. I didn't mean to disturb you. Didn't mean to wake you. I thought I could get to the bathroom by myself. I've got to use the loo."

"No, I think it's better, see whether I can't make it by myself. I have to fend for myself. I have to be *able* to fend for myself. My tummy's rumbling quite badly, I'm afraid. I don't know whether you might want to sit by the window or something. There could be some ... unfortunate noises, let's say. Maybe sing to yourself. Maybe loudly.

"See? I'm coping really rather well, aren't I? I mean, I'm scarcely in condition to run a marathon or anything, but, well, for an old man – for *your* old man's old man – not doing badly. I do think a song would be helpful, sweetheart."

"Well, then, it would be helpful to *me*."

"I don't know, Gerry. *Any* song. Any song, for Christ's sake. Sorry. Sorry, I didn't mean to shout. Sorry, sweetheart. Sorry. Gerry, please. *Please*. I just cannot cope, sweetheart, not with your tears, not on top of everything else. Not just right at the moment, no? I just need you to hum some fucking tune, Gerry – sorry, hum some flipping tune, sing it, dum-di-dum it, save me, for God's sake, some modicum here of embarrassment. Okay?"

Are you going to leave me any dignity, God? Any at all, I mean? Is there any other humiliation you'd like to yoke me with? Any at all, I mean?

"Well, I guess that was fairly graphic. Not too much there left to the imagination. Sorry. Sorry about that. I'm sure it's something psychiatrists, whatever, would think was very good for 'bonding'. I'm afraid, all I feel is embarrassed, and therefore awkward. I shouldn't have shouted at you earlier. I know that. It's not your fault. None of this is your fault, I do know. But I cannot tell you how uncomfortable I am – was – with this whole scene we've just enacted here, this whole mini scenario, whatever it is.

"See. See how much better I'm walking. I don't feel quite as sick either. What did I tell you? They can't keep a good dog down, you know. Not even an old dog. Not if he's good. But down ... I do need to sit down. Lie down, even. I'm going to try not to sleep. You've been deprived of company, I know that, for way too long.

"Help me down, would you, tu'penny? It's so much easier, you have no idea, if I can hold your hands, can sort of ease my bottom back onto the bed. So hugely much easier. I've said I'm sorry, Gerry. Don't sulk on me. I need you to be grown-up at the moment. *Really* grown-up, I mean. Not pretend grown-up.

"Okay, well, I did get to the bathroom and back, mostly

by myself. I was able to slurp for myself. Things are on the up-and-up. And – heavens, I nearly forgot – certainly they are for you. I should have told you earlier, but ... well, with everything else – it's not that I forgot – it's just that I couldn't find the whatever it is (or was) to express it. Nerve, was it? Or energy? Whichever. Or something else entirely.

"They're going to let you go, Gerry. Sometime very soon. Certainly in the next day or two. Maybe in the next couple of hours. So, better hurry up and get yourself packed."

"No, sweetheart, I was kidding. They're not going to kill me. I was only kidding."

"It's some intermediary. Red Cross or something or Médecins Sans Frontières. It's not either of them, but it's some organisation like them. They started gabbling, truth to tell, at that moment. I wasn't too sure. Not too important, is it, either? Not really? Or relevant? You're getting out, that's the important thing. And someone – whoever he is, or she – is acting as intermediary between them and the British embassy. Mummy's already there, already waiting for you. 'Mum', sorry.

"What's the matter? Why are you crying? It's good news, Gerry. They're going to release you. You're going to be free. No, sweetheart, please don't do that." **When you were a baby, is what I want to tell you, when your father and I were still talking, when your grandmother and I, we were still together, still baby-sitting, one of the worst parts of that job – no, *the* worst –, you'd suddenly cry.** "I love you to bits, Gerry, to *bits* – but just now I can't have you dangling around my neck like that, hugging me, cuddling me, whatever. I told you it just hurts too much. It just, Gerry, hurts too much. Sorry. Sorry, for Christ's sake."

And for no apparent reason.

"Don't tell me you're crying about that. You were crying

before you even tried to hug me. For joy, is that it? You crying for joy, Gerry?"

And you would not be comforted. You'd cry and you'd cry and you'd cry.

"Well, what is it, then? What, for Christ's sake?"

And those tears, those sobs, they strobed through me, laser beams of agony. And the torture was that I didn't know what was torturing *you.*

"I'm sorry, I don't mean to shout, but you have to tell me, Gerry. I have to know."

And there have been times, Gerry – there was the odd occasion – when I just wanted to lift you from your cot, your pram, whatever, lift you as Granny taught me to, lift you as if you were Dresden china, protecting the fontanelle or something – whatever the hell that is –, carry you like you were the most fragile and most precious thing on Earth, and simply beat your head against the nearest wall. That's the way it is with children. With all love, maybe.

"Gerry, we need to talk. God, that makes us sound, doesn't it, like an old married couple? What I mean is, *I* need to talk. Before you go. I need to know that anything we might need to say to each other has been said."

"No, it doesn't mean that, Gerry. But it's always good ... One of the few pieces of good advice ... One of the few pieces of advice *my* grandfather gave *me* which was of any use was never to go to bed on a quarrel. And that *is* good advice. Not that I always heeded it. But that's what good advice is usually for: to be ignored. Bad advice I heeded all the time. When I didn't heed that good advice, though, I paid for it. And even when I was busy ignoring it, I was still aware of it, still aware – as I sulked my way to bed – that what I was doing was not wise. Same sort of thing here: We've had quite some time together, and *only* the two of us. Now there's going to be a time (only a short one, I hope) when we're not together. But when we are *next* together, the together we'll be, that's going to be entirely different from the together we have been."

"Well, for a start, we'll have other people around us. Your parents, for instance. I imagine your mother won't again let you out of her sight till you're drawing the old age pension. But the dynamic too, sweetheart, that will have changed. At the moment, we're surviving. Then, we will have survived. Always, always there will be a bond between us – over and above, I mean, the usual grand-father/grandson bond. And that's a strong bond. An enormously strong one. As Freud put it, we have a common enemy. Just like now, in fact. A different common enemy, that is, of course. Still ... But never again will that bond be what it is today."

I never, Ewart, wanted you as my enemy. Never wanted you indeed as anything more than someone to treasure. But you can't keep on – *I* can't – keep on treasuring something which spits back in your face – which *only* spits.

"So, if there's anything you want to say to me, tu'penny, spit it out now." I'd done most things, hadn't I, right until then? Hadn't I?

"No, okay, I agree with you, there *is* no point in talking just for the sake of it. But ..."

"Alright, sure, I talk a lot. Maybe I'm even a bit of a chatterbox ..."

"Fine, a *lot* of a chatterbox, then." I'd been a pretty good father. I'd done most things right. Not everything, of course.

"Anything at all, really." Of course, not everything. But, as parents go, as fathers do, I think I'd done pretty well. Pretty damn well, ask me.

"Let's divide it up into chunks, then. This ... whatever it is ... this event in your life, this cataclysmic event – Oww! Christ! Jesus Christ!"

"No, it's alright. I just leant on my elbow, that's all. I didn't realise how bruised it was." Maybe I should've kept it from you, my love for Valentine. But if I had've kept it from you, how could I possibly have been true to myself? "Do you know what I mean by a rite of passage? It's something that marks your transition from childhood into adulthood. The Jews, if you're male, celebrate it as a 'bah mitzvah'. And it's a huge sort of a birthday party/ first communion/ confirmation all rolled into one. You remember Bela, my business partner?"

"He had, he told me, a lot of Jewish friends when he was at school. And the jealousy he had of them around their bah mitzvah time, all the goodies that were coming their way, he would, he told me one day, have sold his soul to have been Jewish.

"Well, this rite of passage, Gerry, of yours – this somewhat eccentric and unJewish bah mitzvah – this puts all the other comparisons in the shade. All the others, is what I mean to say, pale (by contrast) into insignificance. This has been huge for you, Gerry, enormous. For some time, I should imagine, you won't even realise how huge it's been. And you've coped with it, tu'penny. Not only have you survived, but you've come through your ordeal with colours, not only flying high, flying – Gerry – off the Empire State Building, off the peak of Mount Everest – but off the tail, Gerry, of the Space Shuttle as it orbits around the far side of the moon. And for the rest of your life, you must know that.

"So, let's start there. Is there anything you want to talk about that's happened to you here in the last weeks? ...

"The thing is, if you say it now, it'll be over. It'll have been said. It'll be out in the open. You've heard me tell you, problems hate oxygen. Air a problem and very often it simply evaporates. Same with grievances, Gerry, or resentments. These enormous things which we keep quiet about, voiced become usually quite small things – often tiny and insignificant things. But even if they *are* big things – even if they're gigantic things – the thing about airing them, about voicing them, is that it stops them getting any bigger."

"What do I mean? You're right: I'm not expressing myself well. You're right."

Don't flinch now, Titus. Don't you dare flinch. You've got to tell him this stuff, old man. Got to. This is important stuff. *Important* stuff. You want to die not having told him it?

"I saw a tv programme once about debt. This couple had had a store credit of four pounds. Four pounds, tu'penny! And they hadn't paid it and hadn't paid it. Eventually the store sued them for ... I can't remember ... but something close to five hundred pounds. Well, we pay a sort of emotional interest as well. Compound too. Equally usurious.

"All that British stoicism, that stiff upper lip, grinning-and- bearing-it, that Teutonic emotional Spartanism, all of that stuff which was supposed to be the backbone of the British empire, that's all it did, tu'penny, in the final analysis: It made Himalayan mountains out of molehills the size of zits. And that's why Victorians, as an entire generation, abused their children – and why *their* children abused *theirs*. That's one of the reasons there continues to be the amount of parental abuse around that there is. Abuse is also by neglect. The Press teaches us, the most successful lying is by omission. Parents lacking the time for their children are neglecting them.

"There's always two sides to any deal, though, Gerry, and your side of this deal is that, when I hurt you, you say 'ouch'. I've abused you. I know I have. I'm sorry for that. Sometimes enormously sorry, other times only a little bit.

Not been there for you. No, I phrased that badly. For some of the abuse I am enormously sorry – that day I took you back to the shop when I thought you'd stolen those sweets, which – no – you hadn't; and for other instances of the abuse less so, like when I shouted at you because you would not stop whining that you wanted an Action Man for your birthday. It's completely inevitable, sweetheart – as, when you are a father, you will also know –, that you abuse your children. And then your grandchildren. You can't not. But for every time you do so consciously or malevolently, you do it a hundred times – maybe a thousand – unconsciously or even with very good intentions. And know what? You cannot blame me for that unless, when I hurt you, you say 'ouch'.

"So, what I'm saying, Gerry, what I'm asking you to do – for my benefit, sure, but mostly for the benefit of you and your future – I'd like you to let out now all the 'ouches' you've suffered in silence."

Don't let him worm out of it. And don't, Titus, let *yourself* worm out of it!

"Well, you were angry with me when I was sick."

"It doesn't matter that it wasn't my fault. In fact, you may have been angrier with me precisely because it wasn't."

"Gerry, this is important, tu'penny. Don't drift away from me. Ow! Hell's bells, there doesn't seem to be a single position I can be comfortable in, that's not just lying down or sitting bolt upright. No sort of compromise. That isn't life-like, Gerry. Life is, finally, all about compromise. If you're wise, that is. I think I just wrote a proverb there: 'If you're wise, compromise' or, even better, 'Compromise is comprowise'. No? Alright, suit yourself.

"See, you're angry with me now. It's that kind of thing I'm talking about. This talk is making you feel uncomfortable. Therefore the talker is making you uncomfortable. Therefore I am. But it's not the talker making you angry but the listener. Being angry with yourself, though, is a lot less comfortable than being angry with someone else, so the part of you angry with yourself is angry with me for making you angry with yourself and even angrier with me for making you aware that you *are* angry with yourself.

"Does that make any sense to you? At all?"

"No? Know what? It doesn't really matter. Because emotions and sense are only occasionally cause-and-effect. Oh, if you're a skilled therapist you can usually trace an emotion to some sort of rationale, but the route there is so tortuous as finally to become, almost, meaningless. Tortuous, I should have said, and cyclical."

It doesn't matter that he's not listening. Who knows what might sink in? What may just be absorbed? This is stuff, Titus, for the whole rest of his life. Wouldn't *your* life have been better if you'd heard this stuff at nine? Even at fifty-nine? Or sixty-nine?

"I was furious with my father for his early death. Furious." Sixty-nine, now, there's a thought ...! "And I have traced the path now whereby I understand quite why I was furious – and *so* furious. I'm not sure, though, the effort was worth it. I don't think – this is what I'm trying to say – that knowing why we're feeling what we're feeling is as important as acknowledging that such-and-such *is* what we're feeling. So many times in my life, Gerry – *so* many times – I've made the mistake of thinking I couldn't possibly be feeling what it is I was feeling because it didn't make sense that I was feeling that. Hot in the South Pole, sort of idea. Sense, in that sense, is nonsense. You *can* feel hot in the South Pole. The sun does shine on the day your girlfriend breaks up with you. When you use sense in that kind of way it becomes, well, *non*sense. It's not, then, a sledge-hammer to crack a nut, it's a sledge-hammer to crack a boiled egg – not even that, a sledge-hammer, rather, to fill a rotten tooth, or to whisk a meringue or something.

"Listen, Gerry, it's fine by me that you go back to your 'Patience', but also, tu'penny, you must listen to me. You have to listen to me, sweetheart. ... This ... whatever ... this rite of passage, it doesn't matter what we say here, what we do, it's going to haunt you pretty much for the rest of your life. There's nothing I can do about that, I'm afraid. I don't think, frankly, there's a whole heap that could be done even by an army of shrinks and councillors and therapists in general. But what I don't want it to do, sweet-heart, what I'm trying to avoid here is that it obsesses you, that it becomes the essence of your life, its core. I want you to have the space in your life for love – of women, your own children, your job, your hobbies, of the theatre and books and dance and music, of flowers and cats and forests and armadillos, of ... well, of this whole magical process called 'life'. I also want you to have space in your life for all the problems of that 'life', for all the shit of 'shit happens'. Because, in their own peculiar and perverse way, those problems add to life's fun, and that shit adds to its fragrance.

"This is work, tu'penny. Work that needs to be done. We don't only have to survive this, we have to *survive* it, if you know what I mean. You remember meeting André's father? You remember André? My accountant, the one before Randolph? You thought there was something very strange about his father. And there was, tu'penny, there was. He'd been a prisoner of the Japanese during the war. He'd worked on the infamous railway line, the 'Bridge Over the River Kwai' one. And he'd survived. But he'd only sort of survived. Most of the Japanese p.o.w.'s – certainly of those

I've met – have only sort of survived. I was going to wonder how many would have survived a whole heap better if they'd been given some sort of therapy once they'd been liberated. But (and here, Gerry, I'm going to contradict myself: I make that point, so that, dear one, you don't have to!) I also knew a survivor of Bergen-Belsen. Who, when released, was suspected by the British of being an SS officer in disguise. She was therefore treated by them with enormous suspicion, and no little additional discomfort. This woman has never in her life had an hour's counselling, not ten minutes' worth, and yet she is one of the most together people I've ever met. Together, strong, healthy, resilient without being callous, and determined whilst remaining compassionate. An entirely rounded human-being who has, obviously, seen the very worst of human conduct and, I suspect, the very best; who has also met the very worst in herself and the best – and who is at peace with it all.

"Don't ever worry, incidentally, about contradicting yourself. Life is a very contrary experience. It's only politicians who are always sure. And look at what they've done to the world! And, worse, what they *are* doing to it. There will, whatever theory you are propounding, always be uncomfortable facts or insights which discredit it – even blow it out of the water. That doesn't always mean the theory is wrong. The laws of aerodynamics, finally, do apply even though bumble-bees flaunt them.

"I don't any longer believe in violence. That's another reason why there is so much irony attached to our present situation. Christ, Gerry, that's scarcely news to you. You know how much I don't believe in violence. But if one of those guys – Joaquín or Oswaldo or Juanito or any of them – if one of them was hurting you and the only way I could stop them hurting *you* would be by hurting *them*, would I do it? Would I even *kill* them? In a heart-beat, sweetheart. Without a second's hesitation. Can I then turn around and say that I *still* don't believe in violence? Of course I can. It's an indication of how seriously crass the level of public debate has become that a spontaneous outburst of aggression – of defensive aggression, at that – can be equated to the measured and callous brutality which is war.

"Do you think ...? Would you mind, Gerry, getting me some water? I could manage it. The walk, I mean. Of course I could. But you have no idea, sweetheart, how difficult it is, just moving. Even keeping my eyes open, Gerry, hurts. I'd be grateful, tu'penny.

"Thanks, sweetheart. Thank you."

"Okay, well, let's talk, then, about pre-kidnap life. About issues you might have had around me then."

"Well, like for instance, me splitting up with Granny. Let's take that for a starter. Like me being gay, we could lump those two together, if you like. And don't tell me you weren't angry with me about those things. Even very angry."

"Oh, you're through it, are you? Well, that's good. So, when all your friends are making all their schoolboy jokes about shirt-lifters or ginger beers, you treat all that, do you, with equanimity? You boldly announce, 'Please do not disparage the gay community,' you proclaim, 'my grandfather is a member of it.'

"We still live in a homophobe society, Gerry. You think I don't know that? Christ, I live in it, for heaven's sake. It's just that now instead of homosexuality it is homophobia that is in the closet. But it's a pretty leaky closet, that one. I'd have hated, by the way, – and I do mean 'hated' – for my grandfather to have been gay. I'd have seen it as some kind of betrayal. I can't explain exactly why. I've thought about it a lot. I like to think I've even thought it through, though I suspect I'm flattering myself. I would, Gerry, have *hated* it.

"You remember what I was talking about earlier, about sense?"

"Well, that's another case in point. You try 'sensing' yourself out of being gay. Oh, there were all sorts of theories dancing around, particularly (if I remember rightly) in the 60's and 70's, about what it was that 'turned' a person gay: hormonal imbalance, I remember was one, genetic predisposition, overprotective mothers ... too many corn flakes in puberty."

"Well, no, it wasn't. But it might as well have been. It was flakey enough, if you'll excuse the pun, to have fitted in well alongside most of the others. There was even in the '60's some kind of 'cure' for it involving ingesting large amounts of LSD. The sheer madness of it all.

"I suspect the theory prevalent today is much nearer the mark: that our sexuality is as individual as our DNA, and that merely to separate the world into the gay, the straight and the bi is about as sensible as dividing it up into those with brown eyes, those with green and those with blue. God, the nonsense that was spouted in those days! That it was all, all of it, well intentioned, doesn't stop it being nonsense.

"Dear old Oscar was fond of saying that there is nothing so rare as common sense. I'm becoming more and more convinced that there are few things less relevant. To what we're feeling, anyway. And what we're feeling, eventually that is the only reality. Many Buddhist monks eat only if they are given food. They are even more mendicant than the down-and-out squatting on a street corner in London with his emaciated dog and his placard of desolate cardboard. And yet their two realities are vastly different.

And so is the reality they create around them: The monk is as venerated as the down-and-out is despised.

"You know something I've learnt, sweetheart – I'm suddenly saying that a lot, aren't I? 'Know something'? Sorry. – One of the things, sweetheart, I've learnt in the about three thousand years since I've been alive, I've learnt that something else common to virtually the entire of humanity is that we all have skeletons in the cupboard.

"And I've also learnt that it suits the powers-that-be that that's where we keep those skeletons. It helps keep us compliant – and *pliant*, come to that. Malleable, elastic. If we're scared that one day our guilty secret – or secrets – will be found out, our emotional energies are drained in trying to keep that secret secret. We're not going to make too much noise in case it attracts someone to our cupboard. These aren't huge skeletons – the skeletons of murder, not even of pick-pocketing. The hugeness of our skeletons is only in our heads. That our father might have been gay, for instance, or that Mummy has a drink problem. Not that I'm suggesting, tu'penny, not for a second that Mummy does have a drink problem. Nor, come to that, that a drink problem is not a serious problem. Nor that having a gay father isn't. I've seen 'Friends'. I know the problems Chandler has."

"It's a sitcom, Gerry, an American sitcom. We were talking about problems. Let's not stray from that, from problems. There's no problem, is what I'm trying to say, that is going to be made any easier or lighter – or more copable with – by not talking about it. That specie of problem just does not exist.

"Look at it, sweetheart, like this: Talking about your problems is not only extremely healthy, it is also an act of political subversion. It frees your concerns to concentrate on precisely that which government doesn't want you to concentrate on. And ... know what else, Gerry? ..."

"No, I used it deliberately there ... know what else, tu'penny, I've learnt in my three thousand years on this planet? What government doesn't want you to concentrate on, it's precisely on that, tu'penny, you want to concentrate.

"You're a man now, Gerry. You've been through a rite of passage which will make you a giant among men. This Herculean rite of passage, as it should be called. And like the Bible says ... No, come to think of it, I'm not wild about it, that passage, 'Now I am a man,' that whole number, 'I have put away childish things'. No, that's not what being a man, being an adult is all about. Who knows what Shaw was thinking when he wrote that youth is wasted on the young. I suspect it was that the young lack the experience to appreciate all that youth gives them. And, of course, he's right. But he could also have meant – and he would have been right here too – that the young lack the maturity to understand the maturity already contained within them. And he could also have written that age is wasted on those who have only aged. The man who has only aged is one who shuns his own childishness. The truly adult is the one who recognises that adult is still part child.

"I can hear Hitler saying, 'Now that I am a man I have put aside childish things.' I can hear Stalin saying that. But I can't hear Gandhi saying it, or Martin Luther King.

"It doesn't look like they're letting you go tonight, I'm afraid. Never mind. Pity. For you, I mean. For me ... Well, I hope you know by now that every moment in your company is a joy for me. But I know you must be hankering after ... so many things, I suppose. Seeing Mum again, having a hot bath, sleeping on a decent bed, having something halfway decent to eat. God, besides this stuff even a McDonalds might seem edible. No, probably not.

It's not quite *that* bad."

"I'll miss you too, tu'penny. And I'll be alright. It'll only, anyway, be for a day or two. Then we'll all have this huge party together, no? I think I'm going to order steak. That what you want?"

"You are a strange chap, and no mistake. Smoked haddock, you sure?"

"Fine, fine, smoked haddock it is. Who am I to argue? With? Chips?"

"Mashed potatoes, fine. I'll have chips, I think. But not those thin French friey type things, those thick, chunky ones, you know, like they make at Mario's. You going to have a dollop of butter on your mash?"

"A great big dollop, of course you are. And vegetables?"

"You're no grandson of mine, Gerry. Parsnips? Are you sure? Parsnips?"

"Well, they're parsnippy, for a start. And, in the second place, they taste of parsnips."

"No, no, *you're* eating them, tu'penny, not me. Parsnips it is. Though the availability of parsnips in downtown Bogotá, well, let's put it this way, I don't guarantee it. Starter?"

"Tomato soup? Is that all? You think you should brush your teeth now? Finger your teeth, at any rate? We might as well get some sleep. So you're fresh and bright for tomorrow. The tomorrow, maybe, that'll see you free at last. I think it'd be a good idea, sweetheart. Quite apart from anything else, your old man's old man – your old man's *old* old man, I should say – he's beginning to wilt, tu'penny. And fast."

"I think it would be best. A reasonably early night. Wake up refreshed tomorrow. Ready for all the rigours ...*of* tomorrow. Freedom, let's hope. Let's hope you can have this meal tomorrow night. Sort of a rehearsal for when we have our meal together. So, we'd got to tomato soup. That's all you want? Sure? I mean, sweetheart, the world's your oyster, so you could have *them*, for instance, oysters."

"Well, one day I'm sure you'll love them. And love what they do to you."

"Wait till 'one day', Gerry, and you'll have no need to ask. No foie gras? No escargots?"

"You don't know what foie gras is? I don't believe it. Not escargots? And I always thought your mother was a civilised woman. Clearly she's not, Gerald. The mark of a civilised person is that she brings her children up to be civilised as well. And someone who doesn't know what foie gras is, or escargots, well, they may be described as many things, but 'civilised' would not be among them. Foie gras, young sir, is goose liver. We won't talk about the process that is undergone to create it. And escargots ... escargots are snails."

"You yuch as much as you like, young man. They're delicious. Scrumptious, let me assure you. At *our* meal, I think I'll have escargots. If you're very good, I might let you try one. You can see for yourself."

"There are, Gerald, more culinary delights available to you than are dreamed of in your imagination – and certainly more than just tomato soup. Out of a tin, no doubt."

"Heinz?"

"I have no idea *how* I guessed. Divine something or other, I suppose. Nice and clean, are they? I'll bet that's something else you're longing to do: clean your teeth properly. I know I am. Just, for a second or two, to feel a mouth glistening, you know, the way it does. Pudding?

"Now, what do they want? You know I can even recognise their walks now. Joaquín and Oswaldo, you want to bet? This could be the big one, Gerry. This could be freedom. Their sense of timing was always immaculate.

"*Buenas tardes, caballeros.*"

"Don't cry, Gerry. You're going home. *Muy bien, Joaquín. Gracias. Por favour, dos minutos. Por despedirnos. Gracias. Dos minutos, si. Gracias.*

"I'll be with you in a day or two, tu'penny. And then we can have that celebration meal we were talking about. We never got to pudding! Never mind, you choose my pudding for me. Whatever you decide, that'll be fine with me.

"Let me look at you. Do you have any idea, Gerry, any idea at all of how brave you've been? Truly brave, I mean? Not all the John Wayne, the Alan Ladd nonsense?"

"Well, you have been. And I want you always to remember that. You've been as brave as it's possible for a human being to be. And if you apply that same bravery to the other difficult situations in your life, you'll come through them. Not always well, and certainly not always happily, but you will come through them. I want you always to remember that, and always to know it. And I want you to know and remember that in that same core place I was talking to you about in another context.

"And in that same place, Gerry, I want you always to know – always – how deeply I love you and how enormously proud I am of you. Deeply, deeply, *deeply* I love you; the enormously *enormously* I am proud of you.

"There's so much more to say to you, but there always is. That's life, the way the cookie crumbles. I'll see you soon. We can say all the unsaid stuff then. I ask you once again, though, before you go, is there anything you want to say to me?"

"It's alright, tu'penny, it's okay. There are times when words won't come, times too when words just aren't the right tool. A lot of that stuff you're struggling to say, I know it, Gerry. I can see it in your eyes, feel it ebbing from your soul.

"Take this letter. Promise me you won't open it. Give it to your parents. I'm sure, Gerry, they'll let you see it. Insist, in fact, they let you see it. But I need you to promise me you won't open it till you're with them. Promise me."

"There. Attaboy. What a very special person you are, sweetheart.

"*Okay, Joaquín.* You take care of yourself, Gerry, you hear? Don't worry about me. I'll see you, as I said, in a day or two. I'll be fine. Just fine. Go on, go now. You don't want to keep Mum waiting. She's waited quite long enough, don't you think? Give her my love.

"I love you, Gerry."

* * *

It had to happen, Titus. Jesus, it *had* to happen. How long have you been bottling them up, those tears? Ever since, old mate, ever since the day of the kidnap. Ever since then.

What am I talking about? What are you talking about, Titus? From a lot further back than that. From the bust-up with Emily, probably. No, *much* further back even than that. Christ, Titus, you didn't cry at your father's funeral. How many tears have been stoppered since those days? How many of your tears just now were those from childhood?

You thought it was a grown-up thing to do, not to cry. Where did you learn that one from? You even gloried when they said to you, "What a brave little soldier." You basked in it, Titus. "What a brave little soldier." Glowed in it.

* * *

Jesus, how many tears can the human body contain? That's dawn creeping up over the horizon. The last dawn, I suspect, of my life. Doesn't seem much point sleeping. Not now. Not with the Big Sleep beckoning. What a great film that was. Dear old Bogey at his best, Bacall at her poutiest. And Raymond Chandler ... great writer. And about as likely a thriller author as Emily Brontë would be a columnist for 'Hustler'. Another of life's funny little whatevers. Something, I can't help feeling, more sinister than mere ironies.

It is fun, life. We should be allowed to enjoy it. Will they be allowed to enjoy it, Gerry and his contemporaries? What legacy, Titus, *have* you left? Whatever happened to that adage, I mean, when did it suddenly vanish, that axiom, whatever it was, that way of thinking? That we don't inherit the Earth from our parents, we hold it in trust for our children? Don't you think, kids, it might be time you reclaimed your birthright? Started insisting we, your parents, did something about the sacred trust with which we were endowed?

Just three sheets of paper left. Not going to get too far with three sheets of paper. Oh Christ, I'm going to cry again.

* * *

"*Hola, Joaquin. Buenas días.* You're going to kill me today, no? *¿Hoy, no, van a matarmi?*"

"That was so unconvincing, dear boy, I cannot begin to tell you." Why can I not hate you? I want to hate you. "*No, no, está bien. Gracias por el café, por la fruta. ¿Papel, por si acaso?* Paper? You know, to write on?"

"Okay, no paper. Pity. *Una lastima, Joaquín.*" You want me to hate you as well. Because that would make hating me so much easier.

"*Estamos amigos, Joaquín. ... Si, amigos.*" You want to hate me. I can see that. "Tape-recorder! Could I, *amigo*, use the tape-recorder? You know, Colin and Wictor? *¿Macina de voces?"* You would dearly like to hate me.

"*¿Toca que? ... Toca cintas, si. Si, Joaquin. ¿Yo puedo* borrow it? Borrow ... borrow?: *¡Prestar! ¿La toco centas, puedo prestarla?"* You're trying to suffuse those eyes with hatred. But there is no hatred there.

"*Toca cintas, si. ¿Puedo prestarla? ... Gracias, amigo, gracias.*"

* * *

"Okay, they've lent me their somewhat primitive recorder – the one, Gerry, I used for that letter to Alan Dance. I'm hoping against hope it's recording. I don't dare hear it back to check in case I run the batteries dry. So, there is no rehearsal for this, Gerry, I'm afraid. All I can do is to record the thoughts as I think them and they occur to me, and hope they make some kind of sense at the receiving end – or, if not that, that the sense contained somewhere within them is one which you will be able to unscramble from the surrounding goo.

"And now I'm talking to you, Gerry, because that's what I'm now used to. But, in talking to you, I'm really talking to you all – anyone who is listening to this, or even happens to listen to this.

"Well, if you are listening to this, tu'penny, two things are certain. Three, I suppose, if you count that the tape recorder *is* working. The first thing – and you have no idea how sorry I am to say this – is that I am dead. The second is that our kidnappers have, at least, a vestige of compassion. Because it will only be through their offices that you have got this.

It was the flash of a spark, the burst of a gun. The rat-tat-tat of Gatling. The blink of a cobra's eye. One dead. A hundred dead. In the blink of a cobra's eye. After the first death, there is no other. Not death. Not sensations. Flashes of sensation.

"This tape is bound to invoke a whole host of feelings, a jumble of them, a hundreds-and-thousands assortment all joshing round together like clothes in a tumble-drier. And that's alright. That's all alright, in fact. *They're* all, all of those feeling, alright. Remember what we talked about, the two of us here, around feelings and sense? Remember we decided they had very little to do with each other? Well, actually (you're right) *I* decided that, and you just sort of silently acquiesced – probably, I suspect, as the line of least resistance. In that instance I was right. Sense doesn't come into feelings, nor does obligation. You may try to impose a 'should' on a feeling, but (if you are true to yourself) the emotion will very shortly shrug itself free of that 'should'. It'll just be, that emotion, what it is. I urge you, tu'penny, whatever feelings are thrown up by this tape, acknowledge them, work through them.

"Pain is the Lon Chaney of sensations: it has a thousand faces. Anger is pain, fear, hatred, frustration, intolerance ... and nine hundred and ninety something others – they're all pain. All of them. But all these pains, Gerry, have one thing in common, there's only one way to put them behind you and that's to put them behind you. It's finally that simple.

"The pain of most of humanity today is quite staggering. Relative prosperity has changed the dynamic of Western pain, without question, but it has not allayed it commensurately. And until we start easing off pain it is inappropriate to call what we have got 'prosperity'. We have money, we do not have wealth. And we have affluence, but we do not have prosperity.

"The pain of the poor is obvious. Christ, the sights we saw in Bogotá were enough to chill the blood. And those aren't what the World Bank would even consider the 'desperately' poor. Appalling though their poverty is, they are two or three rungs from the ladder's bottom. These people, Gerry, are just as we are – *just* as we are.

"There was a wonderful photographer in the 60's and 70's, Don McCullin – he may even still be around, but I've not heard of him for a year or two. McCullin took some of the definitive photographs of the Vietnam war. He felt enjoined at one stage to 'inform' (as he appeared to see it) a Western audience that when someone died in a Vietnamese family, that family too, just as Western families, would grieve their dead member. This may have been to counter the words of the general commanding the forces in Vietnam: Westmoreland, as he was called. Who is on television record as saying that 'The Oriental does not see death as we do. For him it is a matter of less concern'. Those may not have been his exact words – you know what my memory is like. But that was certainly what he said.

"Clearly McCullin felt that so many of us in the West shared Westmoreland's view, that we consider ourselves to belong to another species, that caring about family members is somehow the privilege of affluence. That's no new phenomenon either. And I accept that. In Boccaccio's 'Decameron' I remember a basically sympathetic character suggesting that love was much more prevalent within wealthy households than poor ones. But like a lot of myths it's one we've just got to dispel.

"There is no separate species. There just isn't. And yet another thing which unites us is that we are all, all of us, in pain. And finally pain is pain. Our pain in the West may not be the developing world's remorseless pain of hunger. But know what? I think we allow so much of that remorseless pain simply because we will not acknowledge our own.

"Getting rid of our pain is not only something we need to do to make us feel better, it is a responsibility we have to help society function more easily. Pain is, I think, at the core of all anti-social behaviour, of all the manifestations of anti-social behaviour. And you can bring in whatever Draconian legislation you like, you can introduce crucifixion for shoplifting or thumbscrews for not paying your bus fare, but until we recognise how much pain people are in how much of the time – how much pain *we* are in how much of the time –, we will do nothing about delinquent behaviour, nothing beyond the cosmetic, whether that delinquency falls inside or outside of the law, whether its propagators are teenage tearaways or middle-aged company directors, whether the violence is propagated against the old age pensioner and her savings or the planet and its treasures. So often the causes are the same.

"So, how do we get ourselves out of pain? Well, first of all, sweetheart, we ... wait for it ... we talk. We talk and we talk and we talk. That is so much a huge part of it.

"We need to talk more, tu'penny, and chat less. Oh, there's nothing wrong with a chat, with a good conversation, even (from time to time) some scurrilous gossip. There's nothing wrong with it and plenty right with it. We need it for – ghastly word warning! – 'bonding'. And it's great for bonding. But it can also disguise the pain. Which may make us think it has indeed tackled the pain. It hasn't, tu'penny. It hasn't even come close.

"To tackle pain – to really tackle it –, we have to talk seriously. About things which are serious for us.

"A taboo is being created about being serious. (And what I'm certainly not advocating here is a world either without laughter, nor where we take ourselves too seriously, where we can't laugh also at ourselves.) But we do also need to stop being scared that being serious is somehow being ridiculous. We need to learn that talking – real talking – is the sex of the mind: It is that which makes us intimate with each other.

"On which note, let *me* be serious for a moment. And seriously I want you all to know – particularly you, Ewart and Georgina – that Gerry when he was here handled himself with astonishing dignity and courage. Amazing dignity, extraordinary courage. He did you proud. And you should be proud. He is a walking tribute to the way that you brought him up and to the love you clearly showed for him." Pity, really, you couldn't have shown me too a little of that same love.

I'm dying, Ewart. I'm shortly going to die, I have to speak to you before I die. You have to hear me – once – before I die. It wasn't ...

Valentine was a friend. Had been a friend. I knew he was gay. That was never an issue. Not one way, or the other. It was just what he was, like having brown hair. He was gay, not camp. Well, you know. Why am I telling you this? Sexually, I'd never even noticed him. Not even really thought of him as a sexual being. Oh, I knew he had sex. It's not that that I'm talking about, it's that it wasn't there. Not till that night. That glorious night. Yes, Ewart, that glorious *glorious* night. That glorious Thursday night ...

You seem to think it was deliberate, an act of wantonness, of licentiousness or depravity. It wasn't. It wasn't like that. I was just lonely. I was awash, in fact, with loneliness. So lonely, you cannot imagine. I mean that: I really hope you can't imagine it. If you can, you've been through it. And I would hate that.

Your mother and I, we'd left each other, Ewart, years before. Oh, we still slept in the same bed, even very occasionally still had sex together, but the sex was listless, 'dutiful'. And dirty. It was always dirty, shameful.

Just as, from the very first, with Valentine it was always clean. Like Nazneen in 'Brick Lane', I waited, after our first time, for 'disgust to stalk its way over me and into me'. (I remember that phrase so well. It was – oh so much – the story of *my* sex life.) It never did disgust me. In any way. It was so chaste, it was almost virginal. At its most torrid, it was suffused with chastity – and so clean you could have sold washing powder with it.

As for the cohabitation with your mother ... well, it was similar (as we seem to be in literary mode) to the 'Life of Pi' – you know, that extraordinary book about a small boy and a Bengal tiger stuck on the same life-raft together. Drifting in an infinite ocean. Just hoping to survive for long enough that some kind of rescue becomes possible. Watching each other for signs of weakness. Who's going to eat whom? There was so little joy, so little – even – companionship. A kind of mutual suspicion, that's all. A mutual suspicion that we were having less of a life than the other one, and a suspicion that somehow the other was responsible for that. The Bengal tiger and the boy both blaming the other for the ship-wreck. But not voicing that. Just allowing it to simmer. Like acid. Whispers of white fumes snaking from the test-tube.

"He has shown our captors, Gerry, how to handle themselves in adversity, how (in fact) to live. Christ, he has shown me how to live, come to that!" And that's quite enough soft-soap for the time being, thank you very much!

"Those captors, whatever you may be thinking, are not our enemies. Not our real ones. Like the troops in the First World War who met in No-Man's-Land on Christmas Eve, I have played football with these men – obviously, in my case, metaphorically. I know they're not the enemy. And I know we can't be allowed to know who the enemy is. The answer is too close to home. They'll probably be found – Joaquín, I mean, Oswaldo and the rest. Quite possibly shot 'resisting arrest' – akin to the ETA terrorist who managed to commit suicide by shooting himself in the head *twice*! And if they do stand trial, our captors, it will be they who do.

"We'll see no reason to put ourselves on trial. To question *our* part in the offence. And that's one of the reasons why it's bound to happen again. Bound to. It's a variation on the theme that we will continue to have to repeat the lesson until we have learnt from it.

"Some of you will have heard me say this before – maybe you all have. I suppose that's one of the penalties of getting old – another of the penalties, I should say. Every year in Spain, a couple of bulls are spared in the ring from being killed. It's very rare, but the odd one who shows quite extraordinary courage or charisma or something does get saved. That bull never fights again. Mostly because it is no longer fooled. It knows its enemy is not the red cape, but the man waving it – and it thus ignores the cape and attacks the man. Well, that's true of so much of the way today we lead our lives: We are kidded by matadors into believing it is the cape which is dangerous and not the man. I say again, the captors are not our enemy.

"And yet – of course they are. I talked to you when you were here, Gerry, about the President of Chile, Salvador Allende, about how his supporters were tortured by the Pinochet regime. And about how Pinochet's henchmen threatened their victims' children. The Allende supporter would have hated the henchman. Must have done. Clearly. But that henchman, Gerry, was only in fact the cape. The matador was Pinochet.

"Indeed the matador was not even Pinochet but the American Executive. Not even that but the unaccountable CIA. Not even that but what is perceived by that non-accountable CIA as being 'American interest'. And that perceived interest has about it all the intelligence and respect for life of the suicide bomber. It's just a policy enacted on such a gigantic scale that we either don't recognise it as such or won't or don't dare to. It is fundamentally the same thinking because unless the planet's problems are addressed, America too will perish. And it will be then, apparently (and, apparently, only then), that the dollars that are so lauded today will be seen to be the sham that they truly are.

"And, yes, you're right: I'm angry and I'm bitter. You can hear that in my voice. You won't be able to miss it. Nor do I think, frankly, I want to avoid it – being angry and bitter. I'm so pissed off I cannot begin to tell you. Remember what's engraved over the portal of Armageddon? 'Because our fathers lied'? Well, you see, I believed the lie as well. I believed the lie of my fathers, and the lies. The lies which is one sodding great big lie: The fairy-tale lie. The happy-ever-after lie.

"Christ, Hollywood's got a lot to answer for! I believed, you see, believed if I worked hard, paid my taxes, looked after my family, all would be alright with me here and hereafter. Well, who knows about hereafter? If I get any inside track, I'll try and let you know. But here? This is not the end of a happy-ever-after script. I mean, in happy-ever-after scripts, kidnappers have a change of heart in the last reel. Or the whole thing is discovered to be one gigantic practical joke. Or the cavalry arrives or something.

"Oh hark! By what am I being deafened? Well, what do you know? By the complete absence of a bugle call!"

There was a happy-ever-afterness with you, my darling Valentine. For our short time, lover, it *was* ever after that we were happy. That I was. I hope you were.

"It is the obscenity of Hollywood, the happy ending. Far more demeaning and dishonest than any pornography. Oh, not the happy ending per se. But the *insistence* on the happy ending: The hooker marries the millionaire, wife and mistress are reconciled at the deathbed, Bond defuses the bomb. If we're good little citizens, the happy ending tells us, the state or fate will look after us. Or God will. The fairy-story-ending was, I think, an active accomplice in September 11th. And in much of the other horror with which we're surrounded.

"Of course life is hard. For anything that has life, life is hard. For the ostrich or the orchid, for the buffalo or the butterfly. Even elephants have their young killed for meat, tigers get mortally wounded by other tigers, lions starve in droughts. And it's fine, it's absolutely fine for life to be tough. It's the way Nature intended it to be. It's a great experience, well worth some struggle. Indeed often the struggle enhances it, adds piquancy to life, helps you to appreciate it more. But don't we make life so very much harder for each other – and so very much harder than it need be – just by not acknowledging that it *is* hard? By pretending that everything is perfect in a perfect world? By insisting that to the righteous shall come the rewards? And doesn't disabuse inevitably lead to disappointment?

"It's a lie, 'happy-ever-after'. It's that simple. It's a whole host of little lies, wrapped up in a great big one. And I'm really pissed off because I think I should have a happy ending. I think I *deserve* a happy ending. And I'm not going to get one.

"And – think about this one, Gerry – if I don't get one, what makes you think you're going to get one either? We buy into the lie at our peril, we buy the lie at enormous personal cost. Why? So that the rich can get richer. And for absolutely no reason beyond that."

Or was it that we were happy ever after? Had we had the time, lover, to even start 'ever after'? Was the happiness I found in you, Valentine, the joy of novelty? There was joy with you too, Emily. So much joy.

"So many films today are toxic in their allegory. 'It's a Beautiful Life', for instance, or 'It's a Wonderful Life' or something was an Italian film of the '90s. It was the story of a shop-keeper, I think, an unshakeable optimist, who is interned by the SS in a concentration camp and who helps his young son to survive the experience by making a game of it. It was a charming little film, funny and touching, with severe lashings of sentimentality – but there's no harm in a bit of schmaltz from time to time. The allegory, though, stank.

"Hollywood appeared to love the allegory – to the extent it gave the film an Oscar. It encapsulated its position and it validated that position at one and the same time. I'm only surprised that more government ministers did not loudly sing its praises as well. Because the allegory also validated *their* position. It says, that allegory, that if we the government or we Hollywood (Daddy, in other words) consider the truth to be too unpalatable for our offspring (i.e. the electorate/ audience/ son), then it is our paternal responsibility to shield that offspring from it.

"Frankly, I can think of few opinions more toxic than that one. It undermines the entire concept of democracy, and adhering to it further compromises the already scant regard paid today to that concept.

"The Western world today is about as much a democracy as Imperial Rome. The plutocrats have now just got enough money and guile to hide that fact from most of us.

"I think you owe it to yourselves, owe it to your own future and your children's, that you demand the return of democracy. Though 'return' may be a misnomer. As the Mayor of London once entitled a book, 'If Democracy Meant

Anything, They'd Abolish It'. No, you owe it to yourselves rather to demand that those claiming to support democracy put their policies where their mouth is."

We queued, Emily, to see 'Midnight Cowboy'. Remember that? Queued round the block. Leicester Square. Somewhere in Leicester Square. What were we doing in London? We'd moved to Exeter by then. I'm sure by then we were in Exeter. Yes, we were staying in a hotel ... that funny little hotel round the corner from Bow Street. And we went to a midnight screening. Yes, a *midnight* screening of '*Midnight* Cowboy'. Somehow that was funny or appropriate or something. That and we thought for the late-night screening the queue would be shorter. What *were* we doing in London? The hotel was just a spit away, so ... well, the absence of public transport was not going to be a problem. It wouldn't have been a problem – with your company as we were then – if we'd had to walk to John o'Groats. We'd been, that was it, to check out that school for Ewart. *That's* why we were in London.

There was an escapologist busking. He did his act several times whilst we were waiting. We must have queued for some time, for *quite* some time. For well over an hour, it must have been. And I was so enchanted by you, so mesmerised by your conversation, your company, it felt like we'd been there no time at all. I've got a feeling, a vague memory that it was cold, perishing even. But I've also got a memory of never having felt warmer in my life. I was kilned by our love, by the joy I had in that love. We'd already been married, what? Ten years? Maybe twelve. How could I have so misremembered? How is memory such a slave to our hankerings? How does it abuse us? Please forgive me, Emily. Please, Emily, forgive me.

"I really do not believe that there is, finally, anything we experience which cannot be considered as an allegory. It is sometimes curious, sometimes alarming to note how those experiences are interpreted. And because, finally, everything we experience is an allegory, I despair of so much of the output both on the small and big screens.

"There's a show, for instance, where would-be pop singers are subjected by people who would doubtless consider themselves role-models to a mixture of vitriol, humiliation and abuse. And yet we are encouraged to have 'zero-tolerance' for the anti-social actions of our young people. Just where, we wonder in horror, are they picking this behaviour up from?

"The theft of dignity is still robbery. The difference between mugging someone on the street or abusing a wannabe before millions of viewers is only one of degree. And which act is the more violent is, I think, a question that is moot. That children agree to perform pornographic acts before the camera does not make it acceptable. Nor is it acceptable that these 'contestants' are volunteers in their own humiliation. Even the concept is an affront to dignity, even the concept panders to the voyeuristic in the worst way imaginable. The tacky is an attack on dignity.

"Dignity has a very low currency currently. (Sorry about that. Not a deliberate alliteration, promise. It just came out that way.) And that's another reason why anger is as prevalent as it is. Because an abuse of dignity is an assault on the soul. And invokes quite as much anger as physical violence. Perhaps more. Because today the society around us seems to expect us to accept it. So if we complain about it, such only adds to the abuse meted out to us."

Talking of abuse, how are you all now, I wonder? Inside of yourselves, I mean? Oh, I'm sure, publicly, hair is being torn and raiments rent, but, inside of you, are you all secretly glad that the old pouf is off to meet his Maker? Serves him bloody right for being so irresponsible. Who takes a child for a walk in Bogotá?

And I'm just as bad, for Christ's sake. It occurs to me that I've yet to apologise to all of you for this assault on your souls, on *all* your souls – this kidnap, that whole number. All the mini-assaults of your soul contained by the big one. I mean, how idiotic can you get? Taking Gerry for a walk. No, you're right: 'idiotic' does not even *begin* to cover it. Well, let me put that right right away, that lack of apology: I'm sorry – so, *so* sorry – particularly to you, of course, Ewart and Georgina. And, of course, also particularly, Gerry, to you. I wasn't thinking. It was an act of folly, of madness. But I wanted a little time alone with him ... with you. No, no ... it doesn't matter why. It was just insanity.

Just total insanity." Because you, you fucker, you had kept him from me. Kept him from me to punish me. Like, because I was gay, I was likely to be a paedophile. Like I was going to bugger my own grandson or something. Do you know what that made me feel like, Ewart, you bastard? And you, Georgina, for all your protests and avowed liberalism, you let him do that to me. You countenanced it, maybe even abetted it. How *could* you?

"Please don't cry for me, any of you. Least of all you, Gerry. I'm an old man now, tu'penny. I'm ready to die. Death has no great fear for me. I don't say that out of any kind of bravado. Nor yet out of any desperation. That's just the way it is. I've lived my three score years and ten. I've had, as the English quaintly say, a 'good innings'. I'm ready to shuffle off, to pass on the baton. Which doesn't mean that it's therefore time that I died. But it does mean that the time robbed from me is the least significant of time, and the least of time, and the cheapest of time.

"There are things which sadden me about dying. I won't be there, for instance, when you graduate or get married or have children. I won't be there when you get promoted at work or sell your first lithograph or clone your first sheep – or whatever triumph it is that you enjoy in whatever field of endeavour you eventually choose to pursue. And I won't be there either when you fail to graduate or you accidentally blow up the laboratory or your wife miscarries – not that I'd be any use, but we could at least get drunk together.

"It's odd. Now that death is almost upon me, it's lost so much of its edge, its significance.

"In my fifties, suddenly death was all around me – and suddenly hugely important to me. A thunderbolt struck, precisely on my fiftieth birthday: I'd had more of my life than I was going to have. I was in the second half of it. Win, lose or draw there would be no extra time.

"When it first struck, that thought, I was horrified by it. And terrified. And that lasted for some six months, I suppose. Maybe a bit longer. Then two things happened simultaneously: I started fretting about the nothing I'd made of my life, and I started dreading how much of it there still was left. It was a weird game, I think, that I was playing with myself: that the pain of underachievement at fifty, whilst painful, was just about acceptably so. How much greater would my underachievement be at the age of a hundred? And would the thermometer of the consequent pain have now climbed into the red area, from just about bearable to totally *un*bearable.

"That plummeted me into a different kind of depression. (That's something else no-one ever tells you about: the different kinds of depression. They just seem to lump them into one. But there are as many flavours of depression, sweetheart, as there are those of ice-cream. There's vanilla depression and raspberry-ripple depression and pistachio depression. Take it from me. I think I've tasted the whole ice-cream parlour – most of them indeed in the greater London area! There are even flavours like bacon-and-egg ice-cream. Which don't taste like depression at all. But they are, Gerry. They really are.)

"It was extraordinary the ... I'm not even sure what it was ... not quite the tug-of-war enacted by death in my fifties. Not the roller-coaster either. Some sort of complicated Elizabethan dance, rather. A bit like the one in 'Shakespeare in Love' – sorry, you're probably too young to have seen that. But you know, I'm sure, what I mean: all sorts of intricacy, moving in and out of dancing quadrangles, changing partners with every other bar of music. One day I would want death now, immediately, would lust after it, try even to seduce it; and on another, I would try to thrust it as far from me as I could. One day, the previous fifty years would seem no larger than a puddle – not even: a rain-drop – and on others they would seem like a vast, vast ocean. The next fifty years likewise. And on some days I was okay with what I had and hadn't done. And on other days I was so ashamed of myself I just wanted to crawl under the nearest stone.

"And then, one day, it just simply vanished. I suppose I was in my early sixties. Something like that. It wasn't momentous. It wasn't like having a tooth-ache and taking a pill where you feel the pain drain from you like water going down a plug-hole. I just realised one day that I wasn't concerned about it any longer. It was there ... oh, in the way, say, the Grand Canyon is there. And there to be thought of in the way you think about the Grand Canyon. I mean, I'm sure there are those with a particular interest in the Grand Canyon – geologists, botanists, local guides and things – but for most of us (certainly for me) it just is. It's there. It's impressive. You can't miss it. But it doesn't impact on my daily life.

"And the impact on my daily life of death not impacting on my daily life was enormous. It was so ... liberating. So cleansing too. Not dissimilar, tu'penny, to what I imagine you are feeling now. Free and clean. And your life over the next couple of days will taste especially sweet.

"In my 20's, I imagined that the approach of death would be preceded by wisdom, by everything making sense, by all the questions being answered – knocked over like ninepins. No, more like the holes on a golf course: You just sink one question after another. Putt the eighteenth and you snuff it. Maybe the only thing in life I have learned is that the only statement in life is birth. And that death is its biggest question.

"You see, I'm a stupid old man. A really stupid old man. I like to think of myself as John Newton, but I'm actually probably a lot closer to Colonel Blimp. John Newton (in case you don't know) was an ex-slave-ship Captain who finally saw the error of his ways and of his former trade. He found God – the same God, probably, that I've lost! – and wrote the rather beautiful, if now somewhat clichéd, 'Amazing Grace'. I like to think I emulate him – see through all the follies of my youth to truth: a broad truth, a robust one. But much of what I say is, and I do know this, marshmallowed in Colonel Blimpism – a reactionary attitude to anything that's new, simply because it *is* new.

"I'm also a confused old man. I know that there are things 'wrong with the world' which aren't wrong with the world at all, it's just that my age finds them threatening, or they are not to my taste or something. But just because such things undoubtedly exist, it doesn't mean that also there are not things which truly are wrong with the world.

"Musically, I've never really got over the death of Buddy Holly – 'the day the music died'. And I hear myself saying the same things about the 'music' today (which, yes, I put in quotation marks!) as I used to hear my grandparents, and parents!, say about Holly and Little Richard – even of Pat Boone! And I kind of know that is me being curmudgeonly and cantankerous and *old*.

"And there are things like the economic holocaust and global warming where I just know that my hatred of the present so-called 'policies' has got nothing to do with my age. Although it likes to be spun in that way – as if morality and decency and probity were hopelessly passé concepts.

"But between those two extremes there is an ocean of greyness where I just do not know – and which, of course, has elements of both.

"There was a tennis player, for instance, called Ilje Nastase. In his day, he was thought of something as a 'bad boy' because he questioned line-calls. But, it struck me, he usually did so with a degree of courtesy and, above all, wit. Then along came another tennis player, John McEnroe. Who also questioned line-calls, but Mr McEnroe did so violently, abusively, aggressively – and with the same amount of wit as an impacted wisdom tooth. I suspected at the time, and continue to suspect, that his famous tantrums had less to do with spontaneous anger than they had to do with a quite unscrupulous gamesmanship. Even more they had to do with profit. Mr McEnroe, I presume, made an extremely lucrative salary from the advertisements he made – all of which (at least, that I have seen) centred on his bad behaviour.

"I remember Mr Blair famously criticising a 'yob society'. I remember no censure by the Prime Minister of Mr McEnroe's contribution to it. Indeed I seem to remember another pair of yobs – a pop group called 'Oasis' – were on the guest list of one of his first Downing Street receptions. Behaving like a yob is only unacceptable, apparently, if you're broke and unknown. The famous and wealthy are allowed, indeed encouraged, to behave in as yob-like a fashion as they choose.

"Because, whilst I have heard no mention recently of Oasis and imagine they have gone the way of all nine-day wonders, the BBC does now employ Mr McEnroe to comment on Wimbledon.

"Not once have I heard that august commentator express an apology for his previous conduct. Indeed he seems to use his privileged situation further to exalt it. Of course he's not single-handedly responsible for all the muggings in the street – but he did (in my opinion, unquestionably) make a substantive contribution to an ethic where 'winning' becomes of greater importance than adhering to a code of principles. Thereafter, that ambition gets further poisoned by a total misrepresentation of what 'winning' is.

"Now, is this me being old and curmudgeonly? Or telling a truth the powers-that-be (whoever *they* are!) no longer want us to hear? I don't know. Probably, as I said earlier, a bit of both. I suppose, at the end of the day, these are areas where we all of us have to make up our own minds. I suppose finally all I'm trying to say is this: Don't dismiss *all* I'm saying as the ramblings of an old man. Undoubtedly, much of what I have to say is exactly that. But there may just be some truth amidst the waffle, some wheat within the chatter. Because I don't care for (what I think of as) the commercial pap of today's pop music, is what I'm saying, does not mean that global warming is not a very real, a very dangerous danger."

I'd never smelled a man before you, my darling Valentine. My sweet and darling Valentine, my lover. I suppose it was testosterone, but I suppose too I'll never know. I'd never had another boyfriend, never want another. So I suppose never will I know whether what I smelled that night was you or man. I'm sure you never smell yourself accurately. Just as never do you see yourself accurately or hear yourself. Not properly. I wasn't drunk. I wanted to blame the booze later, but it wasn't that. 'Blame', like it was something wrong, like it was something blameworthy, like it wasn't the most glorious sensation of a fairly insensate existence. 'Blame', where did that come from? I felt, in your company, warm. Cherished. I felt safe. Comfortable. I leant over you, I remember, for the remote control. And because I was, well, tipsy, I slipped and collapsed onto you. It wasn't a sexual advance, just the clumsiness of a little too much booze. And, in order to haul myself up, I put my hand on your chest, and I felt you. As something vibrant, I mean. Something organic, and sensuous. For the first time I felt you. More than that, though, I felt your heart. Pumping. Like a galloping horse. And as I levered myself up and started trying to steady myself, so I saw your eyes. I saw the want in those eyes, that desire, that passion. The burning. And I knew I wanted you too. That – I mean – *sexually* I wanted you. I knew nothing. Nothing. Not about the technique or the etiquette, I didn't even know who was going to fuck whom, nor how the question was broached, and know what? It didn't matter. Nothing mattered at that moment. Not Emily nor the children. Not work or money or prestige. Not even health. Not even, curiously, life itself. All that mattered was you, and making you happy. That was the only fulfilment that was possible. Or that I wanted. I've never stopped wanting you, Valentine.

"I know how upsetting, how galling it can be, to be told things you've already worked out for yourself. That's not what I'm doing. I may give that appearance, but, believe me, that's not what I'm doing. I may sound as if I'm sure about everything I say, but really I'm not. I'm not sure about anything, in fact. Least of all, that what I'm saying here has any merit.

"Sometimes it feels like I'm on the deck of the 'Titanic' screaming at the top of my lungs to be careful of the approaching iceberg. And I feel at those times the icy glare of the cruisers who think I'm mad or drunk but, whichever, I'm seriously spoiling their fun. And, because I'm screaming, the band plays louder, and the revelry becomes more frenetic. Which makes it even harder for me to make my voice heard as the iceberg comes closer and closer.

"And there are other times when I think I'm standing up, screaming my warnings, but I'm in a row-boat on a village pond. And I just imagine I'm on the 'Titanic'. And what I think are icebergs are merely willow branches dappling in the water.

"I cannot say it enough, I do not know what is right. I know certain things that are right – like feeding the hungry, for example. But I don't know, in its broader context, what is right.

"I also only know the detail of what is wrong. I do know it's wrong, for instance, to take human life. It's just wrong, and it's that simple. But, again, the general concept of what is wrong, or evil, is too big for me to be able to conceive. But because I don't *know* what is wrong does not mean I cannot *sense* it. And what I sense – and sense with every fibre of my body – the *wrong* I sense is that we're getting *IT* wrong: 'it' – the whole thing, the whole shebang, the whole schmeer, this infinitely fascinating process called 'life'.

"I'm perfectly prepared to accept that 'it' is one it's not possible to get right: Man is, as I think I have already said several times, almost defined by his fallibility. But I also sense that the wrong we're presently getting 'it' is – simply but completely – *devastating.*

"And suicidal.

"More than suicidal,: along with our own species, we will kill off entire species of others, vast swathes of the planet. It's the suicide bomber strapping not TNT to his chest but a nuclear device.

"I desperately hope I'm wrong. Desperately (and the word too I use advisedly) I hope that. But, if I am wrong, you have relatively little to lose by addressing the problems confronting both the planet and the species. This against the enormity of the consequences if I am right."

What is that smell? Where has it taken me? It's taken me somewhere good. The somewhere of the song in 'West Side Story' the 'wait for us, somewhere' somewhere. I'm feeling good. Where is it? Where the hell is it? I'm feeling very good. It's olive-like, the smell. It's not olives, but it's redolent of olives. Where the ...?

Corfu! I'm in Corfu!

In that sweet little flat on the beach. And, Emily, I'm with you. We've just had sex. And the smell of the olive grove is cascading through the flat. I'm there, Emily, with you. In love with you. We haven't just had sex, we've just made love. Wonderful love and glorious love. We're lying, naked (of course), head to toe, like sardines, panting on that rickety bed. Yes, that rickety bed. How we laugh at that rickety bed. How we laugh *on* it. With that cane bedhead. One you cannot sit against without indenting your back. We're sure the fan is going to come off its hinges, its base, whatever you call it. And now, it's now gently screeching, that ceiling fan as it hiccups round its wobbly circuit. We're bathed in sweat, the two of us; there are two – no, three – rivulets running between your heaving breasts. Those come-hither nipples still pert from their arousal; the sun beating on the sand just outside the French windows; the heat shimmering on the glass. But within, we're in shadows, and in a sort of torrid cool – the toes tickled by the fan's breeze, our chests heaving with inner heat and outer, with passion and torridity – heaving too with completeness. I have been so wrong, *so* wrong. That was sex, Emily, which was just as fulfilling and empowering and revitalising as any I had with Valentine. Sex, Emily, that was just as clean. *Any* sex, Emily, I had with Valentine.

"Hola, los dos ... Por favor, una hora más. Por favor, Joaquín. Juanito, una hora. Solo una hora. ... Okay, okay. Gracias. Muchas gracias ... Si, una hora, no más. Gracias.

"You probably heard that. I forgot to switch the machine off. I've got an hour left, in case you missed it, before they come back to kill me. Sixty minutes. Doesn't seem like a lot.

"Still I can't hate these men. I've tried to but I can't. Oh, certainly I hate the system which created them. That's for sure. Or, maybe even, the *lack* of system which created them. The hatred which created them. Yes, that hatred I really hate. I hate that hatred with a hated vengeance." **Oh God, Emily, oh God. How have I betrayed you, my love. How I have, my love, betrayed my love for you.**

"The so-called 'security forces' are part of that system, or that lack of system. Unlike those forces, I don't think (as apparently they do) the phenomenon of suicide bombing is just one of hatred. Well, not the kind of hatred, anyway, they talk about. I suspect the phenomenon is extremely complicated and multi-faceted. There may well be factors which these bombers all have in common, but I'm prepared to bet a fair chunk of money that the real impulsion behind their acts is as individual to them as their fingerprints.

"One thing I suspect they may have in common is a feeling that finally, in a world where increasingly the individual is powerless over his destiny, he (or she) *is* taking some kind of control of their life, albeit only in the ceding of it; that finally they are going to be heard and that they are finally going to achieve some kind of status; that finally what appears to them to be an aimless life is endowed with purpose and meaning.

"And our guys – the gang here – you don't think they're exactly the same? They're going to die young. Since they were capable of conscious thought they've known that they would die young. From disease or hunger or decay. You think the threat of death is a real one to them? They've defied considerable odds even to have lived as long as they already have. The most important thing to them is that they will have lived, that they will have tasted one mouthful of this thing called 'life'. Not even a mouthful of the life they've seen enacted in 'Dallas' or 'Sex and the City' or any other of the zillion Hollywood fantasy products – but, at least, some kind of life. And, failing that, that they will somehow have imprinted their mark on life. That they will at least be remembered.

"If a peasant here, a *campesino*, grows coca on his land and not, I don't know, wheat or bananas or whatever the hell else it is it would be that they do grow (geography, need I remind you, was never my strongest suit) he can earn ten, fifty, maybe a hundred times more. He can embrace the capitalist system. He can take himself and his family out of the poverty trap. His children can afford to go to school. Maybe, with education, they can get legitimate jobs. Why on earth should he care that his product is going to create problems on streets thousands of miles away? (And which, anyway, are less the problem than a means of dealing with it!) And that have nothing – nothing whatsoever – to do with him? This is a country that not in a thousand years will he be able to afford even to visit. And yet America gets very indignant if its desire for a lack of Colombian coca fields is not adhered to immediately.

"Bolivia agreed to American demands. It instructed its peasants to destroy their coca fields. And, guess what? The Bolivian economy therefore collapsed. And guess what else? Guess who was first in the queue *not* to help Bolivia in its crisis? Why, the good old U.S. of A., of course. Proving the adage (if further proof were necessary!) that no good deed ever goes unpunished."

Running out of time, old darling, running out of time. Last words are called for now, final confessions, that whole number.

"Sorry. Sorry, guys, but I've got to cut to chases now. No time for dawdling, for careful turns of phrase, any of that stuff. If I gabble, sorry, too.

"'If': I've mentioned 'If' before, mentioned (at least, Gerry, to you) that there's a remarkable amount of wisdom packed into its few words. The 'Desiderata' had become the cliché it is precisely because there's so much truth in it. And 'de Profundis' is a work by Wilde vastly under-read. I suspect because we want our jesters only to be funny. Far greater than their inability to play Hamlet is our reluctance to let them do so.

"Three axioms as well: the first I mentioned earlier, that we do not inherit the Earth, but hold it in trust."

Tempus is fugitting, old mate. You've got to get on with it, Titus. It's fugitting at an alarming rate.

"The second is that a man is not defined by his achievements but by his choices. God, the differences there would be in the world today if that little aphorism had been taken on board!

"And the third – and most important of all, tu'penny – is, I'm afraid, that old, old chestnut (almost as old as me!), Polonius's advice to Laertes: 'This above all,' I wait for you all to breathe in so that you can chorus together, 'Unto thine own self be true.'

"That is a huge skill. It is a skill which takes a lifetime of dedication to acquire, in fact. But I suspect – I can only suspect because for years I wasn't true to myself – I suspect it's one of those skills where the process of acquiring it already brings rewards.

"You cannot be true to yourself, tu'penny, unless you allow others to be true to themselves. And you cannot be true to yourself if you are starving or in bondage – however subtly you may be in bondage. Yes, another little axiom of my own I've just made up: 'We need more bonding today and less bondage'.

"There's been a television show in the last few years, 'Six Feet Under'. You're still a bit too young for it, but maybe Mummy – sorry, Mum – maybe you've caught her talking about it to friends or something. It's about a family of undertakers in Los Angeles – or funeral directors as, rather pompously, they insist on calling themselves. To be quite honest, I couldn't get into it in the way that other people did. Oh, it was hugely better (we're having a 'huge' day today) ... it was hugely better, as I was saying, than the – yes – *huge* majority of the stuff on the box. But that is hugely not saying much. It would be huge- ... *very* difficult to get *worse* than most of the stuff they screen these days. Whatever the appropriately named Lord Bragg might adenoidly say. I *will* stick to the point, tu'penny, I'm just getting there.

"There was one episode of 'Six Feet Under' when, as usual, one of the characters was undergoing some emotional upheaval, this time wondering whether or not to marry his girl-friend. He asks a rabbi – who, just to underscore the relentless realism of the piece, is as sexy and pretty and female a rabbi as is to be found either side of the Wailing Wall – he asks a rabbi what a soul-mate is. 'A soul-mate,' she replies (words to this effect), 'is someone who allows you to be the most "you" you can be.' I thought it was a rather wonderful description.

"You remember I was talking earlier about dignity? About the lack of dignity there is around today with which the business of living is conducted? Well, that's a pretty good description too of dignity: 'Someone treats you with dignity when they allow you to be the most "you" you can be.' Think what a glorious place we could be inhabiting simply by the expedient of allowing everyone around us to be the most "they" they could be. It's so much less complicated than loving others as we love ourselves. It's a beautiful recipe for life, and I leave it to you, I suspect, as my last bequest. They'll be back any moment now.

"You *cannot* be the most 'you' you can be if you are starving. I know I've said that before. It needs to be said. And it needs to be said again and again and again. Nor can you be the most 'you' you can be if you are allowing others to starve. Finally, it's that simple."

It was the flash of a spark, the burst of a gun. The rat-tat-tat of Gatling. The blink of a cobra's eye. One dead. A hundred dead. In the blink of a cobra's eye. After the first death, there is no other. No other. Except that the millionth death is still the first death. The ten millionth, the ten *billionth* death is still the first death. *Each* death is the first death. And the last. 'And now I lay me down to sleep ...'

"I keep waiting for the clouds to separate and for God to make Himself known to me. Again. Know what? I'm beginning to realise it ain't going to happen. Like the cavalry arriving, or the hooker marrying the millionaire.

"That was something else which fell away with you, Valentine. Oh, you know that, I know. As, Emily, *you* know my faith was never exactly all-embracing or unconditional. I don't think I could claim to have been a regular church-goer or anything. But, yes, I did have a gentle, fairly undemanding, not-too-inquisitive belief.

"But suddenly, with Valentine, the Church told me that what I was doing was wrong. Not only wrong, 'abhorrent,' they told me, in God's eyes. And I knew then that the Church had got it wrong. This, what I had with Valentine, was beautiful. If they thought God would disapprove of something beautiful then they'd misunderstood God. It was that simple. There may well be a God, but that God wasn't that of their religion. He couldn't be. And if He was, I wasn't prepared to pray to that God – a God Who condemned something beautiful as being something 'abhorrent'.

"And what I'm certainly not trying to say, Emily, is that it hadn't also been beautiful with you. But God never found that beauty abhorrent. Only the beauty that existed with Valentine. I am so sorry, Emily. So terribly sorry."

Or am I sorry, Emily? Wow, that's a nasty one! Must gives us long pause over that one. Long pause? Oh, right! Like I've got time for that!

Maybe, deep down, I did want to hurt you. I'd been so hurt at home, *so* hurt – oh, not *by* you, Emily – of course, my darling, not *by* you, but, yes, *via* you. You were, as it were, the conduit of pain. But I don't think, at the time we're experiencing pain, we analyse it that closely. It's Pavlovian, the response. I see you: I see pain. Jesus! Perhaps I did want to hurt you. Perhaps the whole thing with Valentine, that was just one elaborate method of hurting you, a perverse means of torture. Oh Christ!

"Why I watched the coronation of the new pope I'm not too sure. Maybe out of nostalgia or something for a lost faith, or curiosity maybe. No, not coronation, whatever it is. Investiture, whatever.

"I know he was John Paul's henchman, the Vatican's Doberman, but there was – is – something about the new pope, Pope Benedict the something as he now is (I was never too good at numbers), an indefinable something, that gives me hope he may return Charity to God. But I guess, on that one, I won't be around to find out whether I'm right or wrong.

"Christ, I'm completely out of time. Thank God sometimes, huh, for Latin punctuality! Anyway, in his address, the Pope's – his sermon, I suppose – he asked us to pray for progress and the liberation of Man.

"It hit me like a flash. Like, I suppose – and not to be too blasphemous about it –, an epiphany. There it was. The entire problem of the world summed up in those six words, in fact in one: 'progress *and* the liberation of Man'. It's right there. Staring us all right in the face.

"There's the problem: We think of these as two issues. There is only one issue: Progress *is* the liberation of Man. That is the only description of 'progress' which means anything.

"Unless Man is liberated by something that something is not progressive. And, yes – my favourite phrase – it's that simple.

"Globalisation is not liberating. It is a backdoor return to feudalism, albeit in a sophisticated form. It is *not* progressive, it is hugely reactionary."

And am I gay? Really gay, I mean? I mean, certainly I loved Valentine. That's for sure. And sex with him was great. But was that the novelty of the sex? Sex is always great at the beginning.

And would that novelty have worn off? I never lusted after another man, was never aroused by the male body as I had been by the female, the fantasy sex was still, Titus, to do with straight sex. Was it, this whole amour, just a horribly sly way of getting at the whole family? Hitting them where it hurt the most?

"So much of today's thinking is reactionary: management-speak, the pandering to greed, the insensitivity to others, the powers of the multinationals. This does not liberate, but enchains. So many of today's inventions and gadgets: the computer, the mobile phone, the internet have elements of both, of liberation and confinement. And these inventions are good when they do liberate, and when they confine they are not only reactionary but evil.

"Treat everyone with the dignity I talked about earlier, treat everyone with the dignity that person deserves – and that *all* people deserve, ask yourself of any action you are about to perform: 'Do I hereby help the liberation of Man?' and I do not believe you can go too far wrong.

"I did go wrong. *So* wrong. So hopelessly wrong. You're not here to forgive me. So I'm going, as I walk to my grave, to try and forgive myself."

Oh Christ! Wait up. That's something now in the corridor.

"I can hear them now, sweetheart, in the corridor. I'm ready. Sort of. There's still so much more I've got to say. But, then, there always would be. Here they are. ...*¿Momento, huh, Joaquín? Estoy por terminar. Dos minutos más. ...*

"You are a very special young man, my darling Gerry. And it has been a privilege – I really mean that – to have spent the time with you that I did. There's, as I said to you once before, so much more to say to you, but there always is. That's life, the way the cookie crumbles. Please, in all your dealings, remember the word and the question. The word is 'dignity'; the question: 'Is what I'm doing furthering the liberation of mankind?'

"God bless you, my darling boy. I pray to the God I don't believe in that you'll lead a happy life. I just do not believe that is possible unless you do what you can to ensure those around you also have a happy life.

"And if that becomes the case, whilst it is my end, it will, far more importantly, be your beginning.

"I love you.

"And it is a measure of how stuck I am in the groove of happy ever after, that, even as I am being led to my execution, there is a part of me that thinks they are walking me to freedom.

"I will not believe the bullet will kill me till I am dead.

"Listo, Joaquín. Vamos."

The End

'Roni'

"It's 12.02. Two minutes past twelve, Brian. And in twenty-four hours' time you'll be dead.

"My wee laddie, he'll be dead. My wean, my own wee Braveheart. You, Brian, will be dead. You bastard. And you ken what's funny about that ... what's, Brian, ironic about that? In the whole wide world there's only one person I can talk to about that and that person, Brian, is also you. My own sweet one. You heap of shit. Isna it great, the irony? Isna it great, irony itself? You ken *why* you're the only one I can talk to? Because, o fruit of my loins, you'll be the only one not around for those words to have consequence – aye, consequence or *a* consequence.

"Your brother's in the room next-door. He canna sleep either. He got fairly tight tonight. Typical Scot, they'll probably be saying. Typical – even more likely – Glaswegian. But you willna. However little you know him, Brian – and that little is a whole giant heap of little – even you will ken that's unusual for him. To help him sleep, he said. What he didna say, it was also to help him forget.

"I can hear his tele. He's got it on low. He would. He always was the considerate one. Please dinna start on again about how *he* was my favourite; *always* my favourite.

"I had no favourites, you stupid wee bastard. I *have* none. I dinna love any one of you – any one of my weans – better or worse. I love you *differently*. And it's no blind, that love. Because I love you does not mean I canna see the faults in you – in *all* of you. *And* your virtues, Brian, and all your virtues – and all the virtues there are in all of you. And nor because I love you does that mean I couldna also hate you. All of you. Not usually at the same time, 'course. Not, as it were, as a job lot. But *all* of you could do hateful things at times; *did*, for God's sake, do hateful things.

"What you did, Brian, that wasna only hateful. 'Hateful' doesna even begin to cover it, describe it, whatever. And I hate you so much for the hateful thing you did that 'hate' doesna even begin to cover that either, or describe it. I mean the Clyde is a river, isn't it? And so is the Mississippi. They're both rivers, whatever the difference in their size. Well, the hate I have for the hateful things you did, Brian, that hate makes normal hate into a stream a hundred times' smaller than the Clyde and the hate for those hateful things into a hate which is a hundred times' bigger than the Mississippi.

"And yet I still love you so much my heart is bursting – aye, bursting its Mississippi banks – in its love for you; in its love, aye, for *you*. I love you so much, Brian, I can still love you despite hating you so much that 'hate' does not begin to cover or describe it. I love you so pigging much, Brian, that that love sears through the hatred – like some kind of laser or something – whilst leaving the hatred in tact. Aye, like the operation Gran had for her cataracts. You bastard.

"And that leaves space for another hatred. Another hatred almost as intense as the first. The hate I have for you for causing so much pain to your victims, to their kith, Brian, and their kin; the hate I have for you for causing *me* so much pain. And for causing pain to so many others – *so* many others, you wee shit. And who are in pain precisely because they do love you. Think about it. Think about it, damn you – think about it, my darling wean. There's Kenny next door, with his tele switched considerately low, Catherine at home in Glasgow, *her* children – your gran, for God's sake, Brian. Even that waste-of-space that calls himself your father. And *his* friends, and my friends, and *their* friends, Brian – and, Brian, *your* friends. Because you still do have friends. Though God knows why. Do you know how much pain there is around you, Brian? Have you the first idea of the combined ... tidal wave that is that pain?

"And we havena started – no yet – we havena even started, Brian, with your victims' pain. That of *their* families, their friends. We're not talking about the pain of those in the emergency services – the police and the paramedics who had to witness what you'd done, those that had to do autopsies on them, or break the news to their families, or wheel their bodies to the morgue – nor, come to that, the pain of those in the prison who will be there to kill *you*. ...

"To *kill* you, Brian ...

"To take the life from you. ...

"Who are there, Brian, to ... you ken ... you. ...

"You bastard, you worm – my babby, my wean ... my bouncing babby, my bundle-of-joy, my wouldna-hurt-a-fly, rock-a-bye laddie. You are my babby, Brian, and I love you. And you are a murderer and a rapist. And I hate you.

"It's now a quarter past twelve, Brian. There will be no other 1215 a.m. with you in the world. Never again. Ever. And now there will be no other 12*16*. Not a.m.

"Will you be sleeping, my wee babby ? Rock-a-bying for the last time? Getting ready for the big day ahead? Like your birthday? No, like Christmas. 'The Night Before Christmas', do you remember that? Do you remember how each Christmas Eve we would read that? All of us together? You and Kenny and Catherine? Your father, of course, was down the pub. Of course. Didna have to be the night before Christmas for that. The night before tomorrow was good enough reason for that. Do you remember?

'Twas the night before Christmas, and all through the house ...' Hot chocolate and dressing-gowns and those wee slippers of yours with the bear's head on the toes? '... Not a creature was stirring ...' All around that Christmas tree, the tatty tinselly one from Woolworths, remember, that Kenny would never let us throw away? Not till he'd left home! The gold star at the top which you made in Art Class. How old were you then when you made that star? Seven, was it? Maybe eight. '... Whilst thoughts of sugar-plums danced through their heads ...'

"What thoughts are dancing through your head right now?, I wonder.

"No.

"No. What I really wonder is what on earth put memories of Christmas into my head? I mean, goodness gracious, what could be less like Christmas than this? It's a sort – if anything – a sort Christmas in reverse, a sort of *anti*-Christmas. A Christmas where you have to give the presents back. 'Specially, it seems, the special presents; most especially, the most special presents. A Christmas where kings from the Orient turn up saying, 'Sorry. Frankincense, that's too good for you. Hand it back. We should never have given you that. You dinna deserve that.'

"Aye, and I, o laddie o' mine, dinna deserve *this.* Being made to hand my present back, my special present – one of the three bestest I ever had." ...

* * *

"How wise – thinking about it – *were* those wise men? I mean, frankincense and myrrh, what good are *they* to a carpenter? Wouldna new set of tools have been a better idea? Maybe bribing the inn's landlord into letting the new mother have an actual room? I mean, isna that like taking a down-and-out to Saville Row, getting him a tailor-made suit? Instead, I mean, of spending the same money on a pair of jeans and the deposit on a bedsit?

"And why the hell am I worrying about that?" ...

* * *

"That bloody Christmas tree. That wasna your fault. I know that. How many times did we try to get rid of the damn thing, you and me? Remember that time in August one year? He was away. Kenny, I mean. Where was he? Nae matter. He was away somewhere – Scout camp, was it? – he was away and you were rummaging through the cupboard looking for heaven only knows what and you came across it and it was like you'd come across treasure trove and you gave a little shriek which was sort of triumph and sort of vengeance-about-to-come and you came into the kitchen waving it almost above your head and we both agreed this was the perfect time, the perfect *opportunity* finally to get rid of the damn thing. And we took it out to the rubbish. Remember? And the rubbishmen ... what had happened to the rubbishmen? And where did that word suddenly come from, 'rubbishmen'? 'Dustmen' is what I meant to say. 'Dustmen'. What *was* it with the dustmen? It wasna strike. It was something odder than that, something really weird. Puncture, that was it, they'd had a puncture. Their lorry had broken down. The day before. It'd had a flat. They were a day behind, emptying the bins. And Kenny came back from camp. And, of course, first thing he did soon as he got in, he took out the rubbish. Because ... well ... Well, because Kenny always did take out the blooming rubbish and there was that pigging Christmas tree, as bold as blooming brass. Bolder. Remember how he stormed back into the house? Stormin' Norman wasna in it: Stormin' Kenny! *Hurricanin'* blooming Kenny more like. Sort of half triumphant and half furious. He shouted at me. Me, his own mother! He shouted. Kenny, I mean. Kenny shouted. I dinna think I ever heard Kenny shout before. Least of all at me. And that pigging Christmas tree, we had it then for years – *years* – right up, I've said this before, till he left home. And no, Brian, that does not mean I love him more – because he didna shout at me, I mean –, or that I loved him more because of that. In fact, almost the reverse. His not shouting meant, I thought, he was hiding something. There was something shifty about it, about his not-shouting, shifty and underhand. One of the things I did love about you: You were direct. If I hurt you you said 'ow!'. You and Catherine both. You were *both* direct like that. Like me. And Kenny, he was like your father. And look what happened to him, the shiftless, no-good waste-of-time pigging waster.

"I've got to sleep. I've got, at least, to try and sleep. I've got to stop these thoughts dancing through *my* head – doing the Gay Gordons through my head, some kind of frenzied Hokey Cokey with a jive thrown in for good measure. I've got to stop thinking about a day from now.

"This is the present. All we have is the present. All we have ...

"In twenty-four hours from now they'll be placing you in a coffin. Except that they'll call it a 'casket'. In twenty-four hours ...

"There was a song in my youth: 'Twenty-four Hours From Tulsa'. A guy sang it called Gene Pitney. That's, aye, 'Gene' said like the lassie but spelled like, och you know, like Gene Parkinson. I thought he was lovely. Gene Pitney, I'm talking about it. Though I wouldna have kicked Parkinson out of bed for farting either. He was a bit straitlaced, though, Gene Pitney. I fell out of love with him soon as your grandpa approved. Your grandpa! It's a good job he's no alive today: It'd've killed him!

"'I was only twenty-four hours from Tulsa/ Only one day awa-ay from your heart.' I canna sing. Hell, you ken I canna sing. You've pleaded with me often enough, when the radio played what they call the 'golden oldies' which are the only songs I know, 'Please, Mam,' you used to say, '*please* dinna sing.' But you'd laugh as you said it. Those blue eyes of yours rippling with laughter. Not like lakes disturbed by ducks-and-drakes, not that kind of rippling, more, I don't know, more like two puddles made out of ink – blue, blue ink – splattered by the rain. *You'd* laugh and then Catherine or Kenny, they'd join in too if they were there. And then so would I. Because your pleaing with me was not an insult. Not in an insulty way. It was a tease. Aye, a tease. It was a tease of love and familiarity and of being allowed to tease. And the splashes that leapt from your eyes, they were saying 'Thanks, Mam. Thanks for running a home where it's alright to tease you. Thanks, Mam, for being a mam it's okay to laugh at.' And that made me feel good. It made me feel so good. We couldna laugh at my parents. Not as children. Heavens, not even as grown-ups. God, you ken that. You've seen it often enough. What you dinna Kenny, though ... you want to ken how much I wanted to laugh at Grandpa's funeral? I mean, he'd made almost a funeral out of my wedding, I thought it only fair, only *fitting*, that I should, I dinna know, sprinkle confetti over his coffin. And the idea that would give him a heart-attack, post-mortem, as it were, that too was something I found funny. Very funny. Och, I know it was all so silly, so spiteful, so childish in one way but ... Well, if truth be told, I also found it funny that I found it funny. The naughtiness of the original funny, that

(I mean) I found funny. Sure I know the old chestnut – who doesna? – that 'funeral' is an anagram of 'real fun', but they're not places – not *occasions* – are they, where real fun is supposed to be enjoyed, are they, funerals? Not 'do's you associate with gales of laughter?

"'And here's tonight's shipping forecast ... beep ... German Bite, Dogger Bay, Scarfa Fell, and Grandpa's funeral: gales of laughter storm force ten and rising. Visibility nil. Blinded by tears. Blinded, aye, by tears. By tears, that is, of mirth, by howls of *laughter*.' What funny names they have, those sea areas. German Bite, what's that when it's at home? What is it, German Bite? Something you get, presumably, from a German Shepherd." ...

* * *

"Which presumably lives in Dogger Bay." ...

* * *

"And when, thinking about it, did German Shepherds become German Shepherds? When I were a lassie they were Alsatians. I mean, it's not that I mind overmuch. I dinna lie awake nights wondering about it. I'm just curious. Is it political correctness?, I wonder. Or the further Americanising of our whole language. An Americanising which, I suppose, will soon be spelled with a 'z'. And a 'z' that will be pronounced not 'zed' but 'zee'. Where does it stop? Will Yorkshire Terriers suddenly become North East English Terriers? Or Victoria plums become South West London plums? Or South East Australian plums? Do you know, I dinna know *where* Victoria is in Australia. Isn't that shameful?

"'I was only twenty-four hours from Tulsa/ Only one day awa-ay from your heart ...' I dinna know where Tulsa is either, if truth be told. Och, I know it's somewhere here, somewhere in America, somewhere on the mainland of the mighty U.S. of A. But North, South, East or West, you've got me there. 'I hate to do this to you/ But I got somebody new/ What can I do? ...'

"You canna get new weans, can you? I mean, you can get new lovers. One goes out the door, you open another and ... bam! Literally, in most cases. In most cases the 'bam' in 'wham, bam, thank you, ma'am' – 'thank you and good night, ma'am'. No, 'thank you, ma'am, ...' (usually) '... and good*bye*'. You canna do that with weans. What you're given is what you get. There's no taking the babby back to exchange it, no refunds for shop-soiled goods. And, know what?, never have I wanted to, Brian. Never. Not even now. Not even knowing all the pain that I would have to face. No, no for a second. You gave me so much joy, my darling laddie. *So* much joy.

"I wonder if I ever told you that.

"What I know I didna tell you – I ne'er told anyone, not even Father Gillespie ... No, start again ... Ahem, right ... My parents ne'er told *me* they loved *me*. Never. Not once. Not together, no (I mean) as a couple, not either one of them by themselves. No on my twenty-first birthday (as it was then), not when I got married. And what I didna tell you, what I've told no-one including Father Gillespie, is that, when he was dying, you remember, in that awful hospice? Of course you remember, how could you possibly forget? That smell of stale cabbage, it's still in my nose. Still clogging up my nose, still shutting out so many other smells. Well, Grandpa signed to me to come closer to him. It was all he could do then just to whisper. He motioned me to him and I thought, finally, he would tell me that he loved me. That he'd say I'd been a good daughter to him, that he didna know what he would have done without me, that he was proud of me. Thank God, even as I was leaning forward, I told myself no to be silly: that it was much more likely he wanted a sip of Lucozade or something, or to change the channel on the tele. You know what it was he did say? 'You're a disgrace,' he whispered, 'a bloody disgrace.' If he hadna've been dying, I'd've killed him.

"Well, I wouldna, of course.

"Why do I say 'of course'? I mean, *why* wouldn' I have? What's 'of course' about my not killing him? I wouldna is all. I wouldna because I was too staggered, if truth be told, too gob-smacked, too smacked-in-the-face-smacked to be able to do *anything*. Except reel. Oh aye, I reeled all right. And then I reeled a bit more. Reeled like the drunken sailor reeled, you know, the one they dinna know what to do with. Och, how I wanted the bastard to die in that minute. But he didna, of course. All I need to do to make, I don't know, Oxford beat Cambridge in the boat race is to start hoping that Cambridge wins.

"He just lay there, wheezing, an evil, a wishing-me-evil sort of half-grin cracking his stubbly chin. And then – God, how much! – I didna want the bastard to die. No, I wanted the bastard no to die. I wanted him to linger on for a while in degradation and misery, I wanted him to suffer the torments of Hell whilst I was around to see him doing so, I wanted him to want to die and not to be able to, to want to breathe and only to get a half-a-breath; I wanted all Beelzebub's pigging minions to rack him with every torture known to a fiendish brain. And it was that moment – and this time it is 'of course' – that he chose in fact to die.

"And it seems to me, Beelzebub, all his minions, having been, as it were, summoned to Earth, decided to hang around. And affix themselves to me. And to plague me with all the pigging torments I'd wished upon my father.

"Maybe if I'd told Father Gillespie ... Maybe confession *is* exorcism, maybe I'd've been spared in life some of life's tortures. Thumb-screws are nothing. Nothing. What's a couple of broken thumbs between pals? Being burnt at the stake, being hung, drawn and quartered, you know the pain will end. Even for you tomorrow, my lamb. In ... you ken ... you ken the pain will end. End soon. It has to. Soon you'll just faint from the pain.

"You ken almost the worst part of *this* pain, Brian? That you ken it will *never* go away. Och, I ken it will diminish. I do ken that. I ken that in a couple of years there may even be whole days when I willna feel the pain. Or notice it. Maybe even whole weeks. But it will always, *always* be there. Lurking. Skulking. Waiting for a memory to bring it forwards, waiting for a smell, a something on the tele, a snatch of music, some nudge, some wink, some speck of what was Brian, for it to bounce back from the wings to centre-stage all over again. Centre-stage and in its own spotlight.

"And with the memory will whoosh in too memories of all the feelings I'm having now – the burning hatred I have for you that my love for you is so strong it's over-riding – and with that will come new pains all their own: the hate I have for you that the memory of you still causes so much pain. All the different, the opposite – the *opposing* – feelings I have for you today, multiplied and made deeper because I'm both reliving them and feeling them anew – and, aye, feeling fresh ones too.

"Know what? That isna even the half of it. No even the half of it.

"Because there will be times, Brian – there *have* been times – when I regret having had you. When I have – if truth be told – cursed God for having had you, in fact. And then I hate myself for having hated you. It's so against the natural order, I tell myself. How can I possibly hate something which has grown within me? That I have held to my breast and suckled?

"And then I think, well, a turd, that also grows inside of me. No great love lost there. And then I think, that worthless lying bastard of a father of yours, I've held him too to my breast, *and* whilst he's suckled there. Even less love lost there than for my turds.

"And then I think – then, Brian, I think – 'NO,' I sort of half-think and half-scream, 'NO,' I say to myself, my soul splitting in two like a wish-bone just about to split, 'NO. I do not hate him. I *canna* hate him. If I hate him,' I say to myself, 'then it's no wonder he's turned out to be who he is, the murderer that he is, the rapist. If I dinna love him, he had to find love elsewhere,' I tell myself, but willna let me – I willna, I mean, let myself tell myself that. 'I canna not love him,' I tell myself instead. 'For me no to love him goes against the grain, goes against the natural order – like a child dying before the parent.' Like a child, Brian, dying before a parent. Like you about to die.

"It's 12.31 now. 12.32, sorry. The paperwork will have been completed by this time tomorrow. The doctor will have signed the Death Certificate. Cause of death? What'll he put down as cause of death? A mother who cursed God for having had him, maybe? Uncontrolled selfishness run amok? Karma? An inability to take 'no' for an answer? Bad luck? Or just political ... what's the word? ... expedience?

"That would be a nice one, political expedience. Shame this isna Florida. Jeb Bush seems like someone good to blame it on. In Florida we might even be right. I've tried to blame others – other people, other things. Heaven only knows, I've tried to blame others. And doubtless I'll try again. And it's no, I know, that there's *nae* truth in the political expedience of it. It's just that, as they would say in a court of law, it's no the *whole* truth. And probably the reason why it's not the whole truth is that that is just too easy. And the truth rarely is that easy. It's too pat. Too *convenient*, that's the word. Just too damn convenient. If I blame the state for it all – and I'm not talking about the state here, the *local* state, but the state, rather, of America; 'state', in other words, being not a part of the nation but another word for the whole of the nation – if it is the state of America that I blame then I dinna need to look at any blame I might have. Or you might have. Or that your worthless father might have. Or Kenny or Catherine or the tooth-fairy or the Wicked Witch of the North or Uncle Tom Cobley and all.

"I've got to sleep. I've got to try and sleep, Brian. What do they call it, psychiatrists? The time between parents and their weans? The time we're all supposed to work towards? What the hell do they call it? The time too between two lovers? 'Quality time', that's it. Quality, like the chocolates, except no 'street' 'time'. '*Quality* time', aye. Well, it's not exactly as if this is, is it, *quality* time? And the visit this afternoon, that's got to be. Got to be. 'Quality time'. Quality time and with a vengeance. With a capital 'q' and a capital 't'. Quality time without the bitten into coffee creams or orange creams or things, the quality time of noisette and hazel clusters and brittle praline. But this ... this ...? This motel room in the small hours of the morning? I mean, if quality time is a Rolex this isna, is it, even a Timex? This is one of those watches they sell you on Spanish beaches for, like, twenty-three p. Breaks precisely one nanosecond after the watch-seller has vanished – which is precisely one nanosecond after he's pocketed your loot.

"It's a nice room, this. A nice bed. The Americans do

these things so well, dinna they? I mean, I've seen some of the so-called 'guest houses' round Barlinnie. They look grimmer, some of them, than the prison itself.

"Not a lot, is there, grimmer, though, than your prison?

"You read such terrible things about American jails. About all jails, 'course, but particularly about American ones: about the violence inside them, about homosexual rape, gang rape. You try to close your eyes to it – I do – your eyes and your ears, but you canna help it, can you? I mean, it's there, isn' it? All the time? In your face, as it were? The toilet with no seat. And no privacy. At all, I mean. And body searches! I mean, how humiliating is that? Having to spread your arse for inspection? I mean, I'm no prude – I hope I'm no prude – and Chester, your father – damn his worthless soul – he wasna, I mean, averse to pleasuring himself in that direction (something else I ne'er told Father Gillespie) – but that's an act of intimacy, isna it, and of love? Bending over, spreading your cheeks for a complete stranger, that's ... well, 'humiliating' doesna begin to cover that, nor demeaning. It's what I said earlier about the Mississippi and the Clyde. If 'humiliating' is the Clyde then what that is, having your bum inspected by strangers, that's the Mississippi.

"There's not too much, now I think of it, which isna humiliating about prison. Heavens, there isna much that isna humiliating just *visiting* people in prison, being (as it were) on the right side of the bars. Those grim white bars. What it must be like, looking from your side out, I dread to think. I *so* dread to think, in fact, or to imagine that I dinna dare to.

"You know, when I used to visit your father, I used to swear I'd never – ever – again visit anyone in prison. I canna begin to tell you how I used to leave that visiting room. God, you might even remember. I can still remember how I got home, I mean, the state I was in when I got there. Still shaking with the humiliated I felt, wanting a bath to clean myself, wanting a bath for my insides, my soul: They'd been soiled, smudged – no, stained. And next visit your father would bleat on about how I should bring *you*. And the others. On and on he'd bleat. I told him, I couldna think of anything more guaranteed to have our children ending up on the wrong chair at a prison visiting room than taking them there as weans. He said I was distancing you from him. I asked him who had gone out and committed the crimes. He said again I was distancing you from him, you all from him. Said it was being punished two times' over – *twice* over, I mean. Couldna see how much *I* was being punished, how much *you* were – we *all* were – and for crimes we'd none of us had anything to do with. He just couldna see that.

"You'd think, wouldn't you, at least *some* chickens would fly the coop? I mean, do they all – every single pigging one of them – have to come *home* to roost? Do you think if I hadna've sworn ne'er again to visit someone in a prison visiting room I'd be here today? You can bet your life I wouldn't! It's God. He has to have the last pigging word, doesn't He?

"Oh my God! Oh my God, Brian, what did I just say? How can I have said it? How can I have said *that*? Oh my God!

"I'm sorry. I'm so sorry, darling. I didna mean it. Not for a second – not for one second – would I ... you know what I'm trying to say ... cheapen your life, make light of it, not give it the importance which it's due. You know I know how important that life is, Brian. To me, anyway. Remember, sweet, I gave it to you.

"I have got to sleep. Got to try and sleep. Kenny's tele's still on. Is he still watching it, though? Or has he fallen asleep in front of it? Gracious, why am I worrying about Ken? He's a grown man. He kens what's best for himself. Kenny kens what's best for Kenny. Why have I ne'er in all these years thought of that before? *Kenny kens*, I mean?

"And *you're* a grown man, Brian. *Deemed* to be, anyway. Deemed to be responsible for your actions, deemed to be accountable – deemed to be so hopelessly wicked that you can be no more. But, know what? I know better. The orange uniform? That's just a romper-suit. And in it there is no grown man, there's only the babby. And that babby is all the things all babbies are – annoying, exasperating, a pigging egomaniac, impossible to satisfy: clutching, cloying, whiney, grizzling – all, all of those things and more. And yet mine. And lovable. So hugely, scrumptiously, good-enough-to-eatly lovable.

"I'm going to need to be strong. I'm going to need my wits about me. I'm going to need every ounce of courage, every last scrap of strength and will and determination. I'm going to need my love serviced, its filters replaced, its oil changed, its retread tyres replaced with new ones.

"I must sleep. I must. Sleep. I must try to. I canna function any longer without it. You ken that. We had that fight the day before you went. You wanted, remember, to party through the night? Wanted us to pour you direct onto the aeroplane. Wanted *me* to party through the night as well. Me?! Wanted us to go direct to the airport. Do Not Pass Go, Do Not Collect Two Hundred Pounds. Remember I told you it was a bad idea? Remember I told you, the whole trip, it was a bad idea? Do you have any idea how desperately I'd like to be wrong about that? Do you have any idea at all?

"You know what I dinna need right now? I dinna need to get angry with you. I really do not need that. Plenty of time for that tomorrow. And the day after. And the day after that. Ad infi-pigging-nitum. Please do not make any mistake, Brian, my lad: I am mightily pissed off with you. Mightily. No. Another dead-end, Roni. Oh wow, *what* an ... unfortunate expression. Another *cul-de-sac*, rather. Another alley we dinna want to wander down.

"I envy Kenny, you know that? I mean, first of all it doesna matter what sort of mindless garbage is on the tele he can watch it. And then, second, he can fall asleep in front of it. Me, I either get irked by the tele's badness or, if it's good, I get hooked. Either way, the bloody thing, it keeps me awake. How many channels do they have over here, did someone say? Was it over eight hundred? Something crazy like that. I mean, when would you have the time to read the listings? And of those eight hundred, seven hundred and ninety-nine, I'd be prepared to bet, are pure junk. I mean, pure, unadulterated junk. Mind-stultifying stuff. Still ... I wish I could watch it, switch off for a moment or two. Switch on to switch off. Surprised, really, that hasn't been made into a slogan.

"I'd drink the duty-free too, only I'm afraid to. I'm afraid I'll not be able to have just the one I need to help me sleep. I'm afraid the relief of the first drink, I'll want more of it. A lot more of it. I dinna want to be tight tomorrow. Not as well as being *uptight*. Uptight I canna do too much about. Oh God!

"I'll leave it for tomorrow. Which isna tomorrow any longer, it's today. Later on *today*. There've been so many tomorrows. It's hard to believe we've now come to the end of them. It's like when that shiftless father of yours stole all that whisky. Remember? Crates of the stuff. We thought that too would ne'er come to an end. It did, of course. Of course it did. Everything comes to an end. Everything. It's just that some ends come sooner than others.

"You know what I canna figure? How each second feels like a year and yet each ten seconds or so that I look at the clock, or glance at my watch, a whole half-hour has passed. Where's the logic in that? It's now, for instance, almost one. See what I mean? The crowds by this time tomorrow will be starting to go home – both those who want to get rid of ... you ken ... and those who would, I don't know, like to bring back burning at the stake or something.

"And to both lots, know what you aren't, Brian? You arena Brian, Brian. You're no a man, no flesh-and-blood, you're a symbol. And that's why I have nae truck with them, with either one of them. Nae truck at all. But, having said that, I do have sympathy for both lots – some sympathy, aye, and for both of them. Sympathy, though, isna truck. No, Roni, 'lorry' is truck!

"Christ, dearest one, your jokes get any worse, you'll find yourself writing a sitcom! You just be careful, lassie. You just watch yourself.

"No truck, Brian, because that's what you are – a Brian – and no a symbol.

"Symbols dinna have funny tufts of hair, you see, when they were five that used to stick up whatever we did with them, however much spit we used on them, however much we took the hairbrush to them; symbols dinna get excited when they come second in the egg-and-spoon race or look completely miserable when they fail to get the part of Chief Ferret in the school's production of 'Toad of Toad Hall'. They dinna get chicken pox from their brother or diarrhoea from a bad hotdog at a Rangers' match or sun-stroke on the first day of their holiday in Turkey. They dinna play pool well and snooker badly and draw moustaches on their sister's poster of the Bay City Rollers. They dinna love peaches and hate nectarines – explain that one, if you will.

They dinna have funny, spidery hand-writing and a smile that warms like an overcoat. And what neither crowd understands, Brian, what it doesna seem to me either understands, it's no the symbol who's about to die, it's the man. It's the tufty hair and the spidery writing and the sun-stroke ... and the smile – that huge, I'll-protect-you-from-the-world smile. The smile that will be no more.

"I'm just going to lie here, be quiet. Be still. Hope sleep may come. Maybe despite itself. I'm going to lie here, in the dark, not let myself think, boot out any thought that may come, just lie here and let the dark hold me, let it cuddle me, let it drink me in so that the dark and me, we become one. Just let a sort of juddery peace overcome me too – overwhelm me. Let that peace too become part of the dark. Let them both drink me in – the dark and the peace." ...

* * *

"How come, even in the dark, even with my eyes closed, there are liver spots in front of my eyes? I mean, there's no before-my-eyes for them to *be* before. I mean, *is* there? Heavens, there's a mighty amount of questions science has yet to answer. ...

"'Course, why toast always lands butterside down, that's been explained. Been proved too not to be an urban myth or anything, but a scientific phenomena. Phenomen*on*, Roni, scientific phenomen*on*. Aye, right. Got to do with the relative weight or something of the buttered side versus the unbuttered. Or something ...

"I am not going to cry. Crying's no going to help. It'll serve nae purpose. None at all. Crying's like drinking: If I open the bottle, I'll want the lot. Plenty of time tomorrow for crying. And for drinking.

"I canna be *too* strong, though. He's such a babby. You're such a babby, Brian. Well, of course you are. That's why you are where you are. From play pen to penitentiary pen with precious little in between. If you see me too strong, too stiff-upper-lippy, you'll think it's because I dinna care. God, it's a fine balancing act – to be caring but not *too* caring, snivelly but not sobbing. You always were a demanding child, Brian. It's good to see that age has not changed you. From play pen to not-play pen. Aye, right. Very not-play pen.

"Age? What am I talking about, age? You are *no* age. Not to die. Not, for heaven's sake, to die. Dying's what old people do. When they have nothing else left to do. It's not a young person's sport, not a pastime of youth. It should be like driving or something, going to a casino. Or drinking. There should be a minimum dying age. A hundred and sixty sounds about right.

"These, Roni, my dear, are no peaceful thoughts. We're going to think *peaceful* thoughts, remember? We're going to be drunk in by the dark, drunk in by peace. We're going to melt into that peace-dark or that dark-peace, whatever it is, we're just going to evaporate into it. We're going to be, Roni, one with it, indivisible *from* it. We're just going to lie here in the dark and, because we know that thinking happy thoughts is not exactly an option here, we're just going to think of nothing. Black waves in a black sea breaking blackly on a black beach. Blackly and silently. Wave upon wave of still. And of peace.

"We went to Blackpool that time, remember? Sassenach country! How old were you? Twelve, maybe, thirteen? Adolescence, it's such a funny time – well, for both sexes, of course. Funny? No, no funny. Difficult, emotional – funny: peculiar. Particularly difficult, it seems, for the laddies. They're, laddies at that age, like their voices:

sometimes child sometimes adult. And, just like their voices, apparently randomly so. I mean, when you see the mouth opening you have nae idea what sound's going to come out, bass or treble. Man or laddie. And sometimes, for pity's sake, it changes mid-sentence. As the man can become laddie mid-sentence or the other way around. Eying the lassies one minute, the next wanting a ride on the helter-skelter. What to buy with the pocket-money: a condom or a toffee-apple?

"Thinking about it, even at that age you weren't too good, waiting on sex. Thought the lassies were holding out on you, thought they were, as it were, giving out to all and sundry minus Mr Fantastic you. Sulking because Brenda had refused to snog you or Peggy had refused to let you touch her breasts.

"They say, don't they?, of rape, that it's not a sex crime, it's a crime of violence. Violence: violation, sound the same, don't they? Same root obviously. Same whatsit-logical root. Estimalogical? No, that's not right. Och, you ken what I mean. What about viol*in*, then? Or, worse, viola? Heavens, viola, when you think about it, viola's even the first half of violation. It's everything in violation, in fact, except the -tion. Which, judging by the way it is usually played, is no accident either. Ectamalogical? No, it's no good. I canna think.

"And that's the problem, isn't it, Roni? That you canna think?

"These – I dinna want to seem to be difficult, Roni – but these, my dear, are no tranquil thoughts. No silent waves on black beaches.

"Hush, now. Hush. Into the blackness. Into the still. Let yourself, lassie, be absorbed by the still. Gently now. Aye, that's the way. Easy. Easy. There we go now ... Gently, gently.

"You bastard. How could you have done it? You total bastard. How could you possibly have done it? And not only once, you bastard, but three times? Trying to get it right, were you? Practice, is it, makes pigging perfect? You bastard, you unspeakable shit. They were so young. So pretty. So, you bastard, full of life. Their whole lives in front of them. Glorious lives. The lives too of the children they'll now not have. Those lives too that you stole, you shit, that you whipped away. The *pain* you gave them, killing them, you unspeakable fucking ... MONSTER.

"Do you know how painful it is to me, the idea that I could have given birth to such a monster? Do you have the first idea? God, I thought the pain of giving birth to you – the physical pain of that – that was, I thought, my pain ration for a lifetime, there was pain a-plenty in that process to last me, so I thought, my lifetime, Brian, and yours. But that pain, that – not by comparison with this – that was nothing: a Timex to the Rolex of pain now whooshing through me – the emotional pain that is so ... charged that it becomes a physical one – a Clyde to the fucking Missi-fucking-ssippi of pain I feel that I could have created such a monster. Carried that monster – no, conceived the fuc-... pigging thing first – carried it, given birth to the thing, suckled and pulled faces at it, burped it and cared for it, kissed its scratched knees better, cuddled it when its lassiefriends dumped it – or, worse, wouldna even go out with it in the first place – bullied it into doing its homework, washed its football kit for it, cooked for it three times a day, seven days a week, three hundred and sixty-five fucking days a fucking year, Brian. And if I hadna've done all that, they'd still be alive, those lassies. Still today be alive. They'd still be ... och ... worrying about which dress to put on for their best friend's birthday party which some hunk of Heaven is supposed to be attending or how to hide that the-horriblest-in-the-whole-wide-world zit or how to put the squeeze on Dad for him to buy that really neat I-pod for their next Christmas. And sixty-*six* pigging days, Brian, in a leap year!

"Atta lassie, Roni, atta way. That's just what the doctor ordered to help you sleep, help you relax. You do ken, do you, you have to get some sleep? You do remember that?

"Well, maybe that's just what you needed. A good blow-out, sort of thing. You know, like a sultry day needs a thunderstorm to clear away the mugginess. Better now, anyway, than later. If it was going to come out, it's better here, between ourselves, as it were, than later with ... you, is it? I've got myself into a bit of a muddle here. Am I talking to you, Brian? Or to myself?

"See, I'm not at all sure, if truth be told, I want to be speaking to you, Brian. Och, I know I have to later. I am aware of that. That's no what I mean and you ken that's no what I mean. My talking to you later, *that* I'll do. It's sort of the last thing I *can* do for you, isna it? It's not – and I say thank You, Lord, for that – as if there's any doubt about your guilt or anything. It's not – and I say again, praise be to God – that I'm going to have to spend the rest of my life having to prove your innocence or anything, feeling obliged to try to clear your name. So, later on, I will talk to you, Brian, and I will remain as supportive of you as I possibly can, and I'll keep whatever smidgeon of decorum is still allowed me in a totally decorumless situation, but I do not really want to talk to you now as well. I dinna know that there's anything more I want to say to you. It's just that the alternative – me talking to myself – that stigmatises me as a mad woman. And I'm too frightened of that, if the truth be told. I'm too frightened that I might indeed be going mad for me to risk pushing myself over the edge somehow. So it looks like, darling, we're stuck together for a bit. For not-a-long bit, as it happens, but there we go. Such is life, as they say. Life's a bitch and then you die. Aye. Right. You die. We all die. It's only some, that's the thing, who are killed. Just a very few. A handful. An even smaller handful who are killed because *they* killed.

"Would it have killed you to say 'sorry'? Once, I mean? And for anything? For what you did? Or for the cost of the trial? For me having to cash in my whole life's savings, to sell my house to come over? To 'be there for you', as they say? Would it really have killed you, Brian, once to have said 'sorry'? To one person from one of the families of your victims? Even, I mean, if you didna mean it?

"And I dinna like it either that you made me use bad language. That you so irked me, I mean to say, that I was so speechless, so tongue-tied I had to resort to bad language. I hate it, you know that. I hated it when your father used it, bad language, when all the kids around us started using it, when you started using it. Aged three and a jelly-bean. Wasna 'Mammy' that first word that came out of your mouth, or 'Dada', it was 'effing Mama' and 'the "c" word Dada'. Okay, in Chester's case, you could have, that I grant you, had a point – that's *not* the point, though. And in mine you were also wrong, as it happens, on a point of fact. The amount of times your father and me effed, well, you could count them on the fingers of both hands – and three of them led to the three of you.

"I'd go down the hall, get myself a Coke – I could do with an ice-cold Coke. I've got a thirst on me like a man in a desert. But it's got caffeine in it, hasn't it, Coke? More caffeine is definitely no a good idea. Didn' I read somewhere, originally it had cocaine in it? That the two Cokes, far from being merely synonymous, actually at one time were the same substance. I suppose I should be grateful there's not Horsa-Cola too!

"Heavens, twenty past one. Already. 1.23, to be precise. One, two, three, thinking about it. As easy as ... One, two, three. 'One, two, buckle my shoe; three, four, knock at the door ...' Oh God, all those memories of childhood. But, know what?, I'm no too sure whether what I'm remembering is your childhood or mine. It's all getting mixed up in my head just right at the moment.

"One, two, three. Aye, right.

"You know, I dinna know what happens ... you know ... afterwards. I suppose they'll let me know. I suppose it's all routine. I'm no going to worry about it. That's the last thing right at the moment I need to be worried about.

"I suppose, the routine, they have to have that. It's the only thing that makes it bearable. For them, I mean. I mean, I know they get extra money, I think, other perks but, God, it must be so hard, so *harrowing* ... so, aye, punishing. I couldna do it. I know I couldna do it. Great heavens, what must they be like when they get home from work?

"And I suppose too that's why for them I also have to become a number, and Kenny does. We canna be people either. If we're people then there's a welter of pain to be ... well, okay, not suffered, not exactly, not even faced up to ... acknowledged! Aye, acknowledged. There's a welter of pain that they'd have to acknowledge. Not just the visitors' pain, but the prisoners' too: their pain, the inmates' pain, that too. And, Jesus, their *own* pain. Numbers, though, are that, aren't they?: numb. Number is just the comparative of 'numb'. 'Numbers' is the plural of 'number' and numbers are number than people. They don't feel like people feel. And us, the kin of numbers, we may not be as numb as the number but we're number than human beings – than regular human beings. We have to be else we wouldna be related to a number. That's what it feels like.

"It feels like, too, some blame attaches. Like I just had to have been a bad mother else my laddie wouldna have turned into the 'bad-assed mother-fucker' he so clearly is. And, aye, you are that, Brian, I'm afraid. And, aye, I agree with them too that some blame does attach to me. But I dinna need to be reminded of that. Not every second of every minute of my visits there. And know what? I'm damned if I ken what blame does attach to me, and I'm damned if I ken how.

"And, know what else? That's something else I'm no going to worry about just now. It's in fact something that I'm going to do my damnedest ne'er even to *think* about. The answer's unknowable and, even if it was, it wouldna help. I mean, where does blame *not* attach? If, as they say, a butterfly flapping its wings in Brazil leads to a typhoon in China, where, for pity's sake, does blame *not* attach?

"There's a funny taste in my mouth. Sort of metallicky. Sort of tinny, in fact. It's like the taste you sometimes get from a filling after the anaesthetic's worn off. What do you reckon that is? My money's on sleep deprivation. Christ, it's almost 2.

"No more, Roni, not for the moment. Black waves, that's all, on black beaches. Silence. If not peace, if peace is not gettable, at least silence. At least still." ...

* * *

"Oof. That was awful. That was grim. It was like I was drunk. Those three nights that I've ever been really drunk. When the room started spinning on me and when, instead of easing gently into sleep, I was sliding into it – but not either a gentle slide, not the slide of a kiddies' playground or anything, not even the kind of colossal and scary one of an aquapark ... a laundry chute, more like. Abrupt, functional, unsentimental. Laundry's on fifth floor, splat, laundry's in skip in the basement. A stainless steel chute – stainless, though, not painless." ...

* * *

"Heavens, I'm sweating. It's almost a quarter to three. I must have slept. 'It's quarter to three/ There's no-one in the place except for you and me ...' Slept some, at any rate. I have to have done. I suppose that's good. I dinna remember any dreams. I suppose, thinking about it, that's good too. Still got that funny metally taste in my mouth, though. And, know what else? Now I also need to pee. Thing is, though, if I do go off and have one, a pee, getting out of bed, that'll wake me up so much I willna be able to get back to sleep again.

"Will I be asleep at quarter to three tomorrow night?

"I will be able to cry by then. And I'll be able to be drunk. I wouldna mind the laundry chute so much if I *had've* been drunk, if truth be told. And, know what?, at quarter to three tomorrow the pain – I can see that now – it willna even have *begun*. It'll be like placing your hand on a barbecue grill. Remember when I did that? When was that? Six years ago, was it? Do you know, I've got an awful feeling it was closer to, like, twelve! It's still embedded in my memory, though, as if it was yesterday. There was a moment of shock/horror realisation of what I'd done. But then there was, just for a moment or two, a time of no pain at all. There was a still, a 'hiatus' as they call it, as if the pain, you know, was taking a deep breath before bellowing out that it was there. Like it knew someone was in the house, and had tried knocking politely and ringing frantically and this was the last thing the pain was going to do before phoning the police. A deep, long intake of breath. Like the doctor tells you to do. Well, that deep, long breath, that's what my tomorrow is going to be all about. That's my guess. Not the pain itself – the pain willna have got itself together yet, will not have summoned up all its strength – but the pain breathing in long and hard – so hard and so long – before it gives it to me with both barrels, double whammy! Double? Quadruple whammy. Thousandle, millionle whammy!

"And all for you, my wee wean. Are you no proud of yourself?

"Stop it, Roni. Black waves, remember, on black beaches. No, not waves. Anything but waves. Waves'll only make it worse, me wanting to go and pee. Just close your eyes, lassie. Think of Scotland. Too much rain in Scotland. Think of Glen Sahara, that little known desert South of Aberdeen. Think of all the Highland camels which can go weeks without water. Think of Highland heather, the purply pink of that Highland heather – that almost other-worldly purply pink, the mist over it painted with the same colour but more pastelly, that mist which is almost other-wordly; that mist that is almost mystic." ...

* * *

"Half-past four. Well, I did sleep, then. Kenny's tele's still on. I do hope he's no still watching it. It's no good. Whether or not I go back to sleep, I've passed the point of no return. Any second now I'll have *pissed* the point of no return. It's no good, if I dinna get up to pee, I'll just pee in the bed.

"I read somewhere the executed man canna contain his bodily functions. His bladder opens, and his bowels. They really do take away from you, dinna they, every shred, every pigging vestige of dignity? It's no enough that they kill you, they have to kill your self-respect as well.

"Och, stop wailing, Brian, will you? There was not too much dignity left either in those three lassies by the time you'd finished with them. Their vaginas slashed open, semen all over their faces. You also did not leave them too much dignity. And what about *my* dignity, come to that? Och, stop wailing, Roni, will you?

"Okay, that's better. Damn! What I should have done, same time as peeing, I should have brushed my blooming teeth. Seen whether I couldna get this taste out of my mouth. What is it? A sort-of tin-canny sort of tin. Cheap tin. The tin of Coke cans.

"I read somewhere the biggest mark-up in the world is in popcorn. I'm prepared to put money on the fact that Coca-cola's not too far behind. And they call the people in Brian's prison 'criminal'. I wonder how many of the people in jail are seriously bad. And I wonder how many seriously bad people are still out there in their parliaments or their board-rooms ... or just walking in the pigging street. The powers-that-be, they'd all like us to believe that Haughey and Nixon and de Lorean, they're just rogue bad apples in a barrel of luscious and butter-wouldn't-melt-in-their-mouths Granny Smiths. But I've got a feeling that they're just – Haughey and Nixon and de Lorean – the very tippiest tip of a mighty, mighty iceberg. I've got the feeling that the main thing that separates them from their colleagues is only that they got found out.

"Know what, Brian? I'm no talking about you there. You are one of the seriously bad people. There is no getting away from that – absolutely no getting away from it. And as for politicians' and their corruptability ... Roni, 'twas ever thus. And thus, for sure, 'twill ever be. And you fretting about it is not going to make one scrap's worth of difference, lassie. Not one single scrap's worth of difference. Whereas getting some sleep, that will make a difference. Okay, maybe not to the planet as a whole, but at least to you, to how you're feeling. You're going to be feeling rough enough, anyway, Roni, you dinna need on top of that the worse you'd feel from no having slept. Black waves, lassie. Black waves on a black beach. Sleep, Roni, sleep.

"Are *they* sleeping, I wonder, the mothers of those lassies? Lassies?! Young women. Knowing their killer is going to die soon, is that going to help them sleep? You know something? If I thought it would, if I even thought it *might*, then this whole process would become a little easier. No, let's no exaggerate here: It *might* become a little easier. I'll never know. Och, I'm not claiming any haloes for myself, anything like that, I'm not going to say, I'm not *saying* it'd be *easy*, not even bearable. But it might just be a wee bit *easier*, a gnat's more bearable. But my problem is I dinna believe they *will* be sleeping better. I doubt they're even sleeping.

"Goodness knows, I've tried it often enough. Often enough and hard enough. I've tried putting myself in their place, I've tried to feel what it is they might be feeling.

"Och, and I've felt their hatred for you, Brian. I've felt their hatred for you so well I've even felt their hatred for me. I've hated you so much I've even hated anyone who's *ever* been nice to you – the man who smiled as he sold you a newspaper, the lollipop man who saw you across the road in front of the school, the team-mates who slapped you on the back when you scored a goal. I've hated you so much, I've hated any prison officer who's able to open your cell door without spitting at you. I've hated the ground you've walked on, the air you've breathed, the chair that's supported you, the food that's nourished you. I've hated the farmer for growing your food and the carpenter for shaping your chair. All farmers, all carpenters, just in case. I've hated you so much that my internal organs curdled into a cauldron of hatred; so much that I was hatred in person – a breathing, walking, waking, sleeping hatred-on-legs, that were also of hate. I've wanted you dead. I've so wanted you dead.

"I've so wanted that ... no ... it wasn't as the cliché would have it that I could *taste* that want ... if anything, it was the other way around. It was that that *was* the taste, everything was flavoured with it. Ice-cream tasted of wanting you dead, roast beef, pizza with extra pepperoni, chicken vindaloo – all of them tasted of that taste.

"I've wanted you to die long, slow and horrible deaths – from excruciating pains that could not be treated, and that would not be eased by drugs; lingering deaths, of particularly vicious Motor Neuron disease, perhaps, or Mad Cow disease: illnesses which would pulp you before they crushed you, disable you before they destroyed you.

"I remember back to an interview with Roman Polanski. He'd been asked whether ever he'd wanted Manson executed. And I remember being surprised – I think I was even appalled – that he didna. I remember wondering whether he'd ever really loved his wife. No that much. If you loved someone, you had to want their killer killed. Didn't you? I mean, *didn't* you?

"It was only when I was in their shoes – *imagining* myself, rather, in their shoes, the shoes of your victims' mothers – it was only then that I understood that that was in fact no contradiction. None at all. That they wouldna be sleeping because what they had been promised *would* make them sleep was doomed to fail. And at some level I think they must know that.

"You see, what I couldna understand when I was wearing their shoes was why I still didna want you executed. I wanted you killed, that was for sure. I wanted you dead, even less question about that. But I still did not want you executed. I couldna work it out. It had nothing to do with that usual chestnut, Could you pull the trigger yourself? It wasn' about squeamishness, not in *that* way. Even when my hate for you took over all of me, even then I didna want you ... you ken

"And then suddenly I realised: there was a difference – a basic difference – between wanting you dead and wanting you killed – and an even more basic difference between wanting you killed and wanting you ... you ken.

"Och, if you'd been killed – if another inmate had gone berserk or something or if you'd have killed yourself – I'd have given a rousing cheer. It wasna, my friend, about the sanctity of life, any of that other good shit. But what it *was* about, it was about reducing me to your level.

"Executing you ... God! I find that word so hard to say ... *executing* you ... well done, Roni; well done, girl ... executing you is stripping *me* of *my* dignity. And that's the difference.

"If someone else kills you, if some bug, some virus does, *my* hands are clean. With an execution, though, that's different: There aren't *three* thumbs on the buttons releasing the poison, there are there the thumbs of everyone of us. It turns us all into killers. And somehow that, if it doesna ... what's the word? ... 'exonerate' you, at least it somehow lessens the total awfulness of your crimes. The shop-lifter canna point a finger at the bank-robber. By ... executing you, I am robbed of my right to condemn you.

"And that confiscation is made worse – just to make matters worse – by compromise. *I* am compromised. The worthiness of my humanity and my worth as a human, those are both compromised. And it's less therefore that an injustice is being done to you than that (as a mother of one of your victims, I'm talking about), a further injustice is being done to *me*. It's not enough that I've lost someone I love, lost something in my life that's completely irreplaceable, but now even the essence which is me is being dented, chiselled away from the outside. I am that sculpture, 'The Thinker', and my arms are being hacked away.

"The crime that it is, the vandalism – capital punishment – is not in the first place of the condemned man's life but of mine. And the 'mine' that that 'mine' is is of *everyone* who isna the person being executed. The vandalism that it therefore is is one, not of the murderer's life, but of society's soul.

"Know something, lassie? You'd have been better off watching the mindless dross on the tele. The 'tube' as they call it here. Why do they do that?, I wonder. I mean tube: underground train, you can see where that came from. But pictures dinna snake through corridors, do they, to get to the screen? You want to tell me, Roni, how much you know about the internal workings of a television set? I mean, how long would it take for you to tell someone the lump sum total of that knowledge? Three seconds? Five? Certainly no more than ten.

"Sleep, lassie, sleep. Worthy thoughts though these all may well be, my dear, you really now have to get, as they would say hereabouts, some 'shut-eye'. And the truly magnificent part about having had a pee is that now I can again think of black waves breaking on black beaches.

"In your teens, Brian, I can remember ... och, a whole host of people saying 'You'll break a few hearts when you get older.' A whole *host* of people – your dotty aunt Diana, the woman at number 24 with the miniature poodle who we invited (goodness only knows why) to your sixteenth birthday party, that long streak of intellectual piss I dated for about seven and a half minutes – and what was *he* called? I dinna think when they said it they had any idea just how truthful their predictions would turn out to be. Nor just how violently you would break those hearts. Nor the manner in which you would. Heaven knows what made me think of that. What *did* make me think of that? What did?

"'Breaking', I suppose. Waves breaking, breaking hearts: I suppose that must have been it. 'Waves breaking': sounds like a crossword clue, doesna it? For an anagram or something. And it probably would be if there was such a word as 'savew' or 'vewsa'. ... Or 'awves'. Black beaches. Silence, lassie. Still. Slee-eeeeeeeeeeep." ...

* * *

"Ten past five. I did sleep. Hallelujah. Not enough. Not nearly enough but, hey, at least something. What is it with this bladder of mine today? Why does it need emptying suddenly six times an hour? Was that what the hell woke me up?

"Teeth, Roni. Remember the teeth this time. Let's get rid of this tinny taste, hey? Once and for all?

"Breakfast is at five, I think. In jail, I mean. In the big house. Five, is it, or five-thirty? Some quite unimaginable time, that I do know. I remember, rather. Another punishment, I remember thinking to myself. And for the staff too, for heaven's sake. I mean, if they're serving breakfast at five, five-thirty, what time do the prison officers themselves have to start in the morning? Four? Three-thirty? Which means they've got to get up at home at what? Two? Doesna that make them night-shift workers?

"There is something about Americans and rising early, isna there? Something built into their culture? Like they take that old proverb literally, 'Early to bed, early to rise …', like they think the earlier they rise the wiser and, far more importantly, wealthier they're going to be. If they start getting up any earlier, Americans, they'll be rising before they go to bed. Which would, thinking about it, probably be the summit of the American work ethic.

"You ken what I find most ironic? That Americans find no irony at all in the fact their civil war was fought in order to abolish slavery. Whoa there, Roni. Their problem, Roni, nothing to do with you, lassie. That's *their* stuff and only theirs.

"I've never liked the super-rich. Och, Brian, you know how I've never liked them. Greedy, grasping little toe-rags that they are. But Getty did once say something which endeared himself to me. Did I ever tell you this? No matter. If children aren't there to hear you tell the same stories once in a while then there's really no purpose in having them. He was asked, John Paul Getty – hey, it's just occurred to me, John Paul, like the Pope – … Getty was asked by a journalist – in the usual ultra-original way of journalists – what he believed the secret was of getting great wealth. "Three things," Getty replied: "rise early …" (which was what made me think of it) "… rise early, work hard, strike oil." A man with that type of wit, I thought, canna be all bad. Though, of course, it being Getty who said it, I canna help wondering whether he thought of it or just bought it.

"You willna want to eat, my darling one. Try to. Do try. You ne'er did want to eat breakfast on 'big' days – exams and such, your driving test, even Catherine's wedding. But you'll need your strength. You'll need – and I know this sounds bizarre, but I also know I'm right – you'll need, Brian, every ounce of strength you can muster. It's going to be a tough day. For you too. And people are going to feel sorry for you. Even you. And, my, you're just going to *love* that one, aren't you? Like a cat loves a dog! You willna even like being the centre of attention. It wasna in that way that your selfishness showed itself. No, you were never a show-off in that kind of a way. You'll also need strength to cope with that, my darling one – with the sympathy and the spotlight.

"And you're going to need courage, Brian. Another of your not-longest suits. Not the swagger, not the machismo, not that frantic 'what-are-you-looking-at?' aggression, but *real* courage, Brian. *Moral* courage. The courage, if you like, of James Cagney at the end of 'Angels With Dirty Faces', the courage of a man acting against his own grain because he kens that's the right thing to do. Aye, and the courage too of people like George Bentley's sister who fought for his pardon and his acquittal for decades after her wee brother had been hanged. I dinna even know, Brian, if you *have* that kind of courage. But I do hope you do. And I hope, *if* you do, you have the further courage you'll need to use it.

"But if you're going to be in with a chance, sweetheart, of using it, you're going to need to nourish it, you're going to need to eat. So ... Eat your breakfast. In Britain, of course, in the old days, in the days when it too used to kill its criminals – the Bentleys of this world, the Timothy Evans's and Ruth Ellis's – breakfast was the last meal. Executions were at eight in the morning, or something like that. Something mighty early as well. But I dinna think, even on your last day in Britain, they roused you from your slumber at five-thirty to give you breakfast. At that hour of the morning, it's not *even* breakfast, it's rather more a late supper." ...

Derek, I mean. Derek Bentley. *Derek* Bentley is who I mean. George? Where did I get that from?" ...

* * *

"Well, I had to cry sometime, I guess. It was the word 'late' did for me. 'Late supper'. Innocent enough, you would have thought. But that soon ceded to 'last supper' and ... well, 'and'. And there we were. Blubbing away and like a good 'un. So, if I did have to cry (and I did!), it's as well I'm crying right now. Whilst I'm alone. And Kenny's tele's still muffling any sound. He has his own grief. I dinna need to make his grief worse by adding mine. He doesna need to be further upset, I mean, by knowing that I too am upset ... by knowing *how* upset I am. And you know what, Brian? I dinna even ken what I'm crying *for*. Or *who* I'm crying for.

"Och, 'course there's a bit for me. Of course there is. I feel sorry for me. I know I shouldn't, but I do. There. I've got to, it seems. It seems there's precious few others feel sorry for me. And if that's not a classic example of self-pity, then I dinna know what is. That's almost, thinking about it, the biggest problem with self-pity, the way it feeds on itself, the way it sucks you into its own labyrinth where, seeking to escape from it, you are in fact only drawn deeper within it.

"And, of course, there's part of those tears that are for you. Mostly, if I'm honest, for the you you were, for the you I first saw, first held in my arms, first took to my breast; for the tidal wave of love that washed over me at that point for you and which has continued to cocoon me all these years; for the you that was as innocent as a lamb, that didna have a bad thought in your head – for the you that wouldna hurt a fly.

"And there's another part of those tears that are for you as you are – for the monster that you have been and that your crimes show you to have been, but, for all that, there are tears too still for the innocent within that monster, for the frightened little laddie clad in a monster's garb who knows he's done something wrong, who knows he's for the high jump, knows he's about to get six of the best – and on his bare bum – but who's really, *really* sorry, sir, and who'll never do it again, sir, and who's learnt his lesson, sir, only, please, sir, not six of the best, sir, not, sir, on the bare – three, sir, three strokes of the cane, three whacks with the tawse, and with my trousers *on*, sir, *please*, sir. And who, even bending over, even told there is no other punishment available, even with his trousers around his ankles, his bum mooning at the stick, who, even then, is telling himself the head'll finally relent. He willna go ahead with it. He'll give me one stroke – a nasty sting, no more. He'll relent then. Tell me to stand up. Pull up my trousers. Tell me I took my medicine like a man. Shake hands. And leave his study united by a bond. And, know what, Brian? You'll be telling yourself something similar when the second stroke streaks across your arse.

"Maybe that will save you. Please God. Maybe, by the time the fifth stroke arrives and the sixth, your chief emotion will be surprise. Surprise that you could have been so completely wrong. And maybe that surprise will shield you from the pain of the fifth and sixth strokes. Maybe by then you'll already be dead.

"Because there *is* an end for you, you bastard. You unspeakable shit. However terrible, however awful, for you tomorrow – later today – there is closure, there is an end. Whereas for us ... For those of us still living, there is *none*.

Tomorrow is no end at all for us. It's not even the *beginning* of an end. If it's anything at all, and that's very far from certain, Brian, it's only, maybe, the end of the beginning.

"And for them, too, your victims. For them too it's only the end of the beginning, for all the Kenny's and Catherine's and ... me's of *their* families.

"And so part of the tears, they're also for them. For their families, friends, the local greengrocer's, the gum-chewing dumpy peroxide blonde who works Saturdays at their dry cleaner's.

"And part too of the tears, they're for the lassies themselves. For the pain you gave them – that hideous, hideous pain. For the future they'll never have.

"And so part of the tears are for their non-husbands and non-lovers and non-children, for the absence of those sweet first kisses, for the absence of great sex ... and lousy sex and sort of routinely okay sex ... for the absence of rows and divorces and children teething and bunking off school and turning up after a party at three in the morning and for fooling around with drugs and for contracting meningitis. ... For the lack too of misery in their lives there is a part of my tears. Even for what, at fifty, they might have thought the *waste* of their lives.

"Know what? There's no such thing as a wasted life, Brian, not even yours. Know what else? There's no such thing as an *unwasted* life. Not even Gandhi's or Einstein's or Mozart's.

"And there's tears too for that. For the utter futility of life at all, for all the strutting and fretting and pointlessness and meaninglessness, for the whole empty nothing of it and for life-being-a-bitch-and-then-us-dying number, for that too.

"And for not knowing whether or not there's a God and

if there isna one for not knowing who, in that case, to be angry with? Angry? We're back again, Brian, to Timex and Rolex, to the Clyde and the Mississippi.

"Jimmeney! Ten to six. Soon the non-prison world will also be stirring. You've not had enough sleep, lassie. No way have you had enough sleep. You nag your son about eating, but when it comes to *you*, you getting the nourishment *you* need ('cos what is sleep if not nourishment?), then the whole deal becomes mightily different. Yet another example, my dear, of 'do as I say, not as I do'? And should that be a question? Or is it, more likely, a statement?

"Know what? That tinny taste has come back into my mouth. What the hell is that? My eyelids feel so heavy suddenly. Even closed they feel so heavy. How is that possible? I mean, you lift a suitcase and it's heavy, put it down on the ground and it's not. Heavy. Well, it is, of course – of course it is – but it's only theoretically heavy if you want to pick it up again. Not like eyelids. That's what I'm saying, that's what I dinna understand. Eyelids, apparently – even on the ground, as it were –, they're still heavy. Know something, Roni? I think finally the few marbles you ever had to begin with, you're losing them." ...

* * *

"Twenty past eight! Heavens! Twenty past eight? I'm late. Late? What, lassie, are you late *for*? Relax, Roni. Take it easy. Aye, and that's an order. You've *got* to take it easy, lassie. You've just got to. Twenty past eight. Less than sixteen hours. The sixteen longest hours of your life, lassie. Aye, and the shortest.

"Okay, in yours too, Brian. I accept that: in yours too.

"Kenny's television's off. He'll be awake then. It'll only

anyway be full of your execution. Rubbing salt into your own wound, that really is stupid. Actually, I'm starting to notice it now only when other people notice it. News, I'm talking about, about your ... well, you ken... your execution. Most of the time, it's just moving wallpaper. Normally, anyhow. But ...

"We were in the hotel bar the other night, Kenny and me, and the news came on and there was something on it about there being three days to go or something before your ... execution ... and about crowds starting to form outside the jail and there was this, like, frantic scrabble for the remote control. And the barman eventually found it and changed channels to, I dinna know, some golf tournament or something. One of his customers came to complain. 'I was watching that, buddy,' sort of thing. And then ... well, he couldna have *recognised* us, not as such, I mean, where would he have recognised us *from*? A few blurs once in a while on the tele ... but somehow or other the barman signed to this guy or something who we were. Or he guessed it or something. And there was this embarrassed ... well, not silence, exactly ... sort of fumbling ... a sort of fumbling apology, but wordless ... a sort of shuffling awkwardness, like when a man makes a pass or something at a woman he then finds out is his boss's wife. No. No, thinking about it, it was more like a man making a pass at a transvestite, and then being told what, as it were, lay beneath the covers.

"And, what I'm trying to tell you, Brian, the *irony* is that up till then I hadn't even noticed what had been on the tele. Only later, if you understand what I mean, thinking back on it. It was there but not there, if you ken what I mean. Like the rumble of traffic if you live on a main road. Like the rumble of traffic in that awful place we had in Queen's Terrace.

"Remember Queen's Terrace? Probably not. Except from the stories you've heard about it. And most of them are exaggerated way beyond any belief. The way your father talks about it, you'd think it was a slum in Calcutta or something. Doesna stop him getting all misty-eyed about the place. That peculiar kind of snobbery: about no-one having had it quite as tough as you have. Like luxury was a slice of bread without weevils, and good health was the pause between consumptive coughing fits. And it *was* awful, Queen's Terrace. Awful. But it wasna so awful it was romantic. It was just drably awful. And made the more awful because it *was* so drab, and because it was so completely and utterly normal. Everyone we knew lived in Queen's Terrace, or a Queen's Terrace-alike. Because they *were* all alike: Queen's Terrace, St George's Avenue, Victoria Way – all high-falutin' names, all posh names, Acacia-Gardens-like names, all names that make you think of leafy suburbs and central heating. I suppose there was spin, even in those days." ...

* * *

"That was your brother on the phone. Wanting to know where I was. We'd agreed, he said, to meet at eight for breakfast. I dinna remember that. I'm no disbelieving him. I just have nae memory of it. None at all.

"I've said I'll go and join him. Well, what I said, I said I was so, so sorry, that I'd overslept, that I'd be right there. But, know what? I'm in nae hurry. I'd like to go back to sleep now, if truth be told. If truth be told, I *could* go back to sleep now. This bed now feels so warm, so comfy ... so nestly, really. So like a nest, I mean. And so, thinking about it, also like a bar of chocolate. Like that kind of Nestlé, spelt with an 'e' accent – Nestlé with an 'e' accent.

Sweet, like a bar of chocolate, familiar, comforting, moreish ... even addictive. And filling a hole. Some sort of cosmic hole, a black-hole sort of a hole.

"Five more minutes, hey? Just five minutes more. Of being nestled and blanketed and scrunched up in some kind of ease. A sort of itchy ease, true. Like the sleep of chicken pox. Comforting yet itchy at one and the same time. Still, chicken poxed, the time passes more easily in uneasy sleep than it does awake. Five more minutes, lassie. Kenny'll give you five minutes more.

"Five minutes! They willna give *you* five minutes, will they, my darling one? One minute past twelve, that'll be it. Not one minute past twelve plus five minutes more. Not even one minute past twelve and five *seconds* more. All the clocks, they'll all have been checked a hundred times, synchronised to the exact second, and at one minute past twelve, to the second, they'll start extracting the life from you, the process will have started which is irreversible. They'll be siphoning life from you, like a syringe drawing drugs from a phial ... like pulling out the plug in a bath.

"Bath. That's what I need. A bath. That'll help. No, what you need, lassie, you need five more minutes in this lovely bed. No, you dinna. You dinna need a bath either. Not just now. Plenty of time for a bath later. After breakfast. After Ken. After you've made sure, lassie, Kenny is alright. As alright as he could be. And after too you've called Catherine. Made sure she too is okay. As okay as ... And let's get real here, Roni, for a moment: five minutes wouldna be five minutes. Five minutes more and you'd be asleep again. For an hour. For at least an hour. And what'll Kenny do during that time? How many times can you walk up and down the lobby? How many strangers pointing you out can you ignore? And pacing your own room, well, *you* might as well be in a cell, mightn't you?

You yourself?

"Up we get, lassie. Up we get. 'Walk tall, walk straight, and look the world right in the eye.' We've done nothing to be ashamed of, Kenny, you and me. No need for us not to hold our heads high. To walk tall. And look the whole world – the whole pigging world – aye, right in the eye. The curious and those that condemn us, the blinking press and the protestors. We dinna need to apologise to any of them, Kenny. We dinna need to feel less than any of them. We're *not* less than any of them.

"Coffee. That'd be good. It's be gooder if it were good coffee, but I suppose ... well, you canna have everything, can you? For a country that likes to live well, it does pour some fairly nasty liquids down its throat: the washing-up water it calls 'coffee', the barely flavoured water it calls 'tea'. Their margaritas are good, that's true enough. Surprised they dinna live on *them.*

"How do we look? Wow! *That* not-good. That's not good. Looking that not-good is not good at all. Anyone would think there'd been a death in the family. Och, screw it, I'll come back later, apply then the three tons of war-paint necessary. What's necessary now is coffee.

"Aye, and time too with Kenny. I canna help thinking, on top of everything else Kenny's going through now, there's a part of him that's quite resentful. Och, I'm no trying to say he's not sad about you, Brian, not choked that his elder brother's going to die – and about how it is he's *going* to die. But I still think there may be a part of him quite ... envious, I suppose it is, about all the attention being lavished on you. For all that you're going to die, people now know Kenny for being Brian Lawson's brother. And I think that rankles with him. I'm not even sure he knows it does, but I sense it.

"He's been a good human being, his life long. A good

man. A good husband, I think. From what I've seen, a good – a very good – father. He's worked hard, paid his taxes, contributed towards his pension, supported his children … aye, and helped his aging mum. He's cared about his friends, his colleagues. About most people in a jam, if truth be told. And when Kenny dies there'll be no fuss, no furore. There willna be hordes waiting round his death bed, waiting either to cry or to cheer. And I think there's a part of him, an unconscious – a *sub-conscious* – part of him really pissed off about that. *Really*, I mean, pissed off. Where's the recognition that is his due? Where are the rewards for a life lived rightly?

"And, you know, I think that's maybe quite a common phenomenon in the world as a whole. I think that's why so many good people – people who *are* good people – why they can get so blood-thirsty, so hang-'em-and-flog-'em when it comes to treating criminals. On top of stealing their goods and their peace-of-mind, these crooks, they're also stealing all the attention. The attention those good people have been waiting for all their lives. Waiting for and wanting.

"With Kenny, there's also, I sense, a kind of resentment-in-waiting: that I'll somehow be attentioned out. That I'll have invested so much emotional attention being there for *you* that when and if the time comes that he needs me to be there for him, there'll be nothing left in the account. And know what, you bastard? He could even be right.

"That'll have to do. Here I come, world, ready or not. What am I forgetting? What the Dickens is it I'm forgetting? Got the key, my bag, what else do I need? What the hell else do I need? Sun-glasses! Honest to goodness, Roni, you'd forget your blooming head if it weren't fixed to your shoulders." …

* * *

"Well, that was fairly horrendous. As horrendousnesses go, I mean. Aye, on a horrendous scale there of one to ten, that scored ... och ... about seventeen. And a bit. And almost the most horrendous thing of all was the absence of any horrendousness. Any overt horrendousness, that is. All that horrendous small talk between us, the over-jaunty 'good morning's' from the lobby clerks, the Colegated smiles of the waitresses, the discreet padding around us of all the other breakfasters as if, I dinna know, we were involved in some kind of deep meditation and the slightest footfall might disturb us.

"A quarter to ten ... A quarter *of* ten, as they say round here. Why, I wonder. Why does language get changed in that kind of way? What kind of consensus is it, makes us in Glasgow speak one way and those that live here speak in quite a different one? A quarter to ten, a quarter of ten, it doesna make too much difference. Either way it means you've only got another fourteen hours, Brian, and sixteen minutes left on this planet. ... And fifteen minutes.

"Catherine. I must phone Catherine. Quarter to three is it there? Or to four? Whichever. Talking of crooks outside jail, there's a superb example of legal daylight robbery: the mark-up hotels get on telephone calls. Free market economy my foot, I should pigging cocoa! It's price-fixing on a giant scale. Hey, isna that supposed to be illegal? Aye, there's a lot of things supposed to be illegal: monopolies, cartels – I suppose that's something else that went by the board with Mr Gates. William Gates esquire, he who seems able to redefine legality. So that creating a monopoly is legal, but pushing the wrong button on a computer keyboard, that is illegal. 'You have performed an illegal act,' it says. I really thought it meant it. Really, I mean. I was expecting, the first time I saw it, squad cars to come screeching to a halt outside the front door. I couldna understand how I could *possibly* have done anything illegal – I only pushed a key. I havena seen that sign recently. Am I suddenly not hitting that same key? Or did Microsoft decide this was a quotes 'joke' in, shall we say?, dubious taste, and better to be replaced by language that was, maybe, less contemptuous of the law. Aye, contemptuous, that's just the right word. How come that little slogan was not in contempt of court? In contempt, in fact, of every court in the world? And why then was Mr Gates not prosecuted for contempting the world's courts? Because, ladies and gentlemen of the jury, the prosecution will prove that even if Mr Gates murdered his blinking wife, he would not be prosecuted.

"Where can she be, Catherine? Och, let's not fret. We'll try her again, lassie, after your bath. You do need a bath. You've got to be ready, lassie. A grime attaches itself, doesna it, to a lack of sleep? And to grief, come to that? And to worry? You feel unclean with them all. Well, not unclean in a clean, coal-minery cleanly dirty sort of way. Unclean, rather, in a Lady Macbeth way, trying to wash off blood that isna there; or in a fish-wifey sort of way, trying to drown the smell of haddock below gallons of Chanel. There's a sort of itchiness to the grime of sleeplessness, a permanent beneath-the-skin prickly heat which scratching cannot reach. What is that all about?, I wonder.

"I should not have had that waffle. Something sweet, I'd decided. Get the sugar levels up. I'd have been better off with some fruit. Only trouble is, for all that it looks appealing, it tastes of nothing, American fruit. It's all – all of it – got the taste (the non-taste, I should say) of Golden Delicious apples. Sort of scrunchy blotting-paper, or chewable Velcro. No wonder they have so much trouble persuading kids to eat it. 'Och, Mummy,' you can scarcely hear the kids screaming, 'please give me some crunchy blotting paper to eat. Let me spend five minutes away from my play-station tearing the peel off this chewable Velcro.' The ridiculous thing now is that the synthetic fruit flavouring tastes more fruit-like than the actual fruit – the orange fruit gum or the strawberry ice-cream or the banana milkshake taste more fruity than actual oranges or bananas or strawberries. And I dinna ken why that is. Chemicals, I guess, are more consistent than Nature. But I wonder whether the fruit isna being produced to look good – because that's what urges us to buy it – and never mind the taste. *Seduces* us into buying it. That'll be Catherine, calling me back." ...

* * *

"DINNA SNIVEL AT ME, CHESTER. God in His Heaven, I havena got enough to cope with?! I mean, you went to all the trouble – as you'd see it – of finding out the damn number – phoning, presumably, Catherine – you lifted the heavy receiver all the way to your ear, forced your fingers beyond the level of their endurance to punch in the necessary numbers, you'd have thought your energy might just have extended to asking me how I was, or to asking how I was coping – or how Kenny was. But, oh no, that's be *too* much trouble, wouldna it, Chester? That'd require you to have a thought for someone who wasna you, and *that* apparently is completely beyond your capability.

"You know what, Chester? I know you're feeling like shit. Know what else? We all are, o light of my life. It's not a competition, you know: the person who feels shittiest loves Brian the best. It doesna suddenly, feeling shitty, make you Father of the Year or, as you seem to think, Father of the pigging Century. Not even if you're feeling shittier than I am. You could have been here with me. You might even, Chester, have been able in some way to support me.

"You've been drinking on it for years. I know. I'm no blind, you ken, or deaf. Not in an obvious way, 'course. Just dropped lamenting words in the right ears, perfected the art of looking desolate – that sort of Basset Hound look that's lost its favourite bone. The 'Turk's Head', the 'Crown and Anchor', the 'Ship'. Became something, didna you, of a name, aye, a wee celebrity? People wanted to buy you drinks. They wanted to be able to say to their chums the next day, 'I was drinking with a chap last night whose son is on Death Row'. It enabled them to think they were being the good Samaritan whilst satisfying the prudrience of their curiosity. Not 'prudrience'. What's the damn word? Purience! Do I even mean 'purience'? Know what? I dinna ken. I dinna ken what 'purience' means, thinking about it. It's just, that's what curiosity is, isna it? Purient.

"When was the last time you *bought* a drink, Chester? For anyone but your-miserable-self? Aye, and when was the last time, Chester, you drew a sober breath? A breath, I mean, that was completely free of booze?

"Know what? I'm not even, Chester, appalled by you any longer. You canna be appalled by the pathetic. And I suppose it's difficult to be appalled by anyone whose parents named him after the place he was conceived in! I'm only surprised, as that was their thinking, they didna call you 'Back-seat-of-a-Ford-Anglia' Lawson. Thank goodness they hadn't gone to Thailand on holiday. You could have been called Phuket Lawson. Or, as someone once said about Chelsea Clinton (whose parents had the same idea), 'Thank God she wasna conceived in

Scunthorpe!' Personally, I was never too convinced about your parents' explanation. There was a comedian in their time, Charlie Chester. I'm not convinced you weren't named after him. You are, after all, a clown. Albeit a sad one. The saddest, Chester, clown of all: the clown only to be laughed *at*, Chester, not *with*. Not ever *with*.

"How is it that it always ends up with me consoling *you*? I mean, even with us, Chester – even, Chester, when you deserted us. Och, I wanted shot of you, no question. I dinna deny that, not for a second. There's only so much time even Job, even the good Lord Himself, can put up with a drunk. But finally *you* left *me*, remember? And yet, within ... what was it? A fortnight? It was you on the phone grizzling to me about how unhappy you were, how cold your new bedsit was, how cheerless, how lonely. And it was *me*, o light of my life, me assuring *you* that everything would be okay, that it'd all work out for the best. You know something? Now I can scarcely believe myself.

"And know what else? None of this is helping me to get a bath. Baths, these days, they're the only erotic experiences I have. It's the only reason I have to take my clothes off. I canna help thinking I got rather short-changed in that department.

"Four lovers, that's no much, is it, for a lifetime? And as I see no orderly queue forming outside my front door I'm assuming it *is* for a lifetime. No, no much, Chester. The more so, given the fact that one of those lovers was you. And you should definitely be counted as a minus. But then so, I suppose, should John also be counted as a minus. *And* Graham, now we're about it. Which just leaves Robbie. Aye, Robbie. Like the Burns. And there was poetry in Robbie. Poetry just not in his words but in his touch. He *was* a lover, Robbie. I wish I'd known then, in those three months with him, I had, squirrel-like, to store up the orgasms I'd need to last me a lifetime. If someone'd told me, I might have been more careful with them then, not taken them so much for granted, have stored them better, put cling-film around them or something. It seems to me that's another of life's little perversities: By the time you're old enough to know better you're too old to *do* anything.

"How many times did you rape me, Chester? Okay, maybe not at gun-point, maybe only at the line-of-least-resistance-point. Still ... if rape is what rape is, sex without consent ... how many times, Chester, did you rape me?

"And when you weren't raping me, how many times were you concerned about my orgasm? What am I talking about, orgasm? How many times, Chester, were you concerned about my *consent*? It's such a fine line sometimes, rape. You know how hard I've tried to convince myself, Chester, that what your son did was genetic? (You notice he became your son, then?) And the genes, the rape genes, they would all have been as well *your* genes, Chester, yours not ours.

"And you know why, finally, I persuaded myself that wasna true. Because if it was, that would be too easy. That would be too close – way too close for comfort – to me giving some kind of absolution to myself ... and some kind of absolution to Brian. But I could have been wrong. It could have been genetic – or, at any rate, genetics could have been a factor – and that still wouldna absolve Brian.

"Or me.

"Or, Chester, you.

"What did you ever teach our son about right and wrong? What mention even did you *ever* make of it? Except to undermine me, that is, when I tried to teach him right from wrong. And for why? To gain some kind of momentary popularity, to make up, in some way, for having missed his football match for the umpteenth time or for having shouted at him in your cups or for having cuffed him round the ear because you couldna pay the gas – and why could you no pay the gas, Chester? You sought to buy his love with a cheap grin of us-against-her. Well, they say cheap is expensive, my dearest one. What do you reckon now to be the cost of those cheap grins, Chester?

"Catherine! This time it has to be Catherine." ...

* * *

"What's she done, Catherine? Taken an ad out on prime time television or something, announced to all and sundry what the phone number is here? Still, it was nice of him, Father Gillespie. Good of him to call. It canna have been easy for him. I mean, what do you say to someone in my situation? Not easy, is it? And I do hope it's the blinking Church paying for the call, not him. Poor sod. Aye, right, *literally* 'poor' sod. Not two ha'pence to rub together has he got. That was a funny way of putting that: 'Not two ha'pence to rub together has he got'! Where did that one come from?

"Know what else, Brian? He said he'd call again tomorrow. So much for your opinion of him, that he was a phoney. As straight, you used to say, as a three-pound note. They're not all tarred with the same brush, you ken. *We're* not. Not all Glaswegians get tanked up on Saturday night and are then spoiling for a fight; and not all Roman Catholic priests, Brian, are sadistic child-abusers. There are some good people in the Catholic Church, my dearest one. There are some good people in the world. A lot of both. A lot, billions of very, *very* good people.

"There was that film with one – a nun, I think. That Weaver woman played her. What's her name? Sigourney.

Aye, Sigourney. I've always liked her, Sigourney Weaver. Well, you can recognise her for one thing. She doesna look as if she's just come off some kind of Barbie-doll conveyor-belt. She was a nun in this film, I'm pretty sure, but without a, you know, habit. I don't mean naked, I mean, sort of in mufti. And she was sort of looking after a man on Death Row, that tearaway, the one who used to be married to Madonna. – What am I talking about Sigourney Weaver? It wasna Sigourney Weaver. I wasna even thinking about Sigourney Weaver. Sarandan, I was thinking of. It was Susan Sarandan. Susan Sarandan who does no come off the Barbie-doll conveyor-belt.

"I never cared too much for her – Madonna, I mean, no Susan Sarandan. But that's maybe because any man I knew cared too much for her! Nor did I care much for him, come to that. Sean ... not Connery. You know who I mean. 'Course if Sean Connery was on Death Row, I'd come and nun him any day of the week. And I'd wear no habit either. Well, in that case, habits are only things, aren't they, to get out of? And with Sean Connery around, the sooner you get out of that habit, the better!

"Know what? Even at this distance, I can hear your grandpa turning in his grave.

"He had tattoos – Penn, that's it: Sean Penn. He had horrible, horrible tattoos, I seem to remember, all over his arms and chest. I mean, yours are bad enough, but his ... They were grotesque. 'Dead Man Walking', that's what the film was called. I rented it just after you were sentenced. I thought I should try and find out everything I could, I should try, as it were, to inform myself.

"Know what? Nothing informs you. Not for this. Not for this waiting, these ten million different emotions all pounding around, all taking a different turn to the turn you expect them to take. Each one more sodding painful than the last.

"Sorry. Never an excuse for bad language. Sorry. Goodness, I've said it to you enough times.

"I remember when I was expecting with you, I remember, och, reading Dr Spock, all them, remember quizzing them all at the ante-natal clinic about this huge thing that was going to happen to my life. And I remember the other mums there – those expecting their second wean or their third – I remember my *own* mum – I remember them all saying, '*Nothing,* Roni, will prepare you. You will have no idea of the chaos this wee thing is about to bring into your life. And you willna know till one day you'll think back onto this conversation and you'll say to yourself, "Roni, those lassies were right. I had no idea how big a chaos this wean was going to be."'

"Well, no-one told me about *this*. But it's the same. It's unpreparable-for, whatever the hell the right word is. There is nothing – *nothing* – that can prepare you.

"Bath. I've got to have a bath. Jimmeney, it's five past ten already. I said I'd see Kenny at half-past. Got to get a wriggle on, lassie. Got to get a move on. Who the hell can that be?" ...

* * *

"Norman! Norman who-ja-ma-flip from Reprieve. Something unpronounceable. Dinna you get so high and mighty either, Brian. You canna pronounce it either. And the work they've done for you! And the work too, Roni, they've done for *you*. Do please let's no forget about that. You complain about Brian's ingratitude. Very quick, aren't we, dear one, to cast the first stone? Not too wise, lassie, not too sensible, being as how not only your house but all your furniture, lassie, plus all your household appliances – in fact, every single aspect, Roni, of your life is made of glass!

"They're amazing people, those people from Reprieve. Amazing. And most amazing of all because they're not amazing. There's just ... human. The way all day long Norman is stroking that pathetic excuse for a moustache, that's human; the way he slurps his orange-juice, like no-one's ever told him how to use a glass – glass again! –; the drive-you-crazy habit he has of clicking his pen up and down, that way he looks at you without seeming to blink, all – all of it – human. But the effort he's made on your behalf, Brian, that's *super*human. Aye, superhuman and just plain super. And, know what? I'll be surprised if you even said 'thank you' to him. And, know what else? Somehow I'll bet that very few of their clients do.

"When I think of it, you are surrounded, Brian, by amazing people. Truly amazing people. Even some of your prison officers, if you only but knew it. Correctional Officers, I should say. That's another sadness, another real sadness, my darling one: That the only person unaware of the amazingness of the people around you is you yourself.

"Norman, anyway, has no further news. You'll know this soon, Brian. He's phoning you, he says. Though how *he* is able to be put through to you when I, his mother, am not allowed even ... well, it all seems very odd to me. Still ... You'll know, having spoken to him – to Norman – they're, as he says, 'running out of options'. 'I promised you I wouldna lie to you, Roni,' he said, 'the prognosis isna good.' 'Prognosis', that's the word he used. Like he was a doctor or something.

"And I suppose, in a sort of way, right now he is. I mean, it's a doctor's job, isna it, to keep people alive? And, goodness only knows, that's what he's trying to do right now.

"The doctors tried to keep Connie alive as well. Me, I think they tried too hard. Her time had come way before her time had come. Connie was younger than you're going to be when she died. And she didna harm a fly in her life. And neither did Ivy. And I had to watch as Ivy watched her daughter die. She was just a child. Thirty-four *is* just a child. And, know what else, Brian? Any age is a child if it's you the parent.

"How long was that whole saga? Two years? Closer to three, I'd hazard a guess. Between first diagnosis, I mean, and death. It might even have been more than three. Certainly, if you take into account all the trips to the doctor and that when they couldna find out what was wrong. All the good news that went with those visits and bad, the peaks and troughs. The reprieves, like you, the stays (as it were) of execution. But behind it all, and them all, the remorseless march of time. Tick-tock; tick-tock. The remorseless, aye, march of time.

Some seconds whizzing past. Like the speed of light. Tick-tock, tick-tock, tick-tock, like if the metronome went any faster the arm would come off. Tick-tock, tick-tock, tick-tock, faster than you can say it. And other seconds lugubrious and endless, like Eeyore mulling over the Theory or something of Relativity, or a lion wandering back to the shade from a zebra carcase. But even amidst those endless seconds the knowledge that time marches on. And those seconds too, like now, which are (magically, but confusingly) both the hare *and* the tortoise. At one and the same time. I've mentioned that before. But it's so strange, so *weird* and disconcerting – if that's the right word – I'll like as not mention it again. I canna even describe it. Not really. Not well. Not properly. Not to you, Brian. Not even to myself. It's like there's two metronomes going, one whizzing: tick-tock, tick-tock, tick-tock; the other tortoising: tick-very-slowly-tock, tick-very-slowly-tock. Or one metronome, maybe, with two arms. And the pianist somehow is supposed to play both times at the same time. Both tempos. As confusing as a man using semaphore whose left arm is working three times as fast as his right one. And none of which matters because in the midst of that too there is the relentless march of time. Like those ants in Africa – they're called 'marcher ants', I think – who eat everything in their path and divert for nothing, never vary their speed, just keep on – relentlessly – going: chomp to the left, chomp to the right, chomp straight ahead of them – like the cannons in that poem about the Charge of the Light Brigade. Chomp, chomp, chomp.

"The relentless ... march ... of ... time.

"Tick-.

"-Tock.

"It was a blessing when Connie finally went. Och, it was sad for Ivy – of course it was. She was her daughter. But even for Ivy it was a blessing too. Even for her. Know what, Brian? Know what else, laddie? Know what it is most of all I hate about this whole hateful thing? What it is I hate most about it? That for me too, there will be a part of it which will be a blessing.

"Even though you're healthy – physically, at least. I honestly do not believe that a mentally healthy person would be capable of doing what you did; and emotionally healthy? Emotionally, Brian, you've been sick – and I mean *really* sick – since you were a wee wean. Aye and a wean too since you were one. And even though, though I sort of hate to admit this, there's still so much you could give, even then there's a part of me which thinks there is a part of this which will be a blessing. When midnight's come and gone, I mean. When *you* have. And do you know how that makes me feel? Do you have any idea how hard

I try, and have had to try, not to feel that feeling? Or to pretend to myself it's not that I *am* feeling? And when I canna persuade myself, how trebly terrible that feeling makes me feel?

"Thing is, do I have my bath now? Catherine's bound to phone back. I'm almost surprised she wasna waiting, waiting for me to finish with Norman. I was half-expecting the phone to start ringing soon as I put it down. And I know, second my bum hits that water, she will phone. Thing is, do I wait for her? 'Course if I do wait for her, she willna ring; and if I dinna, she will. Because that's just the way it is. It is like that that the universe is run. That's God's way. That's what it seems like, God, to be honest with You.

"I should redo my nails as well.

"What I'll do, I'll run the bath. I willna get in. A feint to God, maybe. Maybe it'll fool Him. Maybe Catherine will ring, then. *I* could always give *her* another ring then, I suppose. It's no good, now I will have to take the nail polish off. That chip'll worry me the whole of the rest of the day otherwise. It'll start growing. By the time I get back from the prison, it'll be Ben Nevis size.

"Okay, Roni, now let's be really clear about this: We're going to run the bath, take off the nail polish, remember to turn off the taps, phone Catherine, get into the bath, paint the nails. Got it? *Are* we clear about that?

"Jimmeney! It's past quarter to eleven. Thirteen to or twelve to. What happened to *that* hour? Well, forget baths, nails, all that, Roni, first thing you've got to do, you've got to phone Ken. Tell him you'll be late.

"No. No, you've *got* to have a bath, lassie. Without a bath you'll feel ten times worse than already you do. There's the grime, sure, that willna come off – of grief or shock or whatever it is – but there's also the grime that does. And the only thing worse, Brian, than grime that willna come off is to coat it with grime that will.

“So ... run the bath, phone Kenny, remove nail polish ... and then as was. Run the bath. Okay, Roni, no great mystery there. We know how to run a bath, lassie. ... Okay, now the bath is running. You know why? ‘Cos it’s a bath on legs, boom, boom!

“Know what, Roni? That was so terrible, that joke, the only thing funny about it was its terribleness. Funny word, ‘run’, isna it? It’s got so many different meanings. Except I dinna mean meanings, I mean applications. It’s got so many applications – like a bath running, for instance. Why isna he answering, Ken? Could be, lassie, ‘cos he’s in the bath too. ‘Good thinking, Holmes.’ ‘Elementary, my dear Roni.’ Eggs run, colours in washing machines – there’s the run of a ladder. ‘Cept, of course, that properly that’s ‘rung’. Candidates ‘run’ for office. About the only time they do do any exercise. Certainly the only time they exercise their consciences. I’ll tell you what, Brian, if my running bath was running for office, I’d vote for it. It’d be the cleanest thing in goodness knows when that’d have been in Parliament, in the Senate, whatever, and for a good long while. Catherine! It has to be.” ...

* * *

“Kenny. Wanting to know it it’d had been me on the phone. He’d got out of the bath, Brian, to answer it. He was concerned about me, if it had been me on the phone. Would you ever get out of the bath to answer a phone to me? You! You’d sit next to a ringing phone to save yourself the trouble of picking it up, ‘less you wanted to talk, ‘less you thought it was for you. Dinna deny it. You’ve done it often enough. I’ve been there with you often enough when you have done it. Know what, though? That willna stop you denying it. Doesna matter to you that your hand's sealed inside the cookie jar, the other hands got crumbs all over it, your prints are all over the jar, you've been photographed on CCTV, you'd still deny it. Like you've got the power, or something, to change facts; that by continuing to deny it, the fact willna be a fact any longer, but that your version of the events will become the fact. Or something. Deny something often enough or strongly enough – that would seem, Brian, to be your handle on things, your, Brian, philosophy – and it'll stop being one; you will not have done what it is you've been accused of doing. But, know what else? I dinna think you're alone in that. I mean, if that *is* learned behaviour – and even if there are genetics involved then it is *still* learned behaviour – where have you learned it from? Well, apart, let's say, from your dear old dad. Who'll have aggravated what anyway he gave you in his genes by also teaching you, by example, to deny and never stop denying. More broadly, though, than that waste of space and of humanity, you'll have learned that technique from those self-same politicians we were just talking about, the MPs or SMPs or Congressmen or Senators or whatever. They're all, all of them, like so many Casanovas, aren't they, pontificating about the need for celibacy? Where do they find the nerve? It's beyond my ken. Where the hell do they find the nerve?

"Okay, ten naked polishless digits. Time now for a Roni to get herself as naked as they are. The polishlessness we can take as read! Whoops! Whoa, there, lassie: You're supposed to have reminded me, dear heart: phone Catherine. First of all, before the bath, you've to phone Catherine. ...

"Why hasn't she left the answering machine on? She's tormenting me. Aye, right: She's playing with me. She's just timing it now, got her stop-watch ready, waiting for me to take off my skirt ... then my blouse and stuff ... finally my underwear ... test the water with my toe ... decide to add just a wee drop more of 'hot' ... that's it ... put in one foot ... put in the other one ... grip the side of the bath ... lower bottom onto water ... and ...? What went wrong? Why didna the phone ring? Because, Roni, my dear, you weren't doing it for real. God sees these things. He sees everything. And until He sees that unsightly and unsightlily flabby bum actually cresting, as it were, the wave, He's nae going to tip Catherine the wink to phone. And you know why? 'Cos that's the way it is, Roni. Aye, and that's the way God is.

"I'll have a shower. That'll fool Him!

"Five past eleven. Canna afford to dawdle, lassie. Do you want to take the wrist-watch off too? Or are we going to ice the cake of today by also ruining your grandmother's watch? Which was, whilst we're on the subject, a really sensible piece of jewellery to bring on the trip. I mean, we couldn' 'ave brought with us one of the other three dozen watches we own? You ken, the ones with nae sentimental value? Or any other value, come to that? No, of course not. You use your ball-gown, Roni, to put out the rubbish and whenever you get an invitation to Balmoral, all you've got left to wear is your jeans!

"I dinna believe it. I do not believe it. You *are* watching, aren't You? The moment I'm under the blinking thing ... the precise second when the first drop hits my head ... Well, it'll just have to ring. If I dinna have this shower now, I'll *never* have the blooming thing.

"It does feel cleansing, this water. No question. And not just physically. It's something primitive, I suppose, something pre-human, animalistic. Elephants always seem to have fun, don't they, washing themselves? There was that song – och, a wee bit before your time that would have been – about 'mud, mud, glorious mud'. And you, Brian, you used to like your bath. Once you could be persuaded into it, that was. Like you used to enjoy cauliflower. You just felt it wasna very cool to do so. There's a peculiar childhood ... I don't know ... myth, is it? ... which insists – which tom-toms from one wean to the next – that baths are tortures inflicted by grown-ups on their defenceless young, and that cauliflower is flavoured with all the worst parts about aloe and cyanide. 'Cept it wasna elephants, now I think about it, it was hippos: 'mud, mud, glorious mud'. Now I think about it, it was even called 'The Hippopotamus Song'. He used to live in Littlehampton, Michael Flanders. God knows how I happen to know that. Or remember it. He was one of the singers: Flanders and Swan, they were called. They sang 'The Hippopotamus Song'. Or Swan and Flanders, I canna remember now. And he lived in Littlehampton, which is down South, somewhere by the sea. And he was in a wheelchair.

"The handicaps some people live with. I dinna know why I thought of that. Of Michael Flanders, and that song. But the fact remains that the handicaps some people live with ... Well ... And, know what, Brian? The bigger the handicap – or so, anyway, it seems to me – the less people complain about either it or their lot. I wonder whether there's some kind of message in that. Not again! I really do not believe it – Jimmeney, I'm beginning to sound now like what's-his-name, that character off the tele. The grumpy one. Victor Meldrew! I'm beginning to sound like him: 'I do not believe it' – that's what he kept saying, wasna it? Well, I dinna believe it. That'll just have to ring as well.

"Och, that's so much better. They always too seem to have in American hotels such nice towels – large and fluffy. No wonder, Yanks, they get such a shock visiting Britain.

The towels in most British hotels are the size of face-flannels and have the feel about them of somewhat bristly hedgehogs. Goodness, I feel so much better for that. It willna last, of course. Still ... Will you stop doing that, Roni? Please? Worrying about the soon-to-be. Do you feel better just right at the moment? You do? Well, then, let's *not* worry, shall we, about how you might be feeling in an hour's time?

"You never liked that show, did you, Brian? 'One Foot In The Grave'? Or *any* of the other sitcoms, come to that. Not 'Fawlty Towers', not 'Porridge' nor 'Steptoe' – especially not 'Porridge'. Nothing, that I can think of, that made you laugh. Or didna. Just football. Pigging football morning, noon and night. Which is when, it seems to me, it's on the tele: morning, noon and night. Know what? I think that too might be like the baths and cauliflower of your childhood – you know, some kind of absurd myth, or something, that somehow you're less of a man unless all you can care about is football. There's a kind of desperation around the support for football clubs that you canna quite believe. That *I* canna, anyway. It's like they're trying to convince themselves it's really as important as they try to make out.

"Half-past eleven. I've got to go, Catherine. Meet Ken. Maybe we'll both come back, phone you. No. No, I dinna think, thinking about it, that's too great an idea. You dinna need to feel you're sharing me. Well, you know you are but ... och, you know what I mean. I'll ring before lunch. I'll talk to you then. And Mr or Mrs or Ms whoever-the-other-call-was, well, I suppose I'll get to talk to you whenever I'm no in the shower.

"Got the key, got my bag, anything else? Right, then, here we go." ...

* * *

"Catherine. Must phone Catherine. Before even I have a wee, I must phone Catherine." ...

* * *

"Oh, great! Oh, thank You, God. Thank You so very, very much.

"I suppose it was inevitable. It was, I suppose. I mean, kids will be kids, all that. And the Glaswegian grapevine, that makes the CIA look like pigging amateurs. And the kids' grapevine, that makes the Glaswegian one look like amateurs. But, honestly, God, didna Catherine have enough to deal with with her own pain and that of her weans? I mean, did she *really* need the extra pain inflicted on her by the other kids taunting hers? Did *I*?

"Which, thinking about it, probably makes you an American. That'll confirm the rumour they've been trying to spread: God is American. But it is, isn't it?, almost the essence of being American, not being able to leave well alone, needing that extra bit, that extra mile, that extra dollop of ... anything. I mean, Americans canna just have burgers, they have to put ketchup on them; and they canna just have ice-cream, they have to lace sprinkles all over the top of it. Cake apparently isna cake without the icing, fish not fish without the tartar sauce, and salad is just an excuse for the dressing. All of which are terrible examples, because, let's face it, that's what we all do, the whole world!

"My poor wee Catherine. Aye, and poor wee Isla too, and James. Poor wee tykes. They did not deserve that. They *do* not deserve it. And you may not have caused that, Brian, but you did. Cause it. You willna accept it – like Bart

Simpson, 'I didna do it,' you'll insist. Except that you did. If you'd have kept some kind of check on yourself, exercised some kind of self-control or -restraint, this playground bullying would simply never have happened. Not, at any rate, with you as its focus. And that's just exactly how vicious circles first start.

"Wee. Canna wait any longer. Wee." ...

* * *

"Och, that's better. Well, that was a really successful call. That really helped matters, that call to Catherine. Made me feel a whole heap better, that did.

"Know what, Roni? You're looking at it all wrong, lassie. Look at like this: If you hadn'ave phoned, how would they have felt? They'd still have been bullied – which, be reasonable, sounded a bit more like actually they were teased – and they'd all have been left, simmering in their own pain, without being able to talk to anyone about it, beyond each other. And, without you, *would* they have told each other about it?

"Oh heavens, I think I'm going to be sick.

"No, you're not, lassie. Mind over matter. Mind over matter, Roni. You are not going to be sick. You're just not. I willna allow it. Oh Christ! Now, as well as that tinny taste back in my mouth, I've got salt bloody water whooshing round it like they were rapids in Canada or something. Whooshing around, rapiding around, cas-pigging-cading around.

"Sit down, lassie. Two minutes ... say, five. You can afford to give yourself five minutes. Calm yourself. Compose yourself. Just get yourself, lassie, on some kind of even keel. It's no wonder you're feeling a wee bit bilious, the horizon around you, lassie, it's shifting non-stop. It keeps even changing shape, dear. Aye, *and* distance. Five minutes, lassie. You've got to allow yourself five minutes for you, Roni. For yourself. You've got to, doll.

"Try some deep breathing, lassie. In ... that's the way ... out. ... In ... out. In, Roni ... out. Goodness, what was it you sounded like earlier? Och, aye, Victor Meldrew. Well, now, lassie, you sound like the cox for the Cambridge rowing team or something: 'In, out; in, out.'

"I sound ridiculous. Is there anyone here to hear you, lassie? No? So, what are you worried about, then? Deep breaths, Roni. They were beginning to work. In ... five, six, seven, eight ... out ... five, six, seven, eight; ... in, lassie ... out.

"That was the advice they used to give them in the gas chamber: breathe deeply. It'd make it quicker, they were told. Will you, Roni – and for Christ's sake – just stop that?! Stop it right now. In, lassie ... out.

"What is it, do you suppose, about deep breathing that makes it so therapeutic? Why is it, not just in the gas chamber, but when you're in shock or feeling sick, medicos and people, they urge you to breathe deeply? Face it, lassie, you're ignorant – pig pigging ignorant. And let's face it too, it really doesna matter *why* it works. It's *that* it works which is important.

"Oh, Brian." ...

* * *

"Okay, that's it. That's definitely it. That's the last time I cry. Well, till ... till ... well, till 'till'. Which is now – Jesus Christ! – under twelve hours away. You havena even got the time to live, Brian, which it takes for a sweep of the clock. You'll never know another quarter past twelve, nor another twenty past twelve. Oh, Brian ...

"O God, oh, please God – see, I dinna know, God, whether You're there, God, or no – but – and I'm not God going to ask for intercessions – I dinna want miracles, any of that stuff – if You are there then Your will be done, sort of thing – No, no 'sort of thing', just Your will be done – I'm okay, *fine*, with that – but – the thing is – I have to blow my nose, sorry – Christ, I'll have to redo my sodding make-up too – I'M HURTING, GOD. I'M SO FUCKING HURTING – and so, God, what I'd like to say – please, God – please stop me hurting – not totally, I'm not looking, I said it before, for divine inter-do-dahs, whatever they are, -cessions – just stop me hurting, God, quite so BLOODY MUCH, God, quite so bloody much – PLEASE. And, please God, Brian'll be hurting too – help him, please, also not to hurt so much – just, like (if You'd be so good), take the edge off his hurting – and mine – and Kenny's – and Catherine's and James's and Isla's – and, God, so *many* people's – the families of those poor lassies – aye, they'll be hurting too, God. God, *will* they be hurting! *So* badly. – Ease their pain too, God. If You would. – Why must there *be* so much pain, You sadistic son-of-a-bitch? Why must there be – *so* much pain?

"Go on, lassie, if you're going to bawl again, bawl now. Get it all out. 'Cos this, I'm telling you, this is it. Anything you dinna get out now, lassie, that stays in till goodness only knows when. Do you understand me? I'm no saying it again. Do you understand me, Roni? So? Any more tears to be shed? Sure? Any more rants at God? Are we calm now? Quiet? Serene? Okay, you're right, let's not push our luck: 'serene' might be expecting a wee bit too much. Are we, let us say, okay? Able to cope? Able to, as it were, 'walk tall, walk straight ...', all that? Is there any more loo paper anywhere? ... Right. One more nose-blow. A good, big one, mind. Okay. ... Right. ...

"Okay. ...

"Fine. ...

"Let's look at the damage. Could be worse, I suppose. Not a lot, but that – let's be honest about this, lassie – that has got more to do with the structure than the decoration. I mean, one of those shanty dwellings in Rio or some place, not a lot of point, is there, in them being painted with some kind of Dulux ultra-special tip-top super-emulsion or anything. I mean, the paint would be worth more than what it was painting. Same deal here, lassie. Och, screw it. I've got to try and get a wee nap before we set off for the jail. Which means we've got to eat sometime fairly soon.

"And eat, lassie, you've got to. You've just got to get some food down you. Even if it's just some salad, or something. But something. Something, dear one.

"Please, God. You can see I'm not hysterical now ... I'm calm now, God, and quiet ... and I still dinna know whether You're there, but if You arena, then there's no-one there to hear this, so what the heck? And if You are, then I want You to know that I'm very sorry for the wee outburst earlier – well, maybe not that 'wee', now that I think about it, but ... Och, You know what I mean. But I hope You also know what I meant. I mean, I know it's pain and I know I have to go through it, but ... Well, if You could just cut me a bit of slack or something, just (as I said) take the edge off. And if not off my pain, then off the children's. Or off the lassies' families. Off someone's, for God's sake. Aye, off someone's.

"I'm on my knees. There. That where You want me? How typical of a man! And, see, I'm pleading with You, I'm begging You, God, PLEASE ease at least *somebody's* pain. Because that vicious circle I was talking about earlier, that develops too around pain. If I could feel, I could sense or even suspect that *someone's* pain was somehow getting easier, that would ease mine. Please. God. No. No deals. I'm no offering any deals. It's not that if You grant me this I'm going to give up ice-cream or something for Lent, or that I'm going to start going to kirk three times a day. There are no conditions attached either way. I'm also, if You dinna deliver, not suddenly going to definitely *not* believe in You. But ... it would be nice. It would be an act of the sort of charity You're often supposed to, like, encourage. It would be an act, Lord, of some mercy.

"Oof – not as easy getting up from my knees as it used to be. Father Gillespie's a good man, God. I thought I'd just mention it. In case You were wondering. You want to get more Father Gillespies around. He does well by You and Your cause. He has helped. He's helped, frankly, rather more than You have. If You dinna mind me saying so.

"Goodness, I'm terribly late. Again. Poor Kenny. Aye, poor Kenny.

"You'll have had your last lunch by now, Brian. Your last meal before the special one that'll be your last. Meal. All twenty dollars' worth of it!

"If You could, God, just take the edge off of it ... well, I'd be most tremendously grateful." ...

* * *

"Good laddie, Kenny. *Good* laddie. Aye, put the tele on. That's the way. Aye and run the bath. Trying to spare your poor old mum's feelings. You always did. Good lad. That's it. We're in a James Bond movie and SPECTER is bugging the room. You have to drown the sounds. You have now drowned the sounds. Good laddie. Now you can blub like a babby. That's it, son. That's the way.

"You, Brian, you'd just've blubbed. Right now, you

willna be thinking of any pain *we* might be going through, your brother and me – or anyone else. You know, I wouldna care if it was about *anyone* else that you were caring, even if you cared only a microscopic amount for anyone else. But ... If Kenny were the one on Death Row and you'd the room next to mine, would you have tried to drown the sound of your sobs? Like hell. Sob, in your case, is s-o-b. You'd have raised Cain till I came. And then raised some more till, probably, the hotel manager came, even the cops. Because your pain, Brian, was always to do with you. And, maybe because of that, it turned always to anger and then that anger, that had to be directed at someone.

"Och, this is getting us nowhere. I dinna want to hate you. I dinna want to even dislike you. I'd like to put the clock back, is what I'd like, back to when it all started – back probably to the day you were born – start all over again. But, as that's no possible ... Well, as it's no possible it canna be done. It's that simple.

"And it's simple too what I need to do now. Lie on my bed, try to empty my head of any thoughts, close my eyes for a bit, gather myself together ... gather all my wits, all my courage together ... for this one last visit. This final visit. Which canna be special. And yet must be. And which must include, no, incorporate every meeting we've ever had. And yet canna. And which must supply closure and will supply only a closing.

"Och, it's so easy, I say to myself, 'Empty your mind, Roni' and hey, presto! my mind's emptied. 'Cept it doesna happen like that. It's like me standing at the foot of Mount Everest and saying, 'Now, lassie, climb it.' Och, it's doable, it *can* be done. It's *been* done, for goodness' sake, people have climbed Mount Everest. But doable by *you*? At that moment in time? When you've two broken legs? And you've got in your arms a wounded hippopotamus? How is it we're back to hippos again?

“We had that clown for your birthday. Your seventh, was it? Seventh or eighth. Chester thought – no, that canna be right: Chester ne’er had a thought in his life, not about anything that didna affect *him.* But this did affect him, ‘course. Of course it affected him. – Your father thought it’d be a good idea, it’d save us (for ‘us’ read ‘him’), it’d save us a lot of work if we simply employed a conjurer, a Mr Magic-like man who’d ... well, do everything. Except the food, of course. Organise the games, keep the kids amused, leave us just to dish out the jelly and cut the cake and things.

“The cake! I’d forgotten the cake. As had Chester, of course. It was the one thing I’d asked him to organise, to be responsible for and – surprise, surprise – he’d forgotten. And when he remembered – surprise, surprise – he also, of course, immediately found the solution. He knew someone – surprise, surprise – down the pub, whose wife was the best blooming – ‘cept it wasna ‘blooming’ it was ‘effing’ – best blooming cake-icer this side of Inverness. He’d go to the pub, check with his friend that his wife was up for it, pop to the cake shop, pop back to the pub, give the cake to the mate and you’d have the best birthday cake, Brian, any wean ever had since James VI upped sticks and went to England. Hang the expense, nothing was too dear for his laddie. Conveniently, of course, forgetting we’d have had no blooming expense if he’d remembered the pigging thing in the first place.

“Only – surprise, surprise – he never got to the cake shop. He got talking to the cake-icer’s husband and that was what they did: talked about this fabulous birthday cake they were going to deliver to your party. They were still talking about it when the cake shop closed. And Mr Magic? He – surprise, surprise – was someone else your father knew from the pub. He staggered in, reeking of booze. Which was just about okay. As *he* was just about okay. Until, tail between his wobbly legs, your cakeless father returned home and the two of them went into some kind of conflab about how they would atone in other ways for a birthday deprived (for reasons beyond their control) of cake – a conflab which seemed to require the drinking of large amounts of whisky.

"Know what? It's almost funny now, looking back on it. He was – he *is* – such a sad character, your father. What was I thinking, marrying him? Bedding him? Even dating the poor wee sad thing? What on earth was I *thinking*? The cake, that wasna funny then. Then it was just ... Then I could've killed him. And, if truth be told, I'm no sure that's only a figure of speech. No. No, if truth be told, I *know* that's no just a figure of speech. And I wonder, if the rapes were partly your father's genes, the murders, were they partly mine?

"I have been close to killing your father. And no meta-whatsitly, -phorically. *So* close. I'd like to deny it. But I canna. And I've wanted to kill you too on occasions. And I do mean that. Maybe only for instants, for flashes, but I've tasted the desire to kill. I know the flavour. I've even tasted the *need* to.

"Let's rest now, Roni. Now we've got that off our chest, off our conscience, let's try now to empty our mind. Let's try, Roni, to rest." ...

* * *

"God, it's almost three. It's almost three, for God's sake. Almost, for God's sake, three. What happened to the time? A short nap, I said. Twenty winks, ten. No four thousand bloody winks. Why didna someone call me? You'd think, the five hundred phone calls I get each day, *someone* would've called. Why did Kenny not call? He must be asleep too, poor lamb. I should call *him*. Wake him. God, almost three. We dinna want to be rushing. No today. Get behind a truck or something. We want to leave in, what?, fifteen minutes. Nae more than half-an-hour, anyway.

"Half-an-hour'll do fine, Roni. Just fine, doll. Let him sleep. Call him in ten minutes or so, fifteen. He could do with the sleep. I dinna think he's been getting a lot recently. Me either. None of us, I suppose. What'll you be doing, I wonder, Brian? Watching videos, that's supposed to be the favourite. Where did I read that? There was a time I read all I could about it, life on Death Row, that whole number. I thought, somehow ... I thought if I kenned more about it, if I kenned all there *was* to ken about it, that somehow it might be easier. As if that knowledge somehow was going to take your pain away from you. Or mine from me. Only nothing does. Nothing makes any difference.

"Know what, Brian? Know what it is I think you're most likely to be doing? Sleeping! It wouldna surprise me one iota. And know what else wouldna surprise me either one iota? If you'd been the only one of us during this whole long sorry mess who *has* been sleeping.

"Death? That's the *big* sleep, isna it? That's what they call it. Well, that's what you call it if you're Raymond Chandler. Who was English, I think. Not someone you think of as kin to, I don't know, Thomas Hardy or even Agatha Christie or anything. I mean, I canna imagine Tess or Miss Marple referring to death as 'the big sleep'. Not very Wessex, not very St Mary Meade. It was a film, 'The Big Sleep'. Maybe that's one of the videos you are watching. With, if memory serves, Humphrey Bogart and Lauren Bacall. I knew someone once who'd met Lauren

Bacall. He said she was still impressive.

"*Humphrey* Bogart. I mean, what an unlikely name for Bogart, Humphrey. 'Humphrey Bogart sat on a wall/ Humphrey Bogart had ...' In fact, a less likely Humphrey than Bogart is hard to imagine. It'd have been more appropriate, come to think of it, to *Bogarde*. And 'Dirk', come to think of *that*, would have been more appropriate to Bogart. Aye, got that the wrong way round, God: aye, it should have been Dirk Bog*art* and Humphrey Bog*arde*. Aye, much more suitable.

"Aye, and prison too, that's called the 'big house', isn't it? What's with it, Brian, with you and 'big'? You big lummox. In the big house, facing the big sleep. You big, aye, lummox. No, you big prick. You big ... prick. ... Aye, and doubtless you'd like to think yourself the owner of one of those. And why wouldna you indeed? You're a man.

"See, what I dinna understand – oh, it's been explained to me a zillion times, but what I still dinna understand ... They say, rape is not a sex crime, it's a crime of violence. I've seen you being very sexy – this is what I dinna understand – heavens, I've seen you almost ... you ken ... before my very eyes ... almost, I mean, as it were, penetrating. But what I've never seen, I've never seen you be that violent, Brian. Oh – sure – churlish, that a lot of the time. Sulky, most of the time. Difficult, pouty, up-and-downy, all of those things. I've even known you in a tantrum, ranting, raving what you weren't going to do to goodness know who. But they were just words. Only words. Not even as a laddie, I never saw you pull the wings off of flies or torment the next-door's cat or anything. No. No, completely to the contrary. I remember you shooing away that blinking cat when it was about to devour that fledgling. I remember you returning that fledgling to the nest. It was dead, of course. But you wouldna have it. Even though there was a part of you – I'm sure of it – which knew it was dead. Didna stop you from being upset, two or three days later, when you found the thing, again on the ground. Desperately upset you were. Poor thing wasna just dead, it was bedraggledly dead. I mean, I know dead is dead, but this was, sort of, dead underlined or something. And I remember too you no wanting to leave milk out for Santa's reindeer, but water. Milk was too rich for reindeer, you insisted. Och, you'd remembered something from some science class or other some time back. But it had stuck. And the reindeer's well-being, that was really important to you.

"So, where did all this violence suddenly come from? *That's* what I dinna understand. You were never a paragon exactly, certainly never a saint. But a rapist? And a murderer? A sadistic, almost manic murderer? Where the hell did that come from, Brian? And why in the hell, Brian, am I *in* Hell? Why did *you* – *you*, dear one – why did *you* cast me into Hell? And you know what the Hell is, dear one, you've cast me into? It's that my heart should be cleaving. Not breaking, but cleaving. It's that there should be nae ambiguity about my grief, no doubt about what I'm feeling, nae two-edgedness to the sword. And there is. And that's Hell. Because the part of me that thinks you deserve this – I told you that before – that judicial part is being screamed at by the Mummy part, 'How dare you? Call yourself a mother!' it's saying 'How dare you call yourself a mother?!' And the judicial part can only stay schtoom. Because the judicial part suddenly canna think of a single word to say. In its own defence, as it were. So, on top of grieving as a mother, I'm also grieving that I'm nae kind of a mother.

"Nae kind of a mother?! Not any kind of a fucking mother?! How dare you?! How fucking dare you, Brian? We have nae money left, you heap of shit. Not a single pigging penny bean. Hither and thither across the Atlantic, like it was a ferry across the Clyde. Telephone calls, motels, meals ... och aye, and fags for you. Mustna forget your precious cigarettes. 'They're like currency in here, Mam.' Aye, and outside here, that's what they cost, you ungrateful pile of shit, they *cost* currency. It's what you buy them with. *My* pigging currency, in fact.

"I'd call you a bastard, know that? I would. You only missed it anyway by six pigging weeks. I'd also call you a son-of-a-bitch, but why put myself down in that kind of way? I'm no bitch. I'm not. In absolutely any sense of the word.

"Och, and then all the whines whenever I had to go home. *We* had to. *Had* to, Brian – Kenny and me, or Catherine and me. Nae word of thanks for having schlepped all this way to see you, of course. Or to support you or any of that. Know how hard the work was, Brian, which I had to work to buy that place of mine? Do you have any conception, o wee one of my womb, just what those few bricks represented, and that postage-stamp of mortar? Which is no longer mine.

"You know how Kenny's kids've suffered? They could have gone to private school, you know, with all the money that he's shelled out courtesy of you? You have any idea how he must feel, having to house his antique mum? No privacy ever for him and Dee. Not for them and their kids. Not unless I'm away pestering Catherine for a change. I have no home ... Kenny only has half-a-home – because a home without privacy *is* only half-a-home. Catherine spends her life in terror that some kind of genetic mutation – no, some kind of moral mutation, rather, passed on through the genes – is going to infect her weans. And that tears her apart. I think it does. Because she thinks those thoughts are unworthy thoughts for a sister to have.

Which shows what she knows about sisters!

"*My* sister just gloats. Spends her whole time gloating, I shouldna wonder, your aunty Margaret. She's someone else I canna figure, Brian. I mean, what the hell have I ever done to her that she should gloat in the way that she does? I mean, your uncle Brian, Brian, he would have some reason to gloat – to smirk, even. I was no kind to him as a laddie, growing up. I have to admit that. He'd never, I'd say to him, amount to a row of beans. All the way through his 'A' levels, even through university. Yes, he'd have some kind of right to gloat, Brian would. It wouldna be exactly endearing, but at least it would be understandable. Your aunty Margaret, though ... What the hell have I ever done to her? What have *you* ever done? To her, I mean?

"It was her, you know, who stopped me writing to the Prime Minister. Well, her and that husband of hers. And, though their reasons were wrong, they were right. Of course they were right. Och, and how that rightness helped her gloating along – and for months to come! What a waste of time that would have been, writing to the Prime Minister. She, the Prime Minister's wife, is a great one for making speeches against the death penalty. But never in America, though. Never where it might be a problem. Like her husband, she has no moral ... what's the word? ... rectitude. Or consistency. There are no moral principles left today in Downing Street. There is therefore nothing to appeal to. He's perfectly happy, our ever-smiling PM, to sacrifice British blood to safeguard American interests. And our soldiers, most of them, have *not* gone out and raped people. Murdered and mutilated them. How would you be any different? If he's prepared to sacrifice British who are innocent, what possible chance is there he would make a stand on behalf of someone who is guilty? I mean, what would I appeal to?

"American interests? That's a joke too. Not *even* American interests. *So* not even American interests. Not of the waiters here, or the chambermaids, or of the guests; not even, Brian, of your guards at the jail. Not even the warden's interest! The interests, that's all, of a *handful* of Americans: the super-rich and the super-scared. Och, dinna let's get started down that road. Sorry, Kenny, you've had your lot. Got to wake you now, my darling laddie. Up and at 'em, Kenny." ...

* * *

"Oh, Christ! Oh, Mother of God! Oh, Jesus H. Christ! Where do I start? Where do I even pigging start? Oh my God! My Christ! Oh my Go-o-o-o-o-o-d! ...

"Right, okay. Okay, now. Right. Aye. It's now seven-thirty, Brian. Near as dammit. And I'm having my first drink of the day. It's seven-thirty and I willna see you again. Ever." ...

* * *

"Am I cried out now? I'm cried out now. It's now ten to eight, Brian. I'm now having my second drink of the day. And you ken what? Soon I'm going to be having my third. You ken what else? I'm still finding it hard to breathe. I'm still snatching at my breath. They're not coming, my breaths, naturally or spontaneously. It's almost as if I'm here forcing myself to breathe, forcing my lungs to work almost.

"Fuck! Fuck me!

"Not swear? Me not swear? After what the fuck I've just been fucking through?

"Christ, I'm still shaking. Another drink. I need another drink. God, make this pain go away! Okay, okay, no, I dinna mean that, no, dinna make it go away, but please – PLEASE, FOR CHRIST'S SAKE – please make it easier, more manageable, God, more – God – copable with. More copeable with, God, than this. This pain, this isna even pain any longer, this isna even the Rolex to pain's Timex, not the fucking Missi-fucking-ssippi to the Clyde of pain, this has entered an entirely new dimension. This isna even Hell. This is completely new territory. This is, I dinna know, a stratosphere of pain, or something. It's a pain which has nothing to do with any pain I've had before. Not having you. Not that slipped disc. Not the first time that fucker your father was sentenced. Nor, thinking about it, the first time he was released! Not when he left, not even when *you* were sentenced. This is not even a stratosphere of pain, not even another dimension – not even, like Hell, another world. It's like it's a completely different experience, a parallel universe, if you like, where *all* is pain. And where pain is all there is. Where pain is this bed and the mattress on it, the legs which support it, the sheets and pillows and pillow-cases on it. Where pain is the sky outside and the air within. Where it is the whisky and the time it takes to drink it and the time between the sips and the glass the whisky's in.

"And I feel like I'm a balloon or something being pumped full not with helium but with pain. And if there isna a release soon of some of this pain, if someone doesna let some of this pain out of me, I'm simply going to burst. I'm just going to explode. Into a zillion pieces. All of which are pain. There'll be little bits of me all over America, a zillion pieces hanging like stalactites of mist from every branch – every twig – and all those zillion pieces, they too will be pain, and all the trees, branches, the twigs, they'll be pain too. Jes-uuusss!" ...

* * *

"No, that wasna a cry. Not a real one. A final splutter, no more. The run of a headless chicken. Oh, Christ!" ...

* * *

"That *was* a real cry. Where the hell did that one come from? I thought I was cried out. Okay, it's okay now. Now I *am* cried out. God, I doubt there's a drop of water now, anywhere in my body. Okay, another drink, that's the first thing called for. Thank God for whisky. Thank You, God, for whisky. I mean, what else would get us through times like these? That's not what I've always said, of course. Not when you, Chester, came rolling home. Aye, like the song. What song was it? Cheers, Roni. Well done, lassie. You did well. You came through it, doll. Didna disgrace yourself. Didna let you down, Brian, or yourself or the whole pigging side, whatever that is.

"Splash some water on your face, Roni. Do it now. There's still water in them, there hills. Goodness knows where it comes from. Cold water, lassie. The colder the ... 'Knick-knack, paddy-whack', that was it. What a ridiculous name for a song. 'Knick-knack, paddy-whack, give a dog a bone/ This old man ...' – You, Chester – '...came rolling home.'

"Let it run, Roni, the water. You want it so near ice, lassie, it's beginning to get solid.

"Brrrr! That's better. More. More. Come on, lassie, dunk your head right in there. Right in. Aye.

"Puffy enough for you, are they, those eyes? And red? Goodness, thank Heavens there's nae bulls around, that's all I can say. And that hair? That hair, Roni, that's a disgrace. A positive disgrace. Where's that blooming brush? I left it here this morning. I know I left it ... Where the bloody hell is it? ... It should be ... What's it doing there? What are you doing there? Making hair-brushes, are they today, with invisible legs? Or retractable legs or something? Naughty hair-brush. You just stay where I put you. You're a really naughty, *naughty* hair-brush. Heavens, your hair, lassie, it's almost pure electricity. It's like someone's put a current ..." ...

* * *

"You cannot, Roni, spend the whole of the rest of your life crying, lassie. That's no going to help anyone. No-one. Get a grip, Roni, my dear. Stiff drink. There. That's better. Okay now? No more tears? Have another splash, lassie. Go on, just a quick one. Treat yourself. Good. That's good. Okay, now, what we're going to do, we're going to take the drink back into the bedroom, we're going to top it up – not too much now, dinna want anyone thinking we've got a problem or anything. We're going to top it up, we're going to get out of this ridiculous suit, put on a pair of jeans, get rid of those horribly uncomfortable shoes, we're going to sit down on that not-as-comfortable-as-it-looks armchair and we're going to go through these last few several hours, lassie, bid them a fond farewell. Only way, lassie, you are going to be able to bid them farewell, fond or otherwise, is by revisiting them. You know that, dinna you? They're graves which are, at the moment, yawning open. Unless you seal them, lassie, their ghosts are going to haunt you forever. Forever. You've got to get back there. Seal the graves. You canna do that any other way. Still not bad, that figure of yours, lassie. That'd still look good looked up at by a lover. Even down at. Aye, Roni, dream on!

"Oops. Tell you what, lassie. I think, maybe, you need to put just a wee drop of water in there. It's maybe getting to the head a little quickly. Those *are* good tits, lassie. No question. Still quite an eyeful. Aye, and a good handful. And that, Roni, is no mean bum either. Quite a handful there too. Even for a lassie half your age. And the fact that men dinna drool over it in quite the way they tongue-hangingly used to is proof only of what fools these mortals be.

"Oof, that's better. That is better. Comfy shoes. A comfy place to park that gorgeous bum of yours. You'll notice, Brian, I've stopped all that malarkey: 'It is whatever time it is and you'll be doing such-and-such.' I'm not playing that game any more. That way only madness lies. It's ten past eight, by the way, and you'll by now have had your last meal. And doubtless I'll read in the papers tomorrow what that was. You willna be aware of it, but all about you the activity will be frantic. They'll be sealing off the prison to the press, the witnesses will be assembling, they'll be briefing the guards, handing out high security passes – whatever the hell distinguishes those from the low security type. God, it's as difficult getting *into* that prison as it is getting out! But I'm no going to play that game. I dinna think my sanity will let me.

"What I am going to do, I'm going out to find me a twenty-two-year-old stud, hung like a stallion, who's going to give me the seeing-to of a lifetime from top, so to speak, to bottom. From top, I might add, to really scrummy and eminently 'eff'able bottom. And, even more important than any of that, who is going to massage these poor abused wee tootsies here.

"Where to begin? Where the hell to begin?

"I'm no a prude, you ken. Plenty of people have made that mistake. But it *is* a mistake, Brian. I dinna want you to make it. It would be nice to think, a few hours before you die, there were some things you understood about me. And one of them is, I am not a prude. In fact (and this may surprise you) to the contrary. That one time in my life, that brief affair when my satisfaction was also important, I couldna get enough of it. Of sex, I mean. Of ... cock. And I was rather good at it, what's more. And not just, you know, effing. I, you know, I ... well, oral, the whole thing. Aye, Roni, thank you, dear, so much for sharing that with us. If we might now, ma'am, return to the subject in hand. ... Och aye, in hand too. I wasna averse to that either. There was nothing really I *was* averse to. Well, no a lot, anyway.

"And where on earth did all *that* come from?

"Och ...

"I think I was thinking children will never understand their parents. I'm sure I never understood mine. Under*stood*? I *do* not understand mine. And that wasna to do with you, Brian. But Ken. I was remembering, you see, I woke him. When I phoned. I did wake him, maybe I should say. He was just so wiped, poor wee lamb. And I woke him. But even though he was only seconds awake he was in a state. He'd been crying, he said, even in his sleep. He needed some comfort. Aye, he did. I went – I *fled* – to his room and we just held each other. It wasna even a cuddle. Not, anyway, what I mean by a cuddle. There wasna any stroking. Not any movement at all, hardly at all. We just were like that, holding each other. Two lonely people on a tiny raft in the middle of a shark-filled ocean. We just held each other because there was nothing else to hold onto. We held each other to have hold of something solid and hold-onto-able that wasna ourselves. We'd been wrestling with ghosts ... no, with demons. We'd both been wrestling with them. Like that play of Shakespeare's, you know the one, when they're all stuck on a desert island. 'The Tempest', that's it. And they're all being knocked about and things, pinched and beaten by fairies and elves and such like – by, aye, spirits.

"That's a good idea. Spirits. A good idea. Plenty of water, hey, Roni? I think water would be good. I dinna think I want to be awake at midnight. I think I want to be dead to the world. Dead drunk to the world. Dead." ...

* * *

"No, I'm no about to cry. Just caught up for a moment in a moment's reverie. I am allowed, you ken. Not everything, you ken, just gets delivered – splat – on a silver platter. Not even on a silver splatter! Och, God, you ken what, Roni? Another dram or three you'll even find that funny!

"We held each other, Kenny and me. He started shaking. No, not shaking. It wasna a fit, no a seizure. It was, no, it was more like a shiver. A shiver, though, that wasna the shiver of a frosty morning. How do I describe it? ... There was a man, came into the 'Ship' – in the days when I sometimes went there with your father. God, the things you do for love! The things you do – even worse – for something that's not love but which you fear is going to be the closest thing you'll ever get to it, to love. There was this man, anyway, a regular punter there, had something – something, I think, rather flimsy – to do with films or something, was – for whatever reason – forever jetting backwards and forwards to Los Angeles – or 'LA', as he would inevitably and loudly call it. Leaving Glasgow, he was always dressed for LA weather – you know, short-sleeved shirts, lightweight trousers, all that. Well, one day, the plane developed engine trouble and they had to make an emergency landing in Greenland, of all places. What's more, from the plane to the terminal building they had to *walk*. The terminal *hut*, more like. Well, the shiver he gave, Kenny, that was like what I imagine would have been that man's shiver, stepping from the plane in his short-sleeved shirt onto the frozen wastes of Greenland. It wasna a little brrr – like when you bring the milk in on a January morning, it was a shiver which possessed the whole of him. It was like a sort of fleshy earthquake that tore through, not just his body, but the whole of him. You ken what I mean. Like his soul too was being torn apart, and his brain and his imagination and ambition, his present, his future – every-pigging-thing.

"But it was also, that shiver, like a sort of exorcism. Like some kind of demon had left him – and left me too. A peace suddenly enveloped him, a calm. And, in a slightly more juddery way, that came over me as well. I canna describe it. Och, Kenny was ... almost serene, almost even ... what's the word? ... seraphic. I wasna that. Neither inside nor out, but the moth I had been became ... I dinna ken, I canna think ... became a something that doesna move too much – oh Christ, that makes me sound like your father – no, a something that moves slowly and with tremendous grace: a ballet-dancer or something – or, better, an ice-skater, I suppose, but in slow motion.

"It was, that moment, a spiritual moment. Even a deep spiritual moment. – I'm only realising this now, I should add. – A bond was formed in that moment. A new bond, I mean. Quite different to the bond of mother and son. Aye, and quite separate from it too. This was the bond ... what was it? ... of trench friends? A meeting, a joining of souls. It was formed, that bond, and sealed. There. In that moment.

"And in that still, we pulled apart. In it and *with* it. We needed – and maybe we knew this or maybe we sensed it or maybe self-preservation demanded that we sense it – we needed to immerse ourselves in that still. No, to coat ourselves in it ... to mummify ourselves in it almost. We needed to do that if we were going to survive. And we knew we had to. Survive. The bond that had just been formed and sealed between us was one of survival.

"I wanted the drive to be drab. I wanted it to be so ugly. A drive, you ken, through steelworks and steel-girded slums and disused collieries, streets of decay and a slime-soaked despair. I knew it wasna going to be, of course. Jimmeney, I've done it often enough, the drive. But I thought, at least the colours might be muted, or the sky overcast or ... well, anything. But it wasna. Of course it wasna. The sky was light blue and silky – like that blouse I saw, you remember, in London? At Selfridges'? The one I couldn' afford. So light on the touch. It aroused me, the feel of it on my breasts – *and* I was wearing a bra – even so, it ... aye, aroused me. The sky was of that colour. And of that same texture as well.

"The colours, they were all so ... living: the greens, yellows, browns, all of them with lives of their own, leaping out at you. The blues and the reds. That gorgeous pink on that tree, whatever it is. Maybe you saw it from the prison bus as you went past. That sort of lilacky pink – as manmade in its gaudiness as the colour of ice-cream and yet, because it's no manmade but natural, bursting with so much delicateness of hue. They were colours that lap-danced over you, which shoved their tits in your mouth and rubbed their pussies all over your groin. In a manner of speaking. But which also Bacalled at you from beneath sultry lashes. They were colours that made you realise how much more life-like a painting is than a photograph. Because they were flagrant and subtle, both at the same time. And I hated those colours for their beauty and their energy and gloriousness and ... aye, life.

"No subtle colours, though, at the penitentiary. No delicateness there of hue. Imposed colour here, blocks of colour. The blinding white of the welcoming arch. It's bizarre, that arch almost of welcome. 'You are now entering Death Row – Have a nice day!' The sun blazing off those acres of razor-wire. The reflection slashing you, a stiletto blade slicing through your eyes. The vision of the state's retribution. The vengeance that is so dreadful that is no longer the Lord's but the state's. The ugliness of it all, the lumberingness. The marksmen in the towers, their sunglasses, and high-powered shotguns, whatever the hell they are. The Hell they represent. The images everywhere of ruthlessness and a kind of bureaucratic – not even sadism – savagery. Because sadism needs some kind of emotion. The sadist gets some kind of kick. However perverted or distorted. But some kind of kick. And this place is too sterile for kicks. The cruelty is faceless. It's not the guards who are cruel – it's not 'Cool Hand Luke', anything even remotely like that – it's not even those who dictate to the guards, it is the machinery which dictates to them all. And it aggravates the cruelty. Because there is no-one to appeal to. There are no eyes into which you can look and beg for mercy. It is the sunglasses of the guard in 'Cool Hand Luke': those that reflect you back to yourself.

"Sell my body? I'd give blow-jobs to every man there – warden, guard, inmate, cleaner, even the chaplain – I'd let every one of them bugger me, cane me, beat the living shit out of me if I thought it would save you. What makes it so cruel is that you know it canna. Och, they're friendly, the guards. Very friendly. Today, *particularly* friendly. Smiles trying to combine 'good to see you' with 'sorry about your forthcoming loss' – aye, and both of those coupled with 'dinna look to me for any sympathy: your laddie's got it all coming to him.' Because they have to think that. If they didna think that, how the hell could they later be doing what it is they will later have to do? And that they know *I* know they have to do?

"Kenny, you were magnificent, my darling wee one. Magnificent. That still that overcame you after the shiver, that seemed to keep you okay. It seemed it had taken hold of you. You'd exorcised the demons, evicted them, and some kind of laid-back angels had found this empty property and had squatted there. You were able to match the guards, rueful smile for rueful smile. I couldna. I couldna look at them in the face – not, anyway, in the eyes. If I had to look in their direction, if politeness or just not-*im*politeness demanded that I did, I'd have to look beyond them or at their mouths or something. Or their foreheads. Just not in their eyes. I couldna look in their eyes.

"There are so many clichés. You think of prison – I do – as being such a noisy place. Ugly noises, harsh noises. That many men all crammed in together, the rasp of a hundred locks, the clang of iron gates meeting iron frames. The smell of stale sweat and piss and just-past-its-sell-by-date fried food. But it's not noisy. It's, in fact, terribly, *spookily* quiet. The quiet, aye, of the grave. And it doesna *smell* of any of those things. It smells a bit, I suppose, like those cars with air-fresheners in them, that sort of syntheticky, slightly ucky, slightly saccharine smell. With an undertone somewhere of detergent or bleach or something. It tries so hard to be impersonal. But it just dehumanises everything. It's as antiseptic and soulless as one of those mazes, you know, which psychiatrists put rats in to see how quickly they can find the cheese.

"Aye, it's that it feels like. Like we're all involved in some kind of gigantic experiment. Like we have no value in ourselves, our only value is in either proving or refuting some high-falutin' psychiatric theory.

"You looked well. God damn you. So well. And so pigging young. Aye, I know that, that's one of the side-effects. I remember someone telling me that. The skin, it's never exposed to fresh air, so it doesna age. You look younger now than when you were first sentenced. Couldn't you be racked with pain somehow, paralysed or something, tortured by a consumptive cough?

"I canna bear to see you in those handcuffs. You'd have thought – I'm not the first mother to have visited her son on Death Row – you'd have thought they might have thought to take those handcuffs off *before* they brought you in. You'd have thought they might have done. They brand you immediately. I suppose they're intended to. They stigmatise you. 'I'm a danger to society,' they say of you. 'Before being a son or a guitar-player,' it says, 'or a smoker or a meat-eater or a brunette – before even being a human being – I am a menace to society. That is the first thing you have to know about me, that is the thing which defines me.'

"They're so unyielding, handcuffs. So ... well, metal. And as for those leg restraints ... those they took you away in from court ... no, Roni, we dinna need to go down that street. That at least they spared me.

"They clink, handcuffs. Not even clink, they chink. A ludicrously light tinkly, Tinkerbelly sort of chink. At total odds with the heaviness they represent – the solidness, maybe even *stolid*ness of the law, the unbreakability of its code, the rigidity of the line on one side of which is right and on the other ...

"On the other, Brian, you.

"The wrong that is you. The fresh-faced, babby-faced,

doesna-even-pull-the-wings-off-flies you. *My* babby.

"And the guards then being *so* discrete – tip-toeing around, 'just ignore us', 'just pretend we're not here'.

"Knowing I had to look you in the eyes, Brian. Knowing, Brian, I had to. Dreading – *dreading* – what I would see there. So scared to look, my darling. So scared to look, you shit. So scared of seeing there my darling; so scared of seeing there a lump of shit.

"It doesna vary very much, life on Death Row. It's not even the same-every-day that school is. It's even more monotonous than the litany of how Miss Galbraith was picking on you, or how Stinky Anderson (or whatever the hell his name was) had, I dinna know, come third in a history test or something. And the move from Death Row to Death *Watch*, well, that, my darling laddie, is, I think, too much detail. Och I heard it all alright, of course I *heard* it, but I didna let it register. Know what? I *couldna*, darling, let it register. And can I remember it? Not a word. Not a single word, if I'm honest. Vaguely, through a glass darkly, so to speak, I can remember noises about appealing to the Governor. Plenty of reference to fat ladies and it never being over till they sing. Well, I've got news for you, laddie. The fat lady's now in her dressing-room. She's lubricating the old tonsils, trilling her scales.

"What time is it now? No, it's not that I suddenly do want to play that game, it's that I said I'd go and see Kenny at nine. In his room. There's no point in even trying to eat. And the atmosphere in the dining room? Well, I could do without it. So, there's nae point, really, in meeting anywhere else. I said we'd meet there, in his room, spend an hour or so together, doesna matter what we do, even if we did nothing – we'll probably do nothing, in fact – just sit there in silence. What the hell else is there to say just right at the moment? And that's okay. Sitting there in silence, I mean. It's that that's okay. After that, I want him to go, I dinna ken, to a bar or something. Someplace where he's less likely to notice the time. I'd really like him to go to a brothel or a lap-dancing place, whatever they're called. Get his mind right off the whole business. But there dinna seem to be too many of those places around, brothels or lap-dancing joints. He's going out, he says, to play pool. To get leglessly drunk and play pool.

"And me, I'll stay with you. For the last two hours you are on Earth I will, Brian, be with you. As much as I am able. I saw you into this world – and that was painful. However zillionly more painful, I would have liked to have seen you out. But the prison authorities think chaplains are acceptable, and mothers are not. If you ask me, you need a damn sight more divine help coming into this world than you do leaving it. And around the ante-natal clinic I canna remember a Liverpool kop of clergy. But there we go ... What do I ken?

"Well, one thing I do ken, it's close to nine. They'll be preparing the gurney now. I'm not sure whether the hearse is yet there, or the ambulance. But if they're no, they're on their way. Their drivers will have had their tea, they'll have kissed their wives goodbye. 'Dinna wait up. I'll be back when I'm back.' They'll be caught up in the ... excitement of it all – almost, God help me, the carnival of it all. In the expectation and ... yes, pregnancy of it all. And aye, it *is* pregnant. And this whole time, this whole enormous period of my life, that has been a time – now I think about it – of gestation. I've been pregnant with death. And this whole scene, this carnival, this whole pigging shooting match, that too is pregnant with death. And they'll get caught up in all of that, the drivers. They willna be able to stop themselves from being. And they're going to try to be blasé about it to their colleagues – and around families and friends, they're going to keep a remarkably low profile about the whole thing because the death penalty brings up strong reactions both sides of the fence and they willna want to provoke an argument unnecessarily. And for weeks, even for months to come, those drivers, they'll enjoy a certain local celebrity – 'he's the man, you ken, who drove the hearse that took Lawson's body from the jail'; 'he was the ambulance driver who ...'

"Almost nine. Just another wee dramette. Plenty of water. Just for anaesthetic purposes. They'll have offered you a sedative by now. I do hope you had the sense to take it. Och, I know the sort of macho ethic of Death Row demands that you dinna, but ... well, honest to goodness, how many examples does the world need that machismo doesna work? How many examples, Brian, do *you* need? What part did machismo play in your being where you are today, you bastard? My darling. Just take the blooming pill, Brian.

"'Take your medicine ...' – that's what they say, isna it? '... like a man.' Like a *man*? There's a laugh. If you took medicine like a man (a) you'd never take it; (b) if you did you'd need not a spoonful of sugar but a container-load to get it down; and (c) for weeks everyone else'd have to put up with the grizzling about how dreadful you were feeling, how with each passing minute you could hear the approach of the grim reaper getting closer.

"Well, I suppose that's something. I suppose now the approach you can hear of the grim reaper, it's not a figment or anything of your imagination. Aye, lassie, and when gallows' humour *is* gallows' humour, then it becomes something else altogether.

"God, five past nine. Kenny. Kenny." ...

* * *

"Quarter past ten. Ten fifteen. Twenty-two fifteen. And it's just us, kiddo, you and me. Just the two of us. Till death us do part. And I've now had more than enough to drink. A hangover on top of everything else, that'd be *all* I need.

"There was this man, I think I told you about him – och, two, three years ago, maybe more, it was in the papers – he went to see one of those faith healer people. 'Can you,' he says, 'cure a hangover?' 'I can only suggest,' the faith healer replies, 'you drink less.'

"Which was, now I think about it, pretty much the same thing the doctor said to your father when he went to see him about *his* drinking. 'I think I may on the odd occasion,' said your father, 'be drinking just a touch too much.' 'So,' came back the treatment from the medical genius, 'drink less.' As if those words by themselves would act like a magic wand or something, and suddenly cure the problem. Q.E.D. Doctors, what do they know?

"They willna let you have alcohol, of course. Probably frightened it's habit-forming! Probably think it might turn you into an anti-social element or something! I mean, a last meal you're allowed – anything you want up to twenty bucks! Twenty bucks, I ask you! I offered to pay the difference myself. But, no, that's no acceptable. Spending the zillion dollars it's taken to bring you to the scaffold, that's okay, but not an extra ten dollars, say, or twenty, for a decent last meal. And no last glass of beer, of course, no last wee tot of Scotch ... no, that, my friends, is verboten. It's a bit, isn't it?, like the man in front of the firing squad, that old joke, being offered a last cigarette. 'No, thanks,' he says, 'I'm trying to give them up.' It's what you said earlier, lassie: When gallows' humour *is* gallows' humour, it's no the same thing at all. And, talking of firing squads, where's my Goya to paint *your* death, Brian?

"I could have a cup of tea. Aye, and know what, lassie? I think I will. Have a cup. Oh God, who's that?" ...

* * *

"Catherine. She wanted to know how I was. Sure she did! She wanted me, more like, to ask her how *she* was. She's a selfish wee madam too, Brian. You're no the only one. Even Kenny, on his day, even he can be quite ... what's the word? ... 'thoughtless', I suppose, 'self-absorbed'. Och, get real, Roni, who in the world isna from time to time? You, for instance??? Even Mother Teresa, I'm prepared to bet, had her moments.

"At least I got to talk to her, I suppose. I suppose there's something in that. 'Least I know, well, they're not alright, but they're kind of coping. Still breathing, anyway. You said *you'd* be able to phone later. I wonder if you will. I even wondered at one stage if I'd take the call. But of course I will. Of course I would, whichever. Know what, though? I'm not sure your making it would be an act of love. 'Angels With Dirty Faces' again. I'm not sure, if you really loved me, that you wouldna do something at the end which would make me despise you. Even more, I mean. Which would make this kidnap of you from my life more acceptable. Och, what do I know?

"You're caught on this one, Brian – and I can see that –, between a rock and a hard place. Whatever you do now, or dinna do, could be construed in time to come as an act of love or an act of hatred. Depending on my mood. My mood, I'm talking about, when I'm remembering it, not my mood now. If you do phone or you dinna, if you write me a last letter ... Or if you dinna. And know what? At some time in the future, whatever you do, that'll be an act of love; and on others whatever will be an act of hatred. Or vengeance.

Or retribution. Or cowardice. Or selfishness. Or ... or ... or ... Because sometimes, Brian, you will be my darling son. And sometimes you'll be a shit. And sometimes, just to ice the cake, you'll be both at the same time.

"I remember years back reading an interview with the father of the guy accused of letting off those nail-bombs in London – what was his name? ... Cobham, was it? No, not Cobham. Cooper? –. He said of his son, if he had perpetrated these awful deeds, then he too would totally condemn him – Cope ... Cope- something, *-Land*, Copeland, that was it. I remember being struck then by the word 'totally'. It wasna that American word it is today, when we are all, I dinna know, 'I am so "totally" in love with you'ing all over the place; or when 'I so "totally" dinna want to talk to you.' It's even become a verb now, hasn't it? And not just meaning adding everything together. I mean, they say today, dinna they, not 'the car was wrecked' but 'the car was totalled'. Then we didna use 'totally' except to mean what it means.

"And I also – amazing, isn't it?, the way these almost incidental details of life come back to you – remember reading an interview with Peter Sutcliffe's father – Peter Sutcliffe, he's the Yorkshire Ripper: a serial killer like you, Brian, a serial rapist. But alive. In prison, but alive. No, not in prison, in an asylum. Not 'asylum', Roni, 'secure hospital'. Not Bedlam, that's the old one ... Broadmoor. Aye, Broadmoor. – Sutcliffe's father said, 'He's still my son.' In this interview I read: 'He's still my son,' he said. I wasna sure I knew then what he meant. I do now. Now I understand what they both mean, Daddy Copeland and Daddy Sutcliffe.

"But, then, maybe they said nothing of the sort. I *had* to give that interview, Brian. You have no idea how desperate those financial straits were. Och, you've heard it, you even sympathised about it, tried to grunt out things about no coming to visit so often if it was causing financial problems. How could it *not* be, you heap of shit? How on earth could it *not* be? What? Did you think my trips were being sponsored by Pan Am or something? Or British Airways? 'Want to visit your son on Death Row? Do as Roni Lawson does, fly BA!', that kind of thing? So, that interview – the one which you objected to so much, the one you said was a 'betrayal' –, that wasna an ego-trip or something, it was to pay – you bastard – for some of those trips, to buy you yet another carton or two of Lucky Strikes. Where the hell did you think all the money came from, Brian, to pay for it all? Not just the big stuff, the air-fares and the motels, but the soap and the lipstick and the toothpaste and, for goodness' sake, even the knickers that I wear, they all – all of them – have to be paid for, darling one. Och, it's too late now. The damage is done. Beside the fact that I never said three-quarters of the things I was quoted as saying, and the things I did say I didna say in the way it made me look like I'd said them. Not that you believed me. But, know what? That's your problem, Brian. No mine. Know what I thought about the whole thing? I just wondered why journalists, they even bother to meet you. I mean, why dinna they just ask you to send a photograph – so they can describe you – and then just invent what it is you have to say. It's what they do anyway. And it would save all the cost and energy travelling.

"I'm sorry, Brian, it offended your delicate sensibilities, but know what, my darling one? I'd do it again tomorrow. In a heart-beat. Even knowing they're never going to publish what it is I do say. Even then. What does it matter? It's not that I've anything important to say. It's not, I mean, as if I was a great thinker or anything. But, then, who being interviewed *is* worth the time it takes to read their words? Whether it's theirs or those of the person interviewing them? Maybe, just maybe, someone who'd triumphed against cancer, say, or someone who'd spent years invisibly trying to find a cure for it, a volunteer maybe for the NSPCC or Save the Children. No-one in the public eye, though. Almost no-one in the public eye.

"It's like the public eye, I dinna know, contaminates or something. People who might otherwise have worth have that worth whipped away from them. I mean, who would you point at today and say to your child, 'Work hard at such-and-such and you could be like him'?

"I do have that advantage. I know I have no worth. What I dinna need, though – thank you very much –, is you and your father constantly reminding me I have none. So, give an interview? For a couple of thousand? Without, my dear, even thinking about it. Even for a couple of hundred. God, at the moment, even for a couple. For the price of a cup of tea.

"Which you were going to make for yourself, lassie, a wee while back. Till you went and forgot. It's also a cliché about the middle-aged and their memories. Well, maybe some of us have to be clichés. We canna all be one-offs, can we? Originals? There's some of us have to be normal, we have to be boring and predictable and conformist – hives, to work, have to have their drones. How many times do you hear at funerals, 'When they made him – or her – they broke the mould'? Well, there's a place too, you know, for the likes of us, those who are moulded from the same press as a zillion others. And relatively proud of it. And, if not exactly proud, at least at peace with that. We canna all be extraorindary. Let's hear it, I say, for the chips off the old block – the old tried and tested and reliable block. Without us ordinaries, there'd be nothing to define all you extraordinaries.

"Except that it isna, is it? Reliable? That block? Reliable blocks dinna have chips flying off them which mother serial killers. Or serial rapists. Their chips dinna mother sons who die by lethal injection. Who die in a little over an hour by lethal injection. ... Tea!

"Look after my laddie, God. Please. *Our* laddie, maybe I should say. Aye, *our* laddie – Yours, God, and mine. You are, after all, aren't You, *our* Father? ...

"Aye ... '*Our* Father, ...' Well, we'll just have to hope, Brian, your heavenly Father is something of an improvement on your earthly one. Not that that would be too hard, of course. 'Our Father, Who art in Heaven, hallowed be Thy name, Thy kingdom come, Thy will be done on Earth as it is in Heaven ...' Thy will??? Thy pigging will? When has Thy will *ever* be done on Earth? Is it Thy will that this wee laddie should be taken prematurely from me? That those three women, the women that he killed, that *they* should have been prematurely snatched away? 'Thy will be done on Earth', that's almost a sick joke. Was the Holocaust Thy will? The Russian Gulags? The First World War? The Black Death? Were these all Thy will? And if so, are we praying to a demented, a psychotic sadist? Are we praying, Brian, to you? Or to the likes of you? Is it indeed 'The Life of Brian'?

"It's the whisky, lassie. The whisky talking. Get that tea down you. No, put plenty of sugar in it, lassie. You need to put plenty of sugar in it. You need that sugar. ... Oh, God. That's Brian. That has to be Brian. Even the ring says it's Brian. Oh, God. You couldna, could you, *no* have phoned? You had to, did you, put me through this one last torment? Oh, God." ...

* * *

"Breathe, lassie. You've got to breathe. In, Roni, out. In ... three ... four ... five ... six ... seven ... eight. ... Out ... two ... three ... four ... five ... I'm going to be sick." ...

* * *

"Well, I suppose, thank heavens, I had no dinner. What a waste of money that would have been! Did you *have* to cry, Brian, did you? Did you? Did you have to tell me that you loved me? And did you have to wait till *now* to tell me? Couldna you – I mean, once in your miserable life – have told me that earlier? Oh, Christ." ...

* * *

"See? See what you did to me, little shit that you are? Got me crying too! I was cried out. Bastard. Son- ... aye ... -of-a-bitch. Oh God, my poor, poor darling laddie." ...

* * *

"Fine. Right. That's it. No more. No more of any of that. Tears, deep breathing, throwing up. All of that, that was all just the whisky. Tea. Get that down you, lassie. It makes no mind that it's cold. Just drink it. Tea? *Tea*? Who am I kidding? Who am I trying to kid? You must be out of your skull, lassie, out of your tiny mind. Tea? At a time like this? Out of your mind, aye, and not in a good way. Not in the way you *should* be out of your mind. Like *pissed* out of your mind. Tea? I should cocoa. Whisky, lassie. Whisky. And a dram, what's more, not so wee. There. That's better. Skol, Roni. Lechayim. Down the blinking hatch.

"'*Tea*! I should *cocoa*!' That's quite funny, really. Aye, *quite* funny. Jesus Christ! Each time you think, that's it, I've got to the end of it, there canna be a pain greater than this one, each time that happens – whammo! – another floor introduces itself. It's like you're in a lift or something, but the buttons showing the floors only light up once you've got there. You think the bottom is Level 3. Until you get to Level 4. Which you then think is the bottom till, lo and behold, you're at Level 5. Je-sus! Jesus H. Christ! It's like a horse has kicked you in the guts or something. A whole cavalry regiment has danced the cha-cha-fucking-cha all over your tummy. It hurts. My God, does it hurt!

"And, aye, I remember, I remember when Ivy was watching Connie die. I do remember – I remember so well – the full horror of that. I remember how Connie was praying for her to die. I remember trying to imagine the agony that was, to pray for your own daughter to die, to pray that she would be saved any more pain. But that wasna this. That was not this. Not even close. You're perfectly healthy. Perfectly. Well, in your body, anyway. Your death isna going to bring those poor women back to life, it's no going to make unpainful the way that they died. Nothing can do that. *Nothing*. And nothing, you bastard, can atone for that. Least of all – you hear me, Brian – *least*, Brian, of all –, your own death. If it could, I'd be all for it.

"And also what will not atone for it is me watching – tick, tock – whilst they put you to death. The Supreme Court of America have, apparently, and in their apparent infinite apparent wisdom decided that capital punishment does not constitute cruel or unusual treatment, or whatever the phrase is – cruel or unusual, I think the phrase is, 'punishment'. Well, what – dear justices of the Supreme Court of America – about the punishment being meted out to *me*? How come that's not cruel or unusual? Aye, and you know what they'd come back saying, they'd say, 'But, shucks, Mrs Lawson, you ain't gone and done nothing wrong here. And, shucks, we dinna punish people when they done nothing wrong. Therefore we're not punishing you. Therefore whatever it is you're undergoing right now, well – hush my mouth – that ain't punishment, lady. And therefore the adjectives simply do not apply. So the concept, lady, of you undergoing "cruel and/or unusual *punishment* " is completely irrelevant.' They have an interesting way of judging, judges on Supreme Courts – whatever those courts are called – be it the Supreme Court of America or Britain's House of Lords or the European Court of Justice or the all-highest, most-magnificent court of Abyssinia or some place. All of them, apparently, they start with the verdict and then work backwards to see how to get to it.

"Twenty past eleven. Twenty-*one* past eleven. Forty minutes. Forty goddamn minutes.

"No kidding now, God. You can hear it in my voice, how still I am, how calm. No kidding. Now I need You to hear me. I really need You, God, to hear me. Christ, You saw Your own Son pigging executed. You know what's it's like. And even He, Your Son, in that moment of crisis, He thought You'd abandoned Him. His mother was there. And one thing I do know, God, I do know *She* was the one being tortured. Not Your Son but Her. She suffered ten times the torment He did. Ten thousand times that torment. And Her pain didna vanish, either, with the Resurrection. However pious She was, however unshakeable Her faith. And know what else, God? The fact that He died to save the whole of humanity, at that moment was something She didna give a toss about. Maybe never did. As far as She was concerned, the whole of humanity could remain unredeemed if that saved Her laddie from execution. And She'd have swapped places with Him in a heart-beat. In less than a heart-beat, for God's sake. Because, know what? The pain of dying, even the pain of crucifixion is nothing – *nothing* – next to the pain of watching someone be crucified. And if You dinna know that, God, then You've no right creating the universe.

"Please be gentle with him, God, when he gets to You. This was a beautiful peach – turned, aye, very bad indeed. But it was – *he* was – a *beautiful* peach. 'Our Father, Who art in ...' Jesus, You dinna need me to pray to You to know I'm praying to You. Cheers, God. I suppose there is a kindredness of spirit between us now: two parents, as it were, who have watched their son being killed ... their son being executed.

"No, no, this isna right. You're my son, Brian. Whatever you've done, however terrible the crimes, you are my laddie. God doesna need my company. God's got company enough. All those people praying to Him and such. He's even got Popes and Archbishops and Dalai Lamas to keep *Him* company. But you – my dear, my darling one – you do. 'You are my dear, my darling one/ My dah-dah and beguiling one ...' Well, maybe not 'beguiling', maybe that's going a wee bit too far.

"I said, my darling one, I said we'd do this together. And we will. I'll be there with you, my own sweet wean, every inch of the way, holding your hand, squeezing it if you want it squeezed. Just lean on me, my precious, I've strength enough for the pair of us. Lean on me, Brian. You drift with the wind. 'All your trials now, soon be over.' Remember that song, Brian? Joan Baez used to sing it. 'All your trials, babe, soon be over.'

"So, they're strapping you now to a gurney. That's okay. There's nothing too upsetting about that. They're taking you to have your appendix out. Nasty wee appendix. Been rumbling for a bit of time now. Rumbling? Growling, more like, like ... You remember that Corgi? Lived at number twenty-two? You remember when we were in Sunderland Drive? Nasty, bad-tempered wee brute that it was. Well, it's been growling, your poor appendix, just like that Corgi. Got to get it out. It's going to make you feel so much better. 'You are my dear, my darling one ...' You know you are, my very dear, my very darling one, Mammy's oh so precious one. Take my hand, Brian. Hold it. 'Hold my hand, I'm a stranger in Paradise ...' Remember when you were tiny, how we used to sing that together? Aye, we'll walk that way together, Brian, you and me, walk towards Paradise together. It's just a wee operation, my babby. Not even an operation, a 'procedure', they call it. Going to make you all better, my wee one. Going to take you away from all your pain. Just think, sweetheart, no more pain. No more pain, Brian, no more pain.

"Och, they're just wee straps. They're just strapping you like that, just to make sure you dinna bruise yourself on the trip. Make sure you dinna fall off of it. You know what a wriggler you are. Dinna you? No, you're having me on. A right wee wriggler you are. And you know it. I canna believe you dinna know it. When you climbed into bed, remember? In the old days? When you'd had bad dreams? Bad dreams! I should cocoa! Just excuses, they were, those famous 'bad dreams', excuses to snuggle into bed with your mammy. Excuse to wriggle and wriggle. Just like that wriggly worm. Remember that panto we went to see? Where was it? Somewhere in Wales. Whatever were we doing in Wales? And around Christmas time?

"I'm just going to take a wee dram, darling. Mammy's medicine, okay? Just two minutes. Not even two minutes. Less than a minute. I've just got to go and fill up the glass. Know what? I think I'll spend a penny at the same time. That way, there'll be no need, not any more, to leave you, not even for a second, not till you're asleep. Just think Sunderland Drive, my own sweet one. Think Sunderland Drive and wriggling in bed. Remember, 'You are my dear, my darling one ...'" ...

* * *

"There, that wasna long, was it? Miss me? And I missed you too, my babby. You alright? 'Course, you're alright. Snuggled up in your mammy's bed, wriggling away. Are you going to be okay? Of course you are. Not long now, my own wee one. Not too much longer now.

"Dinna you fret now about what they're doing to your bottom. That's just medical stuff. Stuff that has to be done. Stuff it's maybe better we dinna know about. And that? That's just what they call a 'catheter', my own sweet one. In case, you know, you want to wee or anything. As you're drifting off to sleep, I mean. It's nothing to worry about, my lamb. Nothing that need concern you.

"Well, of course they're praying over you, sweet one. You are so precious, *so* precious. Anything as precious as you, it has to be prayed over. It's a sign we cherish you. That's all, sweet one – an indication, no more, that we cherish you. Is that light shining in your eyes? Just close your eyes, then, Brian. Close your eyes and hold my hand. You dinna need to think of anything else, sweet pie. Think of nothing but holding Mummy's hand. You know, like the Beatles: 'I want to hold your ha-a-a-and/ I want to hold your hand.'

"There's bound to be all sorts of noises, Brians, whirrs and buzzes and such like, that's medicine for you. They dinna give you leeches any longer, you ken. Not for growling appendixes. Look. Look around you. No. No, dinna do that. You dinna want the glare of the light in your eyes. Those precious eyes of yours. No, dinna look around you. I'll be your eyes, Brian. Let me be your eyes.

"There's maybe a dozen people here – immediately here, I mean – visible, almost touchable. All looking out for you, all making sure, Brian, you feel no pain. And even here you can sense there's a whole lot of other people, also all looking out for you. You are the star. They're all – all of them, Brian – there for you.

"'Rock-a-bye, baby, on the tree-top ...' Hush, now, my babby one, my own sweet wean. You just keep holding Mummy's hand. There! That's the way! 'Speed bonny boat, like a bird on the wing ...' Soon be there, my treasure. Soon, so soon now, it will all be over.

"Let your mind, my babby, drift. You're seven-years-old. We're in that forest. You know, the one by Dumbarton. It's March. And one of those summery March days you sometimes get. Takes you by surprise. It's really hot. T-shirts and ice-cream cones and a glow. The kind of glow that steals all over you, creeps up on you, somehow revitalises you. You've just seen a snake. You say it's a viper, but it's more likely a grass snake. You've ne'er seen a snake before. Not in the wild. And you're entranced by it, mesmerised by it. You canna stop talking about it. Not to me, not to Kenny or to Catherine. Even your father is with us. He's even sober. You canna stop talking to him about it either. That blooming snake. And we're wondering around, not a care in the world, the sun thrusting through the trees, not allowing the trees to stop its progress, dappling the light underfoot. And we're wandering down ... no, you canna call it a 'lane', not even really a 'path', not enough feet have worn it in order that it could be called a 'path'. And, no a care in the universe, we swing round a bend in that sort-of path and ... Well, a bit, I suppose, like Wordsworth coming across his cloud of daffodils, we come across bluebells. A whole sea of bluebells, a whole ocean of them.

"You stop, Brian, and you just gawp. There's no other word, no other expression for it: you just gawp. And it's like you've found Valhalla, Brian. Valhalla: that's the warrior's resting-place, no? And you gawp, Brian, and you gawp and you gawp. And then you start jetting into the middle of them, Brian – pretending you're a jet, I mean, arms stretched behind you – and suddenly, and without warning, suddenly you fling yourself on them. Like you're a soldier or something, finally home after decades at the crusades. Or a dog abandoned, you know like in 'Incredible Journey', and then finding its owners thousands of miles away. You start rolling around in those bluebells, Brian, rolling and rolling ... like you're swimming almost – aye, a dolphin frolicking in the sea. There is bliss in you now, my darling one. No, rather it is that you *are* bliss. You have become bliss.

"That, my darling one, is where you are again. You are in an ocean of bluebells, my wee cherub, a dolphin frolicking in the sea. About to arrive home after so long away, about to enter Valhalla. You are bliss again, my dear, my darling one. 'You are my dear, my darling one ...'

"Those are just the chimes of midnight, my own sweet one. Nothing for you to worry about, you're no Cinderella. And dinna you pay any heed – no heed at all – to those curtains opening. They're letting in sun, my dear, my darling one. Letting in some sun that can glisten off the waves ... sparkle off the waves, my own wee one. And dinna you listen to that man talking to you. He's no saying anything you need to hear. You just listen to your mother, you just hold your mammy's hand ... my dear, my darling one. You are in a sea of blue, my darling, an ocean of peace, a dolphin cavorting in an ocean of peace. Time to sleep now, Brian. Time now to go to sleep. Count back with me, my own sweet one, count back with me to the Land of Nod. Hush! My wee one. Be still now. Ten: my darling one ... nine ... eight: Shh! now. Still. ... seven: 'You are my dear, my darling one ...' ... six ... five: Shh! Peace. ... four: Sleep. ... three ... ...

*** The End ***

Also by Gregory Dark

The Prophet of the New Millennium

The God of the New Millennium

Man of the New Millennium

Charming!